Chemistry of the Heart

ROMANCING THE GEEK, BOOK 3

EMI LEON

For those who needed a second chance to get it right!

PHARMA LAB NOTES #269

BY JERRY DAVEY SLANGER

An inside source claims one of the X, Y, or Z pharmaceutical companies is on to something big. As in, for her pleasure big, if you know what we mean. Imagine a Georgia O'Keeffe painting and mentally inhale the sweet orchid scent. According to our source, this product is currently in the third phase of trials, and the results from the second phase are being verified and confirmed by a data specialist. Our inquiries to the company have yet to be answered.

HILDY

I never expected to be in Seattle again. Nothing against the city with a Starbucks on every corner and the best clam chowder at Mo's, but I left more than five years ago on a rainy October day, which was by far the worst day of my life, and there are far too many other places to visit to have ever considered returning.

Well, until this sunny day in August.

Given my mood, the weather should be overcast and dreary, not a bluebird day without a cloud in the Pacific Northwest sky.

With my brand-new employee badge hanging off the equally new lanyard I wear around my neck, I ride an elevator to the twenty-second floor of Zentello Pharmaceuticals. It's too bad I'm not more excited about this opportunity, but in all honesty, a two-week side gig at the cutting-edge company was not on my bingo card for this year—or any year. That's probably why I never would have imagined Nate Lowe, an old friend and one of the co-CEOs, making me an offer I couldn't refuse.

He tried to charm me into doing him this favor for free. That's so typical of his golden boy mentality even though he's on the downward slope to forty, but I held strong. Until he offered me an insane amount of money that will make a huge difference for my younger sister and two-and-a-half-year-old nephew. Once I stopped hyperventilating and picked up my phone from the floor, I caved faster than a nuclear reaction going supercritical.

Fuck that bastard for knowing exactly what it would take to make me say yes.

Now, I'll be able to cover a year's worth of speech and occupational therapy and whatever else my sister, Mathilda, might need for little Flynn. Our father cut her off when his one and only grandchild was deemed "imperfect" with verbal apraxia and sensory processing disorder diagnoses. Flynn's sperm donor had been out of the picture before my nephew was even born.

Nate doesn't know I would have agreed to work for half the amount. I can't wait to tell him now that my contract is signed and I'm officially an employee, albeit a very temporary one. Though having to sign a scary-ass NDA still leaves me with a sinking feeling like I may have just sold the soul of my firstborn to the devil, aka Zentello Pharmaceuticals.

The elevator stops, and I follow the directions to Zelda's office. She sits behind her desk, working efficiently as ever. I haven't seen her since before I left town, but she hasn't changed. A pen holds her auburn hair up on top of her head, stylish glasses sit midway down her nose, and her blouse is buttoned all the way up. She's always been a contradiction, giving off a weird mix of librarian and sex kitten vibes. Not that the two need to be mutually exclusive. Zelda is proof of that.

I still can't believe Nate hired her as his assistant or that she accepted the job, given her education and background. I have no doubt he keeps her around in the hopes that one day they'll get back together. I wish I knew Zelda's thoughts on Nate, but I know he regrets his divorce.

Me?

The idea of working with my ex-husband—or even seeing him again—makes me want to vomit. I'd rather be thrown into an active volcano full of molten lava than reunite with my ex. Without a doubt, he'd agree. No love lost there.

I wait for Zelda to notice me by tapping my foot against the plush carpet, which unfortunately deadens the sound. Whatever she's typing must be fascinating because she doesn't glance my way. She works with an almost frenetic energy that seems to have increased since I last saw her.

Honestly, I don't know why Nate wants her back. They were like acids and bases, endothermic and exothermic reactions, conductors and insulators. People say opposites attract, but in my experience, they repel. It's best to walk away and not look back, which I did.

No regrets, besides not leaving sooner.

Zelda continues to type. At this rate, I'll be late for my meeting.

I clear my throat.

Her head jerks up, and her gaze collides with mine. She does a double take. "Hildy?"

"In the flesh." I force a smile. God help me, but everything about being back in Seattle feels forced.

Remember the money you'll be paid. Mathilda and Flynn need it.

Zelda's frown, however, surprises me. We were never close friends, but our exes did their postdocs at the same lab, so we socialized together over the years. Yet something feels off in a very noticeable way. The tension simmers like a pot of butter and sugar before it reaches the soft ball stage on a candy thermometer. She pushes back from her desk as if to put distance between us and crosses her arms over her chest.

What's up with her?

Her reaction is weird. She's obviously not happy to see me, but I have no idea why. "Nate's expecting me."

Panic flares in her eyes. Again, that's an odd reaction, given Nate calls Zelda unflappable. More than once since their divorce, he's said she had ice water running through her veins, but I'm not seeing that today.

She straightens as if a stick just got shoved up her ass. "He didn't mention it."

Not my problem, but I can't forget I'm here for a reason and flash my badge. "Did he mention today's my first day at Zentello?"

Her face drops—pales—and I feel a little sorry for her. Though I'm totally over my ex-husband, Nate claims Zelda's as hung up on him as he is on her. Given her reaction to me, I'd say he's right, though I'm not sure why she's so put off by me in particular. We'd gotten along fine in the past and never found ourselves at odds over anything. Maybe her job makes her salty, or perhaps it's Nate. I wouldn't want to be in her shoes and have to work alongside my ex-husband every day of the week like she does.

Zelda smiles, a fake smile, but I'll give her points for trying after being caught off guard by my appearance and sudden employment. I hope I haven't gotten Nate in trouble, but knowing him, if that's the case, he deserves it.

"I'm sure he did, and I forgot," she says with enough artificial sweetness to kill a lab full of rats.

Once upon a time, Zelda had a memory elephants envied. We all used to joke about it, so I'm not buying that she *forgot*, which gets me thinking. She's too young for perimenopause to cause brain fog. Nate would have mentioned if she had a TBI, a substance abuse issue, or another health complication that affected the brain. The most obvious answer is usually right, which means she's probably lying.

My skin prickles, which has nothing to do with the air-conditioning.

Zelda has no idea why I'm here, and that's bad because she's Nate's right hand and supposedly the love of his life despite their divorce. So why didn't he tell her I was coming?

A shiver inches down my spine and travels all the way to the tips of my newly polished toenails. What is he up to now?

Zelda stares at me, and I don't look away. Her gaze narrows as if she's trying to size me up. Oh, she should know better.

Whatever game she's playing—it's on. She should remember I'll do whatever it takes to come out on top, even if I have to stand here for the next hour or even the rest of the day. Yeah, I can be a tad competitive, and I blame my sperm donor for that. He wanted sons, but he got two daughters. My childhood was a watered-down version of *The Hunger Games* where we competed for crumbs of attention. Affection was nonexistent, even from Mom, who was too afraid of our father to ever go against him.

As I ready myself for a long-haul stare down, Zelda blinks.

Aw ... That was too easy. "So, Nate?"

"In his office. It's the next one down the hall."

She could have just said that when I arrived. Oh well. "See you later."

I don't wait for a reply and leave.

Nate's office is right next door to Zelda. I hold my badge in front of the digital pad on the wall, and the door whooshes open. Fancy-schmancy, but Nate always enjoyed shiny new toys. I guess he still does.

I step into the office.

It's huge and high-tech, like the rest of Zentello. Nate sits behind a ginormous desk. He sees me, smiles, stands, and walks toward me. *Walk* isn't exactly the right descriptor. The guy saunters up to me like he owns the place. Given he's co-CEO, he sort of does. "It's so good to see you, Hildy. What's it been? Five years? Looking fine, as always."

"Should you say that since you're now my boss?" Yes, I can be a bitch at times, but being a woman in STEM can be difficult. It's a fine dance setting boundaries and sticking to them.

"It depends on your definition of fine. Mine is straight from *Merriam-Webster*. What's yours?"

Nate's as gorgeous as ever. He's dressed more like a business executive than a scientist in his tailored gray suit and flashy red silk tie. Nate kisses my cheek, giving my shoulder a squeeze at the same time. He smells as good as he looks, which is nothing new. Some men are born with good genes or a silver spoon or a MENSA-level IQ. Nate has all three.

We're just good friends, even if I may have had one random fantasy about having sexy times with him post-divorce when I was lonely and horny. The fact he's my temporary boss and still hung up on his ex-wife makes it even easier to keep from proffering my lips now. Which reminds me … "Zelda acted surprised and unhappy to see me just now. Did something happen, or is there anything I should know?"

His mouth quirks, but a smile quickly slides into place. "No, she must be having an off day. It happens to the best of us."

That's reasonable, but his words don't lessen the feeling in my gut. Maybe I'm just on edge from being in Seattle again. "It does."

"What do you think of Zentello?"

"Fancy digs, and that digital security panel is impressive." He beams at the compliment, so I might as well keep going to get on the boss's good side. "But then again, you've always been on the cutting edge no matter what you worked on. I remember that from your postdoc days."

"Good times back then."

Meh. My divorce taints my memories. But I smile instead of saying that.

He leans against his desk and motions to a nearby leather chair.

I take a seat. "So what exactly am I doing at Zentello?"

Nate winks. "Isn't seeing me enough?"

"Not really." I'm being totally honest, but I keep my tone lighthearted so he thinks I'm joking. "You're paying me too much for this to be just a personal visit."

He laughs, a warm sound that's as easygoing as he is. The only thing that flusters him is Zelda.

"That's what I love about you, Hildy," Nate says. "You cut through all the crap and tell it like it is."

He's not wrong, but that's also why I'm in my late thirties and single. Mathilda says my standards are too high. My parents say I'm too difficult. I won't confirm or deny either.

"You know, I have a job waiting for me in New Zealand." A dream job, if only for the next six months to a year. Visas can be hard to come by, but my experience with mathematical modeling and biomedical engineering made me a shoo-in for the position. They don't call me a polymath for nothing. The position has the possibility of becoming a permanent opportunity, but I don't know how long I want to be away from Mathilda and Flynn, even though she told me to go. Giving her all the money I'll make at Zentello will help assuage my guilt. I hope to convince her to move down there if I wind up staying longer.

Nate rolls his eyes. "I know. You told me about it forty-seven times during our phone call, which is why I put a timeframe on your contract. I won't interfere with your plans, Hildy."

He's saying the right words, but something in his casual pose puts me on alert. I can't shake off how much of a surprise my sudden employment was to Zelda.

I cross my arms over my chest. "You're assuming I'd let you."

"Touché." He sounds amused.

I'm not. "The job description was a bit ... vague."

"Like I told you on the phone, we're in the third phase of clinical trials for a new product."

"You didn't tell me the name of it."

"That's because you hadn't signed the NDA. Now, I can tell you." His eyes dance with excitement, and he leans forward slightly. "The product's called Orchid. It's a female pleasure enhancement drug."

I straighten. He's got my attention. "Like a female Viagra?"

"Only better," he admits, and yes, I'm very intrigued. This will look fabulous on my résumé, even if I'm only here for two weeks.

"It's a top-secret project," he continues. "Need-to-know basis only. Our lead scientist in charge of the data needs to verify everything. He could use help."

"So you need another number cruncher?"

"Yes, and with your background, you're perfect."

I'm brilliant. Not going to lie about that fact when everyone knows it's true, but what Nate says doesn't make sense. I'm good, but I'm not the only person who can do this job. "What else?"

Nate flinches, which pleases me because his reaction tells me I've caught him off guard. That isn't something that usually happens with Nate Lowe.

"Excuse me?" he asks as if he's confused. Again, not typical for him.

"There has to be more to this job than data analysis, given the salary and the nice digs you're putting me up in." Not only are my accommodations covered for the two weeks, but I'm also receiving a per diem for food.

His mouth drops open. "I'm shocked you'd accuse me of—"

"Just get to the point, Nate. What's so important I'm the only person who can help you and Zentello?"

He inhales and then exhales as if he's trying to power all the sailboats on Lake Washington. "You're right. I need you to do something else while you're working at Zentello."

Knew it, and that explains the ridiculous amount of money I'll be earning and all the extra perks. I need to trust my gut more. You'd think by now I would. Oh well, it's never too late to learn. "As long as it's not pole dancing for the board of directors ..."

Nate rolls his eyes, grabs a tablet from his desk, taps on the screen, and turns so I can read what's there. "This article was written by a so-called science journalist. He's using a pseudonym. We think he's the same person who's been writing articles about us since the first phase of the Happy Pill last year. Though we know there's a team of them who use similar nom de plumes."

I read the article, which is written in the style of a Hollywood blind item. The not-so-vague references suggest Zentello and their new Orchid project. That's bad if the project is supposed to be top secret. "On our call, you mentioned having issues with reporters trying to publish a story about Bradley and his girlfriend last year. Is this them?"

Bradley Zimmer is one of the good guys and a lead scientist on the project. We met years ago when he, Nate, and my ex all worked together at the same lab back East. You could even say we were friends of sorts until we weren't. I lost the majority of our friends in the divorce, so I haven't spoken to Bradley in more than five years. The one friend I got is Nate. I hadn't seen that coming, and I'm still not sure how it happened, given how close the guys were. But here I am because of that.

Nate nods. "Christina is his fiancée now, but yes, three reporters tried to blackmail Bradley into giving up information about Mr. Z, our other CEO. And a different reporter, James Austen, wanted Christina to spill the beans about the second phase of clinical trials, though he didn't know anything about the actual product being tested. When Bradley finally told me what was going on, we found our mole. A biogenetics scientist named Jennings, who ran a lab here. A bit of a hippie-stoner type who played us all into thinking that he was, well ... stoned all the time. But that was all a cover so no one noticed when he listened in on conversations or snooped around in areas he shouldn't have been."

One mole found, but the new article still refers to an inside source ... "Do you think someone else has taken over that guy's job of snooping?"

"Yes, although I'm not sure they've taken over. Maybe they were working alongside him the whole time." Nate points at the tablet. "Nothing about Orchid has been released to the public. Most at the company don't know about the project either, which means ..."

"You have another mole."

"Someone who must be part of the Orchid project itself. I need you to ferret him out."

Nate has never acted sexist in the past, so I'm surprised by his use of that pronoun. "Him?"

"I'm ninety percent sure I know who the mole is this time. And yes, the person is a man." Nate narrows his eyes on me. "But we need to confirm the identity of this person so I can stop him. If more specifics about Orchid are released and another pharmaceutical company gets there before us, we stand to lose billions."

I blink rapidly. This is so much more than what he told me on the phone. I'm confident in my abilities, but ... "I'm not sure I want to be responsible for something this heavy. What if I'm not able to sniff them out?"

"This isn't all on you, Hildy." Nate takes my hand. "Just do your job as normal. All I'm asking is that you keep your ear to the ground and your eyes open for two weeks. If you can't get proof to take down the mole by the time you leave for New Zealand, fine. But you'll be working with my number one suspect, so it shouldn't be too hard for someone as intelligent as you to get what we need to fire and arrest him."

I'm all about the compliments, but I get the feeling there's so much more to this than Nate's telling me. What's the phrase ... trickle truthing? I'm a scientist and mathematician. That means I need more data. "So I'll be working with this person?"

Nate drops his hand and nods. "An awful lot of data needs collating, Hildy. There's no way only one person can handle it on their own. This will be the perfect cover for you."

"Okay." Though I'm feeling anything but okay. The worry in his eyes hits me right in my core. Nate isn't a worrier. He takes action and makes things happen. "Tell me about the suspected mole so I can devise a plan of what to look for."

Nate takes a breath and then smiles. "I'll do better than

that. You can meet him. You'll get a better perspective on him than me giving my opinion of what the guy is like."

Something still feels off, but I get the feeling Nate won't tell me more right now. "Okay, let's go meet our mole."

"But first, I need you to put this on." He digs in his pocket, pulls out a diamond ring, and hands it to me.

The diamond is huge. This thing must've cost him a fortune. "What is it?"

"An engagement ring," he says the words slowly as if I'm a child.

"I can see that." Maybe I need to rephrase my question. "Why do you want me to wear the ring?"

"Because if we're engaged, my hiring you without an open job req seems more reasonable."

I study him. No tells, but … he's lying. I feel like Alice after she fell down the rabbit hole. "So I'm supposed to be your fiancée?"

"Yes."

"Yet I'm not staying at your house?"

"We can say your sister might visit so having your own place is easier."

The guy is way too smooth, though I'm impressed he remembers I have a sister. "You have an answer for everything."

Nate picks up the ring from my palm and slides it onto my ring finger. "I do, which is why I'm the boss."

The ring feels like a shackle. I haven't worn anything on that finger since the divorce. "Do I get to keep it?"

Nate hesitates and then shrugs. "Sure."

He's not all in on that decision, but this rock is easily worth five figures. More money for Mathilda and Flynn after I sell it. But one thing niggles at the back of my mind. "What about Zelda? Does she know about this?"

"Not yet."

That would explain her reaction to me. "She'll never buy us being engaged. You have to tell her the truth."

Nate huffs. "I'll take care of Zelda. Just trust me, okay?"

I don't trust anyone, but I clench my teeth against any protest. He's paying me enough that I'll play along ...

For now.

CHAPTER 2

SAM

Four minutes and twenty-six seconds.

That's how much time I have left on my lunch break, and if I've calculated my reading speed correctly, I can finish this chapter of the book I bought yesterday. It's a little heavy, but I relate to the main character, who discovers an entity from another universe. It turns out the being is sentient, so he looks for ways to communicate with it. The way the being is described makes me think of black matter, even though that can't be sentient.

Still, the fictional situation reminds me of my ex-wife. When we split, she turned into the darkest of matters, and I was unable to communicate with her in any way, shape, or form. Her lengthy emails about us took me days to decipher because of the tangents she went off on, including lists of my inadequacies as a husband. As I traced each point back to its beginning, the crux of the matter became clear—she wanted a divorce.

I didn't, but that's beside the point. I've been single now for more than five years, longer than we were married, and I rue the day we met.

Anyway, I'm finding it hard to get through my new book, but I'm determined. Finishing this tome will be my own personal Mount Everest. I imagine myself standing on the summit, wearing an oxygen mask because I have nothing to prove about my athletic ability or lung capacity, holding up the book, and then tossing it into the abyss below—not on the climbing route because I don't want to hurt anyone.

But completing things is what I do. No matter how difficult something is, I'll see it through to the end—unlike my ex-wife, who gave up on us far too easily.

Yes, I'm still bitter, but I'll never admit that to anyone because they'll think I still love and miss her.

I don't.

She's the definition of chaos, and I don't mean that in a good way. Me? I'm stability incarnate. On one of her lists, that translated to me being a boring stick-in-the-mud. She also accused me of working too much, not engaging with her or others, not wanting to start a family, and not agreeing to adopt a dog.

Thinking about my past always sours my mood. I try to redeem it by reading to keep my focus on something else.

I glance at the clock. Three minutes and forty seconds left on my break, and I still have the same number of words to read. I've spent far too many seconds thinking about my ex-wife. I wish I could purge her from my brain. That would be the best thing for me. I adjust my glasses.

As I force my attention to the book, I shift in my desk chair, and my reading picks up speed so I can finish the chapter in time.

As I turn the page, my office door whooshes open.

Fuck. I don't even have to look up and turn to know who entered.

Zentello prides itself on being "cutting edge," even with the way the doors open. Only an authorized person with a special badge or palm scan can open the sliding doors. Due to the highly sensitive nature of my project, only one person can access my lab and this office, besides me.

Fuck my life.

I focus harder on the words before me, but the entire page blurs.

Nate's aftershave permeates the air like the men's restroom after burrito truck day, making me nauseous. He's worn the same scent since we met doing our postdocs. But that isn't why the smell is ingrained in my gray matter. I still remember the scent lingering in my ex-wife's apartment when I'd visited her to see if we could try again. Even post-divorce, I'd wanted to reconcile.

"Afternoon, Sam." Nate sounds as smug as usual.

I don't look at him, deciding to double down on my book. "What do you want?"

"I need to talk to you about Orchid."

I hate Nate Lowe with a passion, almost as much as I hate my ex-wife, which makes it even more unbelievable that I've been at Zentello for more than two years now working for the guy. He may have made me an offer I couldn't refuse, but I still can't stand to be in the same room as him.

Why the hatred?

After my divorce was finalized, my ex-wife fucked Nate,

who was my closest friend at the time. I should say ex-friend. He swore nothing happened when I was married to her as if hearing that made the news any easier for my fragile ego. His admission cost me our friendship. No way I could stay friends after knowing he'd been intimate with her and how he'd boasted about it.

As my friend, he knew I didn't want the divorce and was trying to reconcile. His actions felt like an intentional blow, a betrayal. After all of her emails and rants, I compiled a list of my own. I'd gone through each of her points and come up with an actionable plan or response for every one of them, and I'd gone to her apartment to tell her how I planned to change. I wouldn't work such long hours; I would engage with people more; I'd be more open to starting a family; and I'd even consider getting a dog.

I had a plan, and my heart pounded when I walked through her apartment door. It was all I could do not to pull her against me and kiss her. I had to keep reminding myself to be patient and not fuck it up. But then ... I scrunch my nose as if I can still smell the familiar aftershave, knowing Nate had been there with her. The two of them alone. I couldn't say any of the words I'd been rehearsing. I'd mumbled I shouldn't be there, turned around, and walked out. How could we reconcile? She'd moved on from our marriage, leaving me with my stupid list and my pride in tatters.

Just thinking about the two of them together sends my blood pressure spiraling.

But in exchange for the insane money I get paid, the least I can do is be somewhat professional, and that's all I would do.

"No, sorry. I'm on my lunch for another"—I glance at the time—"two minutes and fifty-five seconds. Come back after that, and if I'm not too busy, we can talk."

Okay, maybe that isn't exactly professional, but I am civil when I want to tell him to fuck off. And legally, I get a lunch break. So sue me.

Someone sighs, and I know it isn't Nate. The sound is strangely familiar. I just can't place it, but I'll be damned if I look up. If anything, traveling on public transportation in Seattle has taught me to avoid making eye contact with anyone you don't want to talk to. That lesson has come in handy at Zentello.

"Well, that's tough, I'm afraid." Nate sounds far too chirpy, considering I've basically told him, my boss, to fuck off. Something I do whenever I can, if I'm being honest.

"You need to meet your research partner," he continues.

Whoa! My muscles bunch. He's gotten my attention with that line, but not enough for me to glance his way. Yes, I can be a total prick. He deserves it.

I keep my gaze focused on the book. "I don't want a research partner. My contract doesn't mention one."

When Nate offered me the job at Zentello, I asked for a contract that spelled everything out, including the bonus amount I'll receive once the data is verified. After that, I'll be out of here and onto bigger and better things. I can't wait.

"It's not like I want to work with you either, you a-hole."

Fuck. I know where I've heard that sigh and that voice. My gaze jerks up. "Hildy?"

"Hey, Samuel. Lovely to see you too." Hildy flashes a smile

I recognize from the many times she's been pissed about something, namely me.

The years have been good to her. No gray hair or rotted teeth.

Her dark hair is pulled off her face, so I don't know if it's as long as it used to be, maybe longer, but the style shows off her high cheekbones, lush lips, and flawless makeup. She's got curves that don't stop, and I hate that I notice them. Most men would do a double or triple take. She's that stunning.

I force myself to look away and sit shell-shocked by her appearance until I realize she expects me to say something. "What the hell is going on here?"

Nate grins. "Hildy is your new research partner."

I throw my book onto my desk. As it lands with a thud, I push myself out of my chair. "Nope. Not a chance."

Hildy groans. "Stop being an asshole, Sam. It's not like I want to work with you either."

"So go away." I point at the door. I regret not killing Nate when I had the chance. No jury would have convicted me when they heard how he seduced my wife—make that ex-wife. "I'll be fine on my own. I have everything under control."

"Not an option." Nate comes to my desk, picks up my book, turns over the thick paperback, and reads the back cover. "*The Feelings of Matter. A story of man's journey to find answers.* Hmm ... sounds interesting."

He lifts an eyebrow, and I want to take the book and smash it in his face. *Smug bastard.*

Hildy snickers. She's holding on to a white lab coat. "I see your taste in literature hasn't improved over the years."

"I see your taste in men hasn't either," I throw back. Petty, but I must admit saying that feels good.

She shrugs. "Well, I was married to you, so go figure."

"I suppose it's time we let you in on our little secret." Nate's smile widens as if he's holding the winning ticket to a billion-dollar lottery prize. He puts his arm around Hildy and pulls her against him. "We're engaged!"

My heart slams against my rib cage. I thought Nate had lied about what happened between him and Hildy. Mainly, I assumed they'd been cheating while I was still married to her instead of it being a one-night stand. He's probably been flirting and sending heart eyes Zelda's way since I started working at Zentello to throw me off.

But Hildy and Nate?

My breathing stills. So does time. Nothing could have ever prepared me for this.

I open my mouth and then close it. For the first time in a long time, I'm at a loss for words.

My vision swims, and the room tilts as if I'm suddenly light-headed after not eating enough. But I had a balanced lunch, and …

Engaged.

Fuck.

I force myself to breathe before I pass out.

But the air won't go into my lungs, and the vise around my chest gets tighter.

Oh my God.

Am I having a heart attack?

I place two fingers on my neck to check my pulse.

I always thought I should've suffered a myocardial infarction after the divorce, but now the tightness in my chest suggests I'm actually having a cardiac event. The most likely diagnosis being takotsubo cardiomyopathy, aka broken heart syndrome, which pisses me off.

I'm over her.

I hate her. And him.

As if I'm living my life in slow motion, Hildy holds out her left hand and shows me a massive diamond on her ring finger that sparkles under the bright lighting in my office. It's ten times bigger than the ring I bought her way back when, and once again, Nate Lowe proves he's the golden boy, and I'm … nothing compared to him.

A colorful prism shoots out from the stone.

I blink. I must've fallen asleep reading, and all I want to do is wake up from this nightmare.

When I refocus my vision, Nate, Hildy, and the gaudy ring are still there.

Shit. This isn't a dream. Well, I want it to stop anyway. "Get out!"

"No can do," Nate says, appearing quite pleased with himself.

What the fuck? How can they be engaged? Hildy hasn't been back to Seattle as far as I know. And time hasn't dimmed Nate's feelings for Zelda. It's no secret he wants them to get back together. Unless that's all been for show. Of course, I try to avoid speaking to Nate as much as possible, so for all I know, he and Hildy have been a thing for a while. Maybe for the past five years?

Fuck.

Humor lights Hildy's eyes. "Close your mouth, Samuel, or you'll catch flies soon."

"That's better than the spiders you've swallowed while sleeping with your mouth open." Not the best retort, but she caught me off guard.

Nate rubs the back of his neck, and I fight the urge to punch him.

"Is there any chance you two can play nice for a few minutes while I explain why I've brought Hildy on board?" he asks me.

"Let me guess? You want Zentello to pay her to save you from spending money on her. She's always seen relationships as transactional. Guess you do too, Lowe."

"Come on, Sam. You're being a dick." Hildy huffs. "Listen to what Nate has to say."

Nate nods. "I am your boss, Sam."

I don't care. They've interrupted my lunch break and reading time. Not that it matters. I don't ever want to be nice to the man I hate or the ex-wife I despise. Honestly, the two of them belong together. But I'm not quite to the point of accepting that yet. I might not ever be.

As I narrow my gaze on him, I try to decide whether to take option one and smack him in the face with my book or take option two and tell him to stick his damn job. Quickly considering the pros and cons, I go for option three and ignore them both.

Forgoing the last minute and a half of my lunch break, I turn to my computer and log in. To be fair to Nate, an assistant would be helpful, but I won't tell him that. Especially when the person he wants me to work with is Hildy.

She moves closer and peers over my shoulder. "Looks like a lot of work needs to be done."

Her smell is unrecognizable, but then she's never stuck to one scent. She prefers to swap perfumes, depending on the occasion or the time of year. I'd find it odd when she'd say, "Oh no, I can't wear an autumn fragrance in the summer." And you know what? She was right. She tried an autumn scent in the summer one year, and it just didn't smell right.

"You don't have the authority to look at this," I snap.

"Yes, I do. NDA is signed and in Zentello's possession," she mutters close to my ear as if to piss me off. She's succeeding. "Is this the stuff you want me to help him with, Nate?"

"Yes," Nate says with a bit of laughter in his tone. "As you can see, Sam has a large amount of data to go through. I suggest you each take half and generate profiling groups to get started. With your math background, Hildy, I expect you to find a few things we've not considered before."

I roll my eyes, bored of the "Let's all shoot smoke up Hildy's ass" game, and tap away at my keyboard. "If you've finished chatting, is there any chance you could leave me to get on with my work? I have a lot to do and want to finish on time as I have a date tonight."

Like hell I have a date, but I don't want Hildy knowing I'm basically a workaholic hermit or that my weekly meal plans consist of leftover takeout because I work too much to have time to grocery shop.

"There you go." Nate claps me on the back with a firm hand. "See how useful having Hildy working alongside you will be? More time to socialize."

I spin my chair around, my knees colliding with Hildy's legs. I glance at them, already knowing she'll be wearing stockings with a seam up the back. Where I like to wear a suit, Hildy loves to dress like a 1950s pin-up girl. She's curvy and voluptuous with the most amazing boobs that used to be covered in red or black satin or lace. Her panties would most definitely match. That was her thing. Even on Sundays, when we chilled around the house in our sweats and T-shirts, her panties had to match the bra. Even if they were only white cotton.

For whatever reason, my gaze sweeps up from her legs. My body remembers hers—the way we'd be tangled up in the sheets all hot and sweaty and satiated after a marathon sexcapade—and reacts in my pants. Fuck. Her tight skirt accentuates the curve of her hips to her waist. Her short-sleeved red blouse has black buttons. Enough are undone to show a decent amount of cleavage that only sends more blood rushing where I don't want it to go. She's pulled her glossy brown hair into a high ponytail and covered her pouty lips in her trademark Scarlet Woman red.

Those red lips curve into a smile, and she bends closer to me. "Miss me, did you, hubster?"

She then pointedly looks at my crotch, and I know my nightmare has just begun.

Nate chuckles smugly. "Just remember, Sam, you had your chance. She's mine now."

I wonder how long it'll take to write a resignation letter. What other choice do I have? I can't keep working here. That would be inhumane and cruel to myself.

CHAPTER 3

HILDY

Nate Lowe is on my shit list. It's a very long shit list, and he's every single entry. I thought the fake engagement was crazy, but ...

What the hell is he thinking partnering me up with my damn ex-husband? What's worse, Nate's practically sprinted out of the office and left me not only to work here but also to spy on Sam. And here's the thing ... Sam Grant is a lot of things, but a spy or traitor isn't one of them. The man doesn't take risks. He's chased stability his entire life. I get that people can change in five years. The fact Sam works at Zentello and not his staid government job with a pension plan shocks me, but still ...

My gut tells me Nate is way off base about Sam being the mole.

I sigh, something I'm used to doing around Sam, and I'm already back at it again. I also can't believe after all this time and our past, I still can make him hard. I shouldn't feel as good about that as I do, which pisses me off. I shouldn't care.

I don't care.

I really, really don't. I blow out a breath. Definitely not a sigh. "Well, this is going to be fun."

Sam turns back to his computer and doesn't acknowledge me. He just keeps tip-tapping away at the keys as if I don't exist. Funny, but that's how he treated me most of our marriage when he worked crazy-long hours and claimed he was doing it for us. As if I want to eat my anniversary or birthday dinners alone.

Asshole.

I don't know why I thought he would have gained weight and lost his hair. If anything, he's lost weight and is the thinnest I've ever seen him. All his hair is there, but it's a tad longer than it was and tousled in a messy style. I get the feeling that's not on purpose. His glasses are new but still make him look nerdy, which is still my type, unfortunately.

His taste in clothing hasn't changed. He's wearing a white lab coat, but his suit jacket hangs from a coatrack on a hanger. It's navy blue, not tailor-made, but I bet it fits like a designer label. He always took his suits to this guy who ran a launderette and did alterations. The jacket has a red pocket square, and I would also wager that underneath his lab coat is a matching necktie.

Five years later, Samuel Grant hasn't changed physically. He's still the same six-foot-three guy with dark hair and a wardrobe of snazzy 40s-style suits that make him look like a much more handsome Montgomery Clift. When we were together, Nana called him Mr. Clift. Granted, she had Alzheimer's, but she was so adamant that Sam gave her an autograph whenever he saw her.

Our friends used to comment how well-matched we were. Too bad the compatibility was only in our looks and not our personalities. But damn, I really wish he had a beer belly or a receding hairline. I hate that he's still as attractive as ever.

I sigh again.

Yes, Sam is my biggest achievement yet my greatest failure.

He continues typing. Just call me the invisible ex-wife.

Such a rat bastard.

I wait for him to say something—anything. As expected, he continues to ignore me.

So that's how this will be. I'm not surprised, given this is Sam. Another sigh wells, but I swallow it.

As the minutes tick by, I get more annoyed by the silent treatment.

Enough.

"What happened between you and Nate?" I ask finally. "You were going all dark side of the Force on the guy."

Sam harrumphs.

I have no idea what that's supposed to mean. I try to read his face, but nothing's there. His expression is a blank page, something it had never been when we were together. "What?"

"You know."

"I don't." Even though his two words imply enough to write a dissertation about or send me deeper down the rabbit hole, I really don't. I can't even come up with a feasible hypothesis. The only thing I can do is address this logically using the facts I know. "You and Nate used to be best friends. Now you act like you can't stand the guy. You were rude—"

"Stop playing dumb." Sam shakes his head. "You're the most intelligent woman I know, and working here, that's saying a lot."

"I truly have no idea what you're talking about."

He glances at me for a nanosecond before returning his attention to the screen. "Ask your fiancé."

The cold hatred dripping off his final word would freeze hell. It makes no sense. If something happened between Sam and Nate, why are they working together? "I will."

I expect a smart-ass reply, but Sam merely focuses on the monitor and types. Maybe that's not such a bad thing. But Nate hired me to do a job, and I won't let him stop me from doing it.

"What do you want me to do?" By the time I put on the lab coat Nate had given me before we entered the lab, Sam still hasn't answered. Of course not. "Samuel, I'm talking to you."

"Hildegard," he snaps.

"You know I hate that name." I poke him in the back with my fingertip. He's still as solid as ever. He never had time to go to the gym, but he did push-ups and had a pull-up bar installed on one of the doorjambs. I wonder if that's changed. Knowing him, I'd guess not. "You used it just to piss me off."

"Don't call me Samuel, then. You know I hate that name."

I did know, which is why I said it. What I really wanted to call him is *dick*, but one should remain professional, even though I already told him he's acting like one, which he is. I sure hope he doesn't normally treat Nate with such disdain. If so, Sam will find himself without a job soon.

"Okay, *Sam*." I emphasize his name, letting my inner bitch come to the surface. "I'm not one to stand around and look beautiful, even if I'd rock doing that. So tell me what you need me to do for the rest of the day."

He closes his eyes, and my chest pinches as I stare at his

lashes that nearly brush the lenses of his glasses. Long dark lashes that I used to beg him to let me put mascara on for fun. Lashes that used to flutter against my skin when he kissed and loved me. I push the thoughts from my mind, wishing I could swallow a pill that would remove specific parts of my memory without causing permanent brain damage. Maybe I should mention that to Nate as a product they should investigate developing …

"What I'd like you to do, Hildy, is tell Nate you're quitting and don't want this job."

"Not happening, Sam." My first payment should hit my bank account before I return to the temporary apartment Nate found for me. I'll make an immediate transfer to Mathilda because Flynn has appointments tomorrow. Nothing will get in my way of working these two weeks, including Sam Grant.

I button up the coat, grab a chair, and roll it to his side of the desk. "Show me the data, how you're coding them, and what your current classifications are."

"Seriously?" He sounds dumbfounded, which I take as points in my favor. "You're going to carry on with this damn charade of you working here?"

"I need a job for a couple of weeks. Nate knew that, so he offered me one."

I repeat the story—okay, little white lie—Nate and I came up with when we rode the elevator down to Sam's floor. The story is partially true. I'll be here for only two weeks before I move to New Zealand for a once-in-a-lifetime opportunity, and I can't wait. Of course, I had no idea until a few minutes ago that I'd also be spying on Sam to find out if he was selling information about Orchid. Or that I'm pretending to be engaged to Nate.

"Of course Lowe did," Sam mutters. "The fact I don't need or want you here doesn't matter, I suppose."

"Why don't you need me? It looks like you need me." I scoot my chair closer and tilt his computer screen to get a better look at the data. It's probably better if I don't mention his hard-on, right? "Split some of that off and email it to me. I see a desk with a desktop computer, so I'll work over there. Unless you'd rather share your computer and desk with me? That might be cozy."

He stares at me for a beat. "You've got to be joking."

"You know me, Sam, when I joke it's so funny you piss your dapper pants."

"Having your hands on my data is one thing. But working in my office while you do that is another." He reaches for the office phone, picks up the receiver, and presses a couple of buttons. "If she has to work here, so be it, but I'll not have her working in my ... You have to be kidding me ... This was not in my contract, Lowe ... Yes, I'm pissed, and I'll call you what I like ... We stopped being friends a long time ago, *Lowe* ... I'm so glad you find this amusing ... Oh, go fuck yourself."

He slams down the receiver with such force his desk shakes. I jump in my seat.

"Didn't go well, then?" I raise an eyebrow in a perfect arc since I visited the hair salon yesterday and had them threaded for my first day here.

His jaw juts forward. "You're working here."

"Oh goody. Nate was persuasive, then."

Sam shakes his head. "We need some ground rules for this to work."

He's not wrong, and it's all I can do not to poke and prod to get a reaction out of him. But I am being paid to work, so I shouldn't. "We need to act professionally."

"And not bring up the past."

His tense voice makes me think he does want to talk about what happened between us. That, however, might result in an explosive reaction.

"That's for the best," I agree, and it gives me an idea. "Let's start over."

Lines crease his forehead. "Excuse me?"

I hold out my right hand. "I'm Hildy Russell."

"Russell?"

"I didn't want to go back to Bauer after." We aren't mentioning the past, so I don't say divorce. I'd become Hildy Grant when we married, but since we'd never had kids, I didn't have a reason to keep that name. "I decided to use my mom's maiden name."

He says nothing, so I continue. "I have two PhDs, one in mathematics and the other in biomedical engineering, an MS in biology, and I minored in chemistry."

Sam stares at my extended hand as if it's radioactive, emitting 10,000 mSv, a fatal dose of radiation that will kill him in weeks. "What—"

"Just play along with me for once." I try not to sound exasperated, but I'm not sure I succeed. "Shake my hand and introduce yourself."

He does that thing where he rolls his eyes and shakes his

head at the same time. I'm not sure how he does both simultaneously. I've tried and failed.

"Please," I add, figuring a little politeness can't hurt.

"Sam Grant." His voice is gruff, and his expression is pure grump. "PhD in biology."

"Nice to meet you, Sam." He still hasn't shaken my hand. I wiggle my fingers to get his attention. When that doesn't get the desired result, I clear my throat and shove my arm closer to him.

He huffs and clasps my hand, the brush of his skin against mine igniting a spark. Tingles follow and shoot up my arm.

Sam lets go as if he's about to get burned. I know exactly how he feels.

Hot damn. The chemistry is still strong after all these years and a divorce. Guess that explains his hard-on. But I don't want him to know the effect he has on me. This isn't a two-way street. "Was that so hard?"

He flexes his hand. "No."

That's better than a yes. "Now, tell me what you want me to do."

CHAPTER 4

SAM

I'm not sure how I survive the next two hours with Hildy working six feet away from me. I swear I can hear her every breath, and I still feel tingles from her stupid handshake. At least my dick hasn't gone hard again. Talk about embarrassing myself. But she's a distraction to the nth-degree and is affecting my productivity. I need to get away, if only for a few minutes, or I might lose my mind.

Hildy, however, appears unaffected by me. She's bent over her keyboard, staring at the data on the monitor. My gut wants me to tell her to sit up straight or she'll end up sore later. But she's not my responsibility anymore.

I'm stunned she's using Russell as her last name now. I never thought she'd keep Grant post-divorce, but using Bauer, her original last name, made the most sense. Bauer & Sons Financial Investments is a successful company founded by Hildy's father, Werner Bauer. Granted, she and her dad didn't get along, but that name would open doors for her. Hell, I would have changed my name to Bauer when we married if she'd asked—she didn't.

But with her firmly implanted in my mind, I need to take

my afternoon break. A cup of strong coffee and a cookie might help clear my brain, and I know where to find both. I push back from my desk, the well-oiled chair wheels silent against the floor. "I'll be back in a bit."

Hildy startles. "Where are you going?"

"It's break time. You get two plus time off for lunch each day."

"Still a rule follower." She makes that sound like a character flaw.

I shouldn't say anything, but ... "Rules keep society functioning."

"It would be more fun without them."

"No, it would be chaos."

Hildy thrives upon chaos—it may as well be her middle name—so that would be *fun* for her. We are opposites in so many ways. And on that note ... I step away from my desk, patting my pants' pocket to make sure my wallet is there. It is.

"Don't forget to take your book," she says, but I can't tell if she's being nice or sarcastic.

"I don't need it where I'm going."

Questions fill her expression, but I don't care. Nor do I ask if she wants anything.

I walk out of the office without a glance back. It isn't until I'm out of my lab and standing in the hallway that I can breathe easier. Lauren, who works on the Orchid project, waves my way before she turns the corner. That's odd. She usually doesn't come to this side of the biochemistry floor.

As I make my way to the elevator, my pulse rate slows. Unfortunately, the boulder in my stomach remains. I have a feeling it will reside there until she leaves.

A few minutes later, I pay for my coffee and an oatmeal raisin cookie. Zentello's cafeteria is more like a coffee shop-bistro combo. It beats walking to the deli on the corner, which I do when I need to get out of the building. But today, this will do.

Usually, I take my food to my desk. Not today, with Hildy up there.

I sit, staring at my purchases. Which comes first—the coffee or the cookie?

Alphabetical order sounds like a good way to decide. I take a sip, wince, and swallow. Maybe I shouldn't have bypassed the cream and sugar.

Bradley Zimmer walks up, carrying a coffee. He's wearing a lab coat like mine and underneath I see a tie. It's not some weird color combo or pattern like he used to wear. Christina has been a boon for his fashion sense and his smiling face. He looks happier and brighter and so much less tense.

"Mind if I join you?" he asks.

I motion to the seat across from me. "Feel free."

He sits and takes a sip. "I learned something new."

Bradley is a gamer who prides himself on being a fount of knowledge. He's such a great guy no one has the heart to tell him the knowledge is mainly worthless. "What's that?"

"So you know how people celebrate Christmas in July?"

People? More like a movie channel and big-box retailers. "Yeah."

"Well, the Hallmark Channel has a big celebration, but that got me thinking last month."

"About the Hallmark Channel?"

"No, Norway."

I'm sure this non sequitur makes sense to him somehow. "What about Norway?"

"*God Jul i Juli.*" He bursts out laughing.

I must be missing something, so I take a bite of my cookie.

Bradley raises his glasses and wipes his eyes. "Isn't that hilarious?"

I know a little Latin, and I had three years of Spanish in high school, but I've never been to Norway nor felt called to learn the language. Though I've seen photos of Norwegian Forest cats and those look like some badass felines. "I don't speak Norwegian."

"Oh right." Bradley leans forward. "*Juli* is the word for July."

"Makes sense."

"And *Jul* means Christmas." He chuckles as if cracking himself up. "So *Jul i Juli* means Christmas in July. It's almost the same word twice. I just added the '*god*' for Merry Christmas in July. Isn't that hilarious?"

I laugh, but mainly at him because he's so pleased with this piece of worthless knowledge. "What did Christina think?"

"She laughed, but I think she was humoring me. Sophie and Max thought it was brilliant." Bradley uses a British accent to say that last word. "Oh, and Ruby cracked up."

"Ruby is Christina's friend."

"Best friend." Bradley smacks his forehead. "That reminds me. Do you want to go out with Ruby? Christina thinks the two of you would be a good fit. We can double so it's not an uncomfortable blind date."

"Will you be able to keep your hands off your fiancée during the date? Because if you're making out the entire time that will be even more uncomfortable."

"We can control ourselves over dinner." Bradley winks. "So it's a yes?"

I imagine Hildy with Nate ... "I'm in."

The moment the words are out, I want to take them back. I don't date, but it's not like I had to do much for this one. Still, if Ruby is around the same age as Christina, that means she's a decade younger than me. Maybe more.

"I thought I'd have to work harder," Bradley admits, then takes a sip. "But you'll have a good time with her."

I want to bring up the age gap, but Bradley's eight years older than Christina, and they're doing fine. I shouldn't assume I won't have anything in common with a woman that much younger than me. It's not like Hildy is my age ...

Fuck, here I go again.

Bradley's eyes narrow behind his glasses. "What's that face for?"

"Nate hired Hildy to help me with the data. And they're engaged."

Bradley's jaw drops. His wide eyes tell me he's as shocked as I was. That surprises me because he and Nate are best friends now. "No, that's not possible."

"Which part?"

He rubs his chin. "Both."

At least it's not just me. "They showed up in my office, and she's sporting a huge rock on her ring finger. Nate told me they were engaged."

"What about Zelda?"

I shrug. "I didn't ask, and no one mentioned her."

Bradley shakes his head. "Nate's crazy about Zelda. All he talks about is what'll happen when they get back together. I don't know her side of the situation, but how he makes goo-goo eyes at her is almost pathetic. She doesn't seem to mind the attention."

I can tell Bradley is trying to make sense of the senseless. Been there, done that. Still makes no sense. "I have no idea what's going on, but if you learn anything ..."

"You'll be the first to know." Bradley rubs his forehead. "I'm sorry, man. It's gotta bite with them hooking up after the divorce."

At least he understands. "It does, but what am I going to do?"

Though getting black-out drunk tonight sounds like a good option.

"I'll see if I can get the date with Ruby set up for sooner rather than later. You need a distraction. Fuck. A million of them if you have to work with your ex."

I don't have many friends. Okay, I have none, unless you count the young woman that I've mentored for the past three years. I'm not kidding about being a hermit, but I do get along with Bradley and our other colleague, Max Goodall. All of us worked on the original Happy Pill project that became Orchid. We've gone out for drinks a couple of times over the past two years, but that's it. I have no family. None of my foster families kept in touch with me once I aged out, so I'm grateful for Bradley right now. Fucking grateful. "Thanks."

I eat more of my cookie. I'm not sure if it's the sugar or Bradley that made me feel better, but I'll take it.

Bradley downs the rest of his coffee. "I'm going to swing by the twenty-second floor on my way back. Nate mentioned a meeting with Mr. Z today."

I straighten. Mr. Z is the other CEO of Zentello. I spoke to him via speakerphone during my interview. He was flying somewhere, and his voice was so garbled I could barely hear him. Nate says Mr. Z is a bit eccentric and obsessive about privacy. That's fine, but I would prefer knowing the people I work for rather than a blurry photo with a two-sentence bio on the company website.

"Mr. Z is here today?" That would explain why Nate raced out of my office without saying a word. I thought he might be nervous I'd deck him.

"Yes, and I'd like to get a glimpse of him. And find out more about Nate and Hildy's engagement."

"I'd rather keep my distance from Nate, but I hope you catch Mr. Z. Sometimes I wonder if he even exists."

"Given the way those reporters tried to blackmail me to find out more about him, I'm sure he does. While I would have enjoyed telling them that he was made-up, if that were the case, I'm sure Nate would have told me."

I snicker. That comes naturally whenever I think of Nate Lowe. "You have more faith in the guy than I do."

Bradley stares into his coffee cup, then looks at me. "You know, I always hoped the two of you would be able to repair your friendship, but now ... that won't be happening."

"Nope." Nate knows more about me than anyone else,

including Hildy. Maybe that's why what he did hurts so much. Yes, it still hurts, which is why I act like a total dick to him. Of course, he deserves that. I'd trusted the asshole with my deepest, darkest secret. I'd also shared with him how much I hadn't wanted to get a divorce. I'd even shown him the list of how I would change.

He fucked Hildy anyway.

Bradley adjusts his glasses. "You going to stick around?"

A valid question, given I thought about quitting earlier. If Hildy had stopped watching my every move in the office, I might've typed up my resignation, but she kept sneaking glances at me, so I had to put that on the back burner. Then I remembered my end-of-project bonus and realized I was stuck here.

"At least until I have the data verified."

Once that happens, a huge payout will be mine. I had that written into my contract because I knew working with Nate would be difficult and more than a salary would be needed to keep me there. Turns out, I was spot-on and would need that even more with Hildy here.

Think about the money.

The bonus will allow me to go wherever my next job happens to be. Oh, I love Seattle, and I own a small house here, but I'm willing to go wherever I need to for my career. I'd been satisfied with my stable government job, which allowed me to do research, but this job at Zentello has shown me what's possible. It's the stepping-stone to a more prosperous and lucrative career. Once I catapult into the next level, I won't ever glance back at this place. I'll be laughing all the way to the bank. I can't wait.

"Glad to hear it." Bradley sounds relieved. "We need you to see this through."

"I will." Even if spending all day with Hildy will be like another Formics attack in *Ender's Game*. "I'm not a quitter."

I'm not, but something in me needs reminding of that.

Bradley smiles at me. "I should get back to work."

"Me, too."

"Good luck with Hildy."

"Hope you see Mr. Z."

He takes off, and I throw my cup and napkin away. Some people leave their trash for the cafeteria workers to clean up, but I worked food service all through college. Sometimes two jobs at a time. Three during the summers to pay my way through school. I figure cleaning up after myself is the least I can do because I know how hard they work and, often, for minimum wage.

When I get back to my office, Hildy sits at my desk, looking at my computer. "What the hell are you doing?"

She glances up before returning her attention to the screen.

"Okay, so you're ignoring me now, is that it?" I ask.

"Nope. I'm concentrating on classifying another sample of data."

"How did you get that?" I rush to my desk. "I didn't send anything more to you."

"No, you didn't." She continues to study my screen. "You really should change your password."

Dammit! My password is still Sorento1113—our honeymoon destination and the date of our wedding. Why am I such a stupid idiot?

I shrug. "It's easy to remember the worst day of my life."

She snorts and then makes a clicking noise, the noise she makes when pretending to concentrate. I haven't forgotten that sound. I still remember what her tells are. Her body. What she likes and dislikes. "Don't pretend you're concentrating. And don't ever log onto my computer again."

"Like I said, change your password." She turns in my chair and stares at me. "There's something quite interesting about this data."

God, she's annoying with her perky little smile like she knows something I don't. "How long are you going to be working here?"

"Two weeks and then I'm starting a new job elsewhere."

"Wow," I say brightly. "Two whole weeks to hang out with the man you ran away from and haven't spoken to, bar a few badly worded emails more than five years ago."

"Oh, you got those, did you?" She smirks. "Some of my finest work. Admittedly, I might have rambled at times, but in essence, they said everything that needed to be said."

"Yes, I think the dozens of pages in each one testified to that. I didn't know you knew such words. I thought you were a lady."

Smiling, I motion her out of my chair. Surprisingly, she stands without any fuss. I sit, go to my computer settings, and change my password. Okay, I only change the first o in Sorento to a zero, but at least she'll struggle to log in if she tries again.

"Okay," I say once I finish. "What do you find so interesting about the data? If it's the end score variation in the women aged between forty and fifty-eight, then it's already been identified.

We've discovered Orchid's results change in menopausal women."

"Nope, it's not that." As she leans over to reach my keyboard, her breasts brush my arm. Clothing separates us, but a bolt of heat rushes through me. I bite my tongue and concentrate on the computer screen to keep from getting another hard-on.

She types something, and my email inbox appears. "Take a look at what I sent you while you were on break."

I open the email and read it. She's spotted a correlation in the results of a group of six women who all had breast surgery, either cosmetic or medical. Only two results, but she's correct. They are the same for all six women.

Like I said, annoying. Research data isn't even her forte, but she's a math wizard.

"You're right," I admit begrudgingly. "It's probably something you should examine further."

She grins at me with her head tilted to one side.

"What?" I ask.

"T-h-a-n-k y-o-u," she spells out slowly. "I believe those are the words you're looking for."

"I'm not going to thank you for doing your job," I scoff. "I would have found that."

"But the point is, you didn't, and it took me"—she glances at her wristwatch, and I can't help but notice it's the one I bought her on our first anniversary—"less than a hundred and twenty minutes to find it."

The watch is a chunky silver bracelet and not the Rolex I'd wanted to get her but couldn't afford. I'd thought she only pretended to like it to be nice. Six months later, I got the job as head of research at that government agency. I offered to replace the watch once we had some disposable cash, but Hildy said no. Once again, I thought she was trying to prove a point. Seeing that watch on her wrist makes me wonder if I'd been an idiot even then.

I push the memories to the back of my mind. "Well, aren't you clever?"

"In some aspects of life, I am." She smiles. "Others, like the choice of life partners, not so much."

"I know that feeling." Standing, I slip off my lab coat, seeing as I won't be visiting the lab while she's in my office, and return to my chair to sit.

"Nice tie by the way," she says. "I knew it would match the pocket square."

"You know me so well, Hildy. It's almost like we were married once."

"God forbid," she mutters.

"God never had anything to do with it. Maybe the devil had a hand. But at least the state of Washington saw fit to dissolve the marriage. And I'll be forever grateful for that."

She blinks. Once, twice. And sits and turns so I can no longer see her face. No doubt she's gloating.

Two weeks.

How hard will it be to survive the next fourteen days with her? A part of me doesn't even want to know.

CHAPTER 5

HILDY

Hearing Sam talk about our divorce as if it's the best thing that's ever happened to him cuts deep. I sit at the other desk and stare at the monitor, hoping he can't see me. Not that I'd be able to tell because unshed tears blur my vision.

Damn him.

Okay, I'm the one who filed, but a part of me did it as a last-ditch effort to make him realize we as a married couple were in trouble, that all the times I'd asked him to work less and spend more time together hadn't been me blowing smoke up his ass. It had been my sheer and utter desperation.

They say children of alcoholics often find themselves in a similar situation with a significant other. My dad wasn't a drinker, but he ignored me and my sister as much as possible. Funny, or maybe not so funny, how I fell in love with a man who ignored me, too. I held on to us way longer than I should've trying to get Sam to see I didn't care about his job title or salary. That all I wanted was for my husband to want to be with me. His "soon" and "almost there" never stopped, year after year, until I couldn't take it. Strike that. I didn't want to take it after growing up the way I had.

Oh shit. I'm crying.

Ugh. For the past five years, I've focused on being independent. I don't need a man for anything. Any guy who comes into my life is for pleasure only, though I can take care of my own sexual needs, too.

Which is why I hate that I've been reduced to tears. I don't even know where the restroom is. That leaves me one option.

I need to fake sneeze.

Ka-choo.

I do another for extra measure. Now I have a reason to grab a tissue out of my purse. That will allow me to blow my nose and wipe my eyes surreptitiously. If I was anywhere else, I'd say fuck it and not care that I was emotional, but with Sam …

I can't let him see me like this. He'll know …

Too much about how he can still get to me.

"You okay?" Sam asks to my surprise.

"Probably allergies." I used to get them when I lived in Seattle, so chances are if I stick around, I'll have to deal with them again. I grab the travel pack of tissues and clean myself up. *Goodbye, tears.*

I hate that after all these years, Sam Grant can still make me cry. I thought I'd be indifferent to him by now. "Being back in the Pacific Northwest after so long away must be the reason."

"The bathroom off the lab might have some allergy pills."

Not trusting my voice, I nod. "I'm going to take my afternoon break now."

He nods.

I suppose that's better than him telling me to get the hell out of there.

Trying to backtrack the route I'd taken earlier to Sam's office, I eventually make it to Nate's floor after only a couple of wrong turns. Zelda sits at her desk in the outer office, reading something on her computer screen with a worried expression.

"Hey, Zelda." I try to keep my voice steady, but I'm not sure if I succeed. "Is Nate in?"

Her gaze shoots to me and narrows. "He is. Is everything okay?"

I shrug and wipe my eyes with my hands.

Zelda's eyes widen. "Is that an engagement ring?"

"Uh, yes."

"Who's the lucky guy?" She sounds pleased, which surprises me given her chilly reception earlier. But her question suggests Nate hasn't spoken to her like he said he would.

My throat clogs. "Uh ..."

She leans forward, visibly curious. "Who? I won't tell."

"Nate."

Her face falls, and her shoulders slump. I half expect her to fall back in her chair and faint. "Nate Lowe?" she asks in a ragged voice that I struggle to hear.

"Um, yes." I try to hide the ring, but even if I turn the diamond away, the band still shows. "He said he was going to talk to you about it."

"He hasn't." Her words are staccato sharp and full of hurt. If I wondered whether she cared about Nate, I have my answer. And I feel even worse now than I did after what Sam said earlier.

This is why I never want to have another relationship. Hookups and casual sex are the only way to go. I am an island.

The Isle of Hildy has a nice ring to it. "So Nate ..."

Zelda straightens. She doesn't smile, but she's not frowning either. "He's in his office. I'll tell him you're on your way."

"I'm sorry" sits on the edge of my lips, but would Nate's fiancée apologize to his ex-wife for being engaged? Except we're not really engaged, and this is just getting far too complicated. "Thank you."

Seconds later, the door slides open. Nate sits behind his desk. He stands and waves me in.

As soon as the door closes behind me, I slump. I open my mouth to speak, but nothing comes out.

Nate comes closer and touches my face. "You've been crying."

I swallow around the lump in my throat. "You didn't tell Zelda we're engaged. She asked about my ring ..."

"I meant to, but I got busy. I'll take care of it."

"She's upset."

"So are you, and I don't think it's because of Zelda." Nate's voice softens. "What happened?"

"Sam doesn't want to work with me."

"Too bad."

"I don't want to work with him."

"You signed a contract and are getting paid a lot of money."

Which Mathilda needs. "I know, but Sam's angry and bitter. It's more than I expected."

"I know he's difficult, but I need your help."

I want to tell Nate I'm going to New Zealand early and how badly my sister needs the money. But he's a businessman, and my nephew's treatments won't sway him. I do have something else I can say ...

"I logged on to his computer when he took his afternoon break. He's still using the same password."

"Let me guess, it's *password*."

"No, but I think that was his back in the day. Anyway, there's nothing sketchy there. It's so organized I would've been able to tell if something was off. You're barking up the wrong tree. Sam's not the mole."

"It's your first day with him. Surely, you couldn't do an exhaustive search."

"I know him. He wouldn't sell you out, even though he seems to hate your guts. Why is that?"

Nate half shrugs. "You haven't seen Sam in more than five years. People change."

"Not him."

"He's at Zentello now."

"That is a surprise."

"So maybe you don't know him as well as you think."

"He's innocent, which is why I propose you let me work remotely."

"I need you with Sam."

"He's not the mole." My voice is firm.

"I disagree."

"Then find someone else to be with him during the day. This will drive me crazy."

"You're almost through the first day. You're only here for two weeks, and two of those days fall over a weekend."

My shoulders sag. "You're really going to hold me to this?"

"You signed a contract. Unless you want to cancel it? In which case, you won't be paid."

"No." The word shoots out as if it's propelled by a particle accelerator. "That's not necessary."

I won't mess up my sister's life. Dad already did that when he gave her baby daddy a job after they started dating. To no one's surprise, Dad promoted him after the jerk broke up with a pregnant Mathilda. Now, two of his daughters' exes work for the company, and both are dating women our dad introduced them to.

Thanks, Werner.

At least Sam hasn't been offered a job there, but I think that has more to do with it being a finance company rather than something science-based.

Nate holds my hand. "Sam is a hard man to take. I'd tell him to fuck off if I didn't need him. The same way I need you. There's no one else I trust to do this for me."

I don't want to believe Nate. "So it doesn't matter that it's impossible for me to work with him? To sit only feet away from the man who broke my fucking heart." I suck in a breath, trying to swallow all the emotion the past ten minutes had brought with it.

Nate places an arm around my shoulder.

"I'm sorry the situation upsets you, Hildy, I really am, but I'm desperate." He takes a deep breath. "It's just two weeks. Ten days since you don't have to work weekends, though Sam usually does."

I half laugh because that sounds so much like Sam. He would have slept at the lab more than he did if I hadn't demanded he come home.

"I swear to you, if you still want to go after that, you can."

I frown, not understanding what he means. If I still want to go? Of course, I'll still want to go. My dream job awaits me in New Zealand.

"And since I wasn't exactly up front about what you'd be doing, I'll double what I said I'd pay you."

I'm glad Nate's arm is still around me, or I might've collapsed. The money is so important for Flynn's care, but ... "It's not about the money."

I mean, it sort of is, but that isn't the reason now.

"I know, I know, but I'm not good at the emotional stuff. That's Zelda's thing." Nate shrugs. "Which is probably why she divorced me."

"It wasn't Sam's thing either." I see the same pain in Nate's eyes that I often see in mine when I allow myself to think about my failed marriage. Nate's suffering. Sam's suffering. Zelda is suffering now too. We're all suffering, and sometimes you have to do whatever you can to survive. I need to leave to survive, but Mathilda and Flynn need me to stay. So I'll do what I need to, even if it hurts.

"Two weeks, Nate. Double my fee. If I don't have the information you need by then, well, you'll have to find help elsewhere, because I'll be on my way to New Zealand."

"Deal."

"And talk to Zelda today about the fake engagement," I add because that's the right thing to do. "Or I will."

He gives me a single nod and a sad smile, and I leave his office to return to hell. Back to the man who hadn't loved me enough to fight *for* our marriage but hated me enough to fight *about* it. And there's no doubt in my mind he still hates me.

Maybe even more than he did before.

I hurry to the elevator and when I reach the correct floor, I head to Sam's office. Walking in front of me is a guy pushing a cart of mail. Then I see Bradley coming toward me, with a big smile on his face.

"Sam told me you're now working here," he says, surprisingly pleasant given he chose Sam's side after the divorce. Based on his friendly tone, one would almost think we're back to being in the same social circle.

"Yes, for the next two weeks. I'm helping with the data analysis."

"Well, it's good to see you."

Not knowing what to say, I nod. "I have to get back."

I hurry away before Bradley can reply. I'm not sure whether my badge will open Sam's door, but I give it a try. The door whooshes open, so Nate must have added me to the access list. I know my ex-husband hasn't. Speaking of which, Sam's at his desk when I enter. I expect the silent treatment again, so I don't make eye contact. I take my seat and pull up my data set.

"Have a nice break?" Sam asks.

His question surprises me. I'm not sure what game he's playing with me, given he was never into video games. We would play the occasional board game but that often led to an argument because I wanted to win at all costs. I still do.

I realize, however, if I wait any longer to answer him, he might think I'm ignoring him the way he did me. I've never believed in tit for tat or quid pro quo. Besides, the more hospitable I can be, the better these two weeks should be. At least in theory.

"It was lovely." I use my cheeriest tone. That isn't hard to do when I can't wait to text Mathilda about the additional money coming her way. Knowing my sister and nephew will be set for a while will help me survive the next two weeks. As Nate mentioned, it's only ten working days. "Did you find anything more in the data?"

"No, but I've been reviewing various profiles to see if I can find a similar correlation to what you discovered."

"If you haven't already set up a group for those who've had the BRCA gene test, that would be the best next step."

"That's"—Sam rubs his lips together—"a fabulous suggestion. Thank you."

I wonder how hard it was for him to say those last two words, but I'll take them. "You're welcome."

He rubs the back of his neck. "If you need any more data, let me know."

I nod and turn back to my laptop. "I will."

And so we reach a strained level of peace for the next couple of hours. It's better than the cut-the-tension-with-a-machete atmospheric tension we had earlier.

Suddenly, he turns off his desktop computer and stands.

"Where are you going?" I ask.

"I'm leaving for the day," he announces without even glancing my way.

I check the time, and it's only three o'clock. *Huh*? The Sam I know would no sooner leave work at this hour than streak naked down Pike Street. I wonder if maybe it has something to do with his date tonight, and my stomach churns, even though what he does has no effect on me. At least it shouldn't. I force myself not to pick at the wound in my chest. "Going on your date so soon?"

"Nope." He picks up a folder and puts it inside a walnut-colored leather bag. I glimpse his laptop in there, but he didn't use that today.

"Just goofing off for the rest of the day then?"

"Something like that."

No, this is definitely not the Sam I remember, and if he's not going on his date, I'm glad, though I have no logical explanation for feeling that way. Nor do I plan on revisiting the thought later.

There has to be a reason he's leaving now … Oh shit. What if he's meeting someone to pass on details about Orchid? What if he is, as Nate suggested, the mole?

My head reels. "Do you have a meeting?"

Sam stops packing his things away and pins me with a stare. "What's with the twenty questions?"

I shrug. That'll make me look nonchalant and not desperate for answers. "Nothing, just curious."

"Don't be, because my life isn't any of your concern."

Wow, and doesn't that comment hurt like a bitch. But all I can do is pull up my big-girl panties and recover from the barb, which I do. "It's just not like you."

"You don't know what I'm like anymore, Hildy. You stopped having a right to know anything when you walked out on me."

He picks up his bag, grabs his jacket, and disappears, leaving me to wonder what the hell has gotten into him.

Maybe Nate's right. Maybe Sam is the mole because I don't know who the fuck he is anymore.

CHAPTER 6

SAM

I am a coward, point of fact.

Walking out of work in the middle of the day is not what I do. I've never done that on any day in my working life. I'm the man who turns the lights off on the way out because I'm the last one there. Max Goodall used to stay longer, but now he tries not to work as much thanks to his wife, Sophie. Bradley would also work late, but he no longer does now that he has Christina.

Me? I do not leave early, ever.

The reason I did today ... Hildy. I can't risk being in the same room with her for any longer. When she walked in after her break, I couldn't stop noticing the sway of her hips or the stretch of her lab coat over her breasts. I've always been a boob man, and hers are spectacular. Albeit off-limits, but my dick missed that memo.

I should probably go home and jerk off. After hearing Ashton Lowe, Nate's brother, mention the fleshlight Chloe mistakenly gave him for Christmas, I ordered myself one. Sometimes a hand gets tired. Whatever works, and it's been a long dry spell for me.

Unfortunately, masturbation is nothing like the real thing.

I miss sex. I really miss sex with Hildy. We had issues in every part of our marriage except one—the bedroom. Despite our divorce, I still want her under me, still want to be inside her, and I have no clue how to handle it. Hence leaving work early and buying myself a stiff drink.

I enter the one place I've been for drinks after work, take a seat at the bar, and order. "I'll have an IPA, Eli."

A draft beer from a local brewery isn't that stiff, but it's what sounds good at this hour.

"Coming right up, Sam." Eli is a young guy, smart, with only a few classes to go until he gets his degree, but his uncle owns this place and is in poor health, so Eli runs the place now and school has to wait. I wonder if he'll ever go back to college, but that's up to him. "Where are your friends?"

He means Max and Bradley. I suppose colleagues qualify as friends. And Bradley was a former friend. We lost track of each other until I started working at Zentello. "Work. I took off early."

"That's not like you." Eli fills a pint glass, tipping it just right to minimize the head. "You're not like some of the regular day drinkers who come in here."

"It's my first time day drinking." I'm not even one for mimosas or Bloody Marys at brunch. Mainly because I'm not the kind of person who gets invited to do brunch. It doesn't seem like a meal you go out for on your own. "Had a rough day, so I thought I deserved to skip out early and treat myself to a beer on my way home."

"Hope this helps take the edge off."

"Thanks." I have a feeling only a full lobotomy will do that.

The pint arrives quickly enough, and I take a sip. This brand has a bit more of a hoppy taste, but I must admit it hits the spot, way more than another coffee would. One sip follows another until the glass is half empty.

Do I really want to get drunk tonight?

Yes, I think I do.

I'm not one for drinking alone, but who am I going to call? Bradley and Max? Both are still at work. Tonight, they'll be at home. They are too in love to choose a spontaneous drinking night with the guys over spending the evening with the women they love. Not that I blame them.

I miss having someone to go home to.

But being here helps.

Music plays in the background while the din and movements of the other patrons keep me from feeling so alone. But it doesn't ease the pain in my chest. The spot where my heart should be hurts, and I'm not sure what will cure that other than numbing myself with alcohol.

I take another sip.

This bar might be my new stomping ground for the next two weeks. I get the feeling I'll be driven to drink heavily for the next thirteen days. Unless ...

Can I take an impromptu vacation? Hell, a staycation would work. Zentello owes me so many hours for the PTO I've built up, it's probably illegal. And then I remember Orchid.

Fuck. The data can't wait. That means I can't go away. My liver will just have to pay the price. A good thing the damage won't be permanent once I stop drinking.

Bottoms up.

Not quite, but I take another drink.

My cell phone buzzes with a text notification.

I glance at my screen.

Bradley: *I spoke with Christina who talked to Ruby. We're on for the double-date. How does tomorrow at seven o'clock sound?*

Sam: *Looking forward to it.*

Bradley: *Ruby is too. You made Christina's day, which makes mine, so thank you.*

Sam: *Anything to help the cause. Did you catch you-know-who?*

Bradley: *Just missed him, but I learned one tidbit of info.*

Sam: *Spill …*

Bradley: *He drinks his coffee black.*

Sam: *I prefer mine that way too.*

Bradley: *Well, that's more than we knew yesterday.*

Sam: *True.*

Bradley: *I'm going to figure this out.*

Sam: *If anyone can, it's you.*

Bradley: *Appreciate the vote of confidence. Oh, and Nate implied things with Hildy are new. Hope that helps.*

It doesn't, but I appreciate Bradley's help. Still, I couldn't help but wonder how "new" could it be if they're engaged?

"Another beer, Sam?" Eli asks.

The fleshlight can wait, though if I drink too much, I won't be able to use it. "Yeah, one more please."

Two beers are a nice even number. I have nothing to drink

at home except bottled water, but I can swing by the corner market and grab a six-pack or a fifth of something.

"Sam, really, you left work to drink beer?"

I groan and close my eyes, hoping I'm only imagining Hildy standing beside me with the most judgmental expression ever.

Please let my imagination have suddenly run rampant.

Opening one eye, I turn on my stool.

Fuck, she's really here. I've only had one beer so I'm fully sober. No mind tricks happening. I open the other eye. "What are you doing here?"

"Looking for you."

Her nonchalant tone belies the way her gaze darts around the place as if she's looking for something.

I have no idea what that might be, but I'm pissed. All I wanted is some distance ... and a drink. "How did you know where to find me?"

She shrugs, but guilt flashes across her face.

And then it hits me. She doesn't know my usual haunts. Not that I really have any usual places, more occasional ones, like this place. "You followed me."

Hildy's sheepish smile confirms the truth, but once again, she says nothing.

I imagine her hiding in vestibules as I made my way to the bar. I can't believe my ex-wife would do that, yet here she is.

Why?

We never had the kind of relationship where I ever felt the need to check her phone or not trust what she said. I probably shouldn't have been as trusting as I was, but we're no longer together. What I do doesn't affect her at all. "Why did you follow me?"

"You ran out of your office like a bat out of hell."

That's not a reason. I raise a brow. "So?"

"I was ..."

"Nosy."

"Concerned," she says a beat later. "And given where we are, my instincts were on point."

She really is a pain in the ass. I take a sip of beer, trying to ignore her.

Hildy sits on the stool next to me. "I'll take one of those too, please."

Eli places the beer in front of Hildy and winks. The little fucker will be getting a beer over his head if he keeps that up.

Hildy tilts her head to watch him pour me another beer. "Cute."

"Too young for you. He's practically a child."

She snorts and then lifts her glass to take a sip. "You haven't answered me."

"About what?"

"Did you really leave work to come to a bar? Because if you did, I'm seriously worried about you. Do you have a problem with alcohol?"

"If you're asking if I'm an alcoholic, the answer is no. I'm not."

"This is considered day drinking. You could have a problem."

I look her up and down. "I do have a problem. You."

Hildy laughs, and Eli places the new pint in front of me.

"Is the lady's beer on your tab, Sam?" Eli asks.

I pause. Why the hell not? "Sure."

He grins at Hildy, and my hand clutches the glass of beer. I desperately fight the urge to toss the contents at him. When she turns in her seat to face me, Eli takes the hint because he moves farther down the bar to the book he has open. I'm glad he has enough downtime during his shift to read, even if he stopped taking his college classes for now.

"I'm the reason you're drinking?" she asks, sounding uneasy.

"The one and only reason." I take a long sip. Funny, the beer doesn't taste as good with her here.

"That's no reason at all. Are you supposed to be meeting someone?" Hildy glances around. "Because I can go if you are."

I have no fucking clue how her mind works. "Why would I meet someone at three in the afternoon in a bar?"

"Well, why would you even be in a bar at three in the afternoon?"

I breathe heavily, not sure what to say. "I told you. I'm here because of you."

That might not be the politest thing to say, but it's the truth. Every single bad mood, every day I've spent miserable, every regret I've had is because of her. I'm in this fucking bar because of her. And here she is too.

Fuck my life.

"I just need a break." I try to keep any emotion out of my voice, even though I want to yell. "I've been putting in long hours with the project."

She studies me for a second or two. "It must be hard, being

responsible for whether things continue or not. I mean it's your decision, isn't it? Once you've studied all the data, *you're* the one who has to say yes or no to the project."

I frown. "That's no different from any of the others I've worked on."

She knows the nature of what I do because she's in the same line of business. We'd talked about my job when we were married. She also complained about what I did or rather how much time I spent working.

"I know." She watches her finger slide around the rim of her glass. "But this is a prestigious commercial project. No staid government ones. It's top secret too, so a whole lot of pressure must come with that. Pressure that might push you to make strange decisions."

What the hell is she getting at? Does she really think I have a drinking problem?

"Hildy, I have no idea what you're trying to say, but I don't have an *alcohol use disorder*. I promise you after this beer I probably won't have another drink until the weekend, if then. Sometimes I go out with Bradley and another one of our colleagues after work on Fridays, but only sometimes. It's not every week even." That's because both have significant others, and I'm alone. Sucks to be me in so many ways. I take a sip.

"Nate?"

It's all I can do not to spew the mouthful of beer at that. I swallow. "I'd never do anything socially with Nate. The other person is Max Goodall."

"Your being here drinking just seems odd, that's all."

She narrows her gaze on me, and it feels a little too intense.

I take another long drink of my beer and then slam the glass on the bar. Beer remains, but I don't want any more. The last thing I need is for her to tell Nate I'm a drunk and need an intervention. God, that would be a nightmare almost worse than the one I'm currently living with Hildy.

"I'm going home," I announce.

Hildy stiffens. She glances around as if surprised. "What? I just got here. If you're supposed to be meeting someone, I can go."

"No." I stand, not caring that she sounds upset. Once again, I remind myself she's not my problem. "How many times do I have to tell you I'm not meeting anyone? If I were going on a date, I wouldn't arrange it for the middle of the day."

She draws in a breath. "We used to meet up in the middle of the day."

For sex. My heart thuds in my chest. I remember meeting at our apartment during lunch breaks because we were desperate for each other. Early in the relationship, I'd surprise Hildy with a picnic lunch in the park. Or feign dentist and doctor appointments because we couldn't stand the idea of not seeing each other before we got off work.

The memories and her being next to me are all too much. This is exactly why I'd left the office, and why I must leave now.

I lean in closer. "Ask Nate for your own office."

Her big brown eyes stare up at me through her lashes, and her lips part on a small breath. She looks so damn beautiful my hand goes to the back of her head. I pull her close but stop because one kiss will lead to many more. I would *need* so much more than to only taste her lips. When her eyes flutter close, I regain a semblance of reality.

This is my ex-wife, who is engaged to my boss. Kissing her or touching her is a really bad idea. The worst.

Back away, Grant. Now!

I let my hand drop, pull out two twenties, and toss them onto the bar. That should cover the drinks and a tip. If not, I'll make it up to Eli the next time I'm here. "I have to go."

I turn and walk away.

"You can't keep running out on me, Sam," she calls from behind me.

I stop walking and take a breath before turning back to her. "Just following your lead, Hildy. Just following your lead."

CHAPTER 7

HILDY

I arrive at Zentello bright and early the following morning. Sam's parting shot at me last night at the bar kept streaming through my mind, but I slept fine. I always sleep fine. My brain understands it needs sleep, so I never have to worry about that, even under the most stressful conditions. But I woke up realizing something.

Sam has changed.

I thought Sam Grant would never change, but he has and not in a good way. He used to work nonstop, but he was still pleasant and caring. Now, he's all grouchy and grumpy. Something happened to him since we divorced. I wonder if Nate knows what.

But I don't have time to ponder my ex-husband. I need to channel Mata Hari and get to spying. That's what I do for the next hour, but so far, I haven't found anything to point toward him being Orchid's mole.

At least Sam's ethics haven't appeared to change.

But Nate's paying me, so I can't give up yet.

Glancing at the time, I realize my window of opportunity to snoop around Sam's office is ending. It's almost seven, and

Sam will arrive soon. That is, if he keeps the same hours he used to. Seven thirty in the morning until eight at night or longer. I'll never forget because I was the one waiting at home for him. That means I have half an hour.

The filing cabinet provided zilch, so I open his desk drawer. Only an old science magazine and a packet of gum are inside. I didn't even know Sam chewed gum. He used to hate the stuff, so who knows what that's doing there? I try the next drawer, but it's locked.

Could this be a sign that Sam's the mole?

Or does he keep his desk locked for personal reasons?

Two questions I need answers to. Because questions for questions' sake don't prove anything.

My gut still tells me Sam isn't the one I'm looking for. He acts too flustered around me to be some sort of corporate spy mastermind. Even though I'm sure his actions yesterday had more to do with our history than anything else, Sam is also a loyal man. At least he was to me and his other job, and I can't see him having a reason *not* to show loyalty to Zentello. Whatever his beef with Nate is, Sam prides himself on his work, and I don't believe even my friendship with Nate would cloud that for Sam. He might be my ex, but he's not that kind of guy.

I go over to a cabinet against the far wall and try the handle. Not locked. Thank goodness. I open the door, hoping to find something, but all I see are reams of copy paper and office supplies. This would be the perfect place to hide documents or whatever else could be passed on to a reporter. I must know for sure so I take out things and place them on the floor.

The door whooshes open.

"Shit." He's early, and I'm kneeling on the floor with my back to the door.

"What on earth are you doing?" Sam asks from behind me. "And why are you here so early?"

Taking a deep breath, I glance over my shoulder and plaster on a smile. "Oh, good morning. I couldn't sleep so I decided to come into work early."

"And empty the storage cabinet?"

"I was looking for a pen, and it's a little unorganized." I put everything back and hope Sam accepts my explanation.

When he moves to his desk and doesn't say anything else, I think he's accepted my explanation. I close the cabinet door.

"Why are you really poking around in the cabinet?" he asks. "Don't lie. I know you've been checking my desk drawer too."

My curiosity gets the best of me. "How the hell do you know that?"

"The gum was on top of the magazine. Now it isn't."

Whoa. Talk about attention to detail. Unfortunately, he's correct, so what can I say? I finish putting everything into the cabinet. That's the least I can do, right?

I also need to do some damage control over his stupid gum being moved and the mess I've made. "Like I said, I was looking for a pen. When you didn't have one, I went to the storage cabinet, which is really unorganized. You should work on that."

"Why are you here before me?" he demands. "I don't buy the fact that you couldn't sleep. You could have the weight of the world on your shoulders, and you'd still sleep like a log."

Shit, he's right. What the hell do I say? My mind swirls with something plausible.

"It's you," I blurt. "You've got me all riled up because you're being a coward."

"Me?"

"Yes, you. Who else would I be talking about?"

"I'm not a coward." He pulls his chair closer to his desk and unpacks his bag. First out, his laptop and a file.

He's lying to himself. I know because his nose twitches and his earlobes are pink, the same color they turn when he tells a big old lie.

I'm determined not to let him off the hook. "You leaned into me last night."

"I have wax in my ears; it causes balance issues."

I snort. "Liar. You clean your ears every night after you've showered."

"Well, maybe in the five years since you left me, I've changed my habits."

His earlobes go pink again. The argument also seems to have diverted his attention from the fact I've been snooping— mission accomplished.

"Doubtful." I scoff and hope I appear affronted. "You definitely leaned in for the kiss and then pulled away."

"Well, you do have a fiancé."

"You knew that going in."

He shrugs. "If you want the truth, the smell of garlic on your breath was too much to stand. I needed to breathe."

I glare at him because he knows I have a phobia about my breath smelling badly, which is why I carry those mini-toothbrushes and a mouthwash spray in my purse. Yes, I'm a bit obsessive about dental cleanliness.

"No," I snap, knowing my breath smells minty fresh since I've had nothing to eat or drink since brushing my teeth after waking up. "I didn't have any garlic yesterday. You wanted to kiss me and were being a coward about it."

He shakes his head. "So delusional, Hildegard. Like I said, balance issues. Although, if I did consider it, and I promise you that I didn't, it would have been the alcohol to blame."

"You weren't drunk, and you know it. And don't call me Hildegard."

"Whatever." As he pulls papers out of the folder, he turns his back to me. "Believe what you want, but don't think I've forgotten you've been poking around here. If you think you can find something to beat me with, then you'll be looking for a while."

"What's that supposed to mean?"

"You, snooping around. You're clearly looking for something to give me shit about while you're working here. Well, there isn't anything." He glances up from the papers and slowly twirls his chair to face me. "You aren't looking for clues as to how to get me back, are you?"

I burst out laughing. "No. What the hell gave you that idea?"

"Because you're up to something, Hildy. I know you well enough to know that much." Sam returns to his papers and then pulls a set of keys from the pocket of his pants. Taking them, he bends and unlocks the drawer I hadn't been able to open. He removes a sealed brown envelope with red tamper tape along the flap. I try not to stare for too long, but that has definitely piqued my interest.

Is that the information he's giving to the journalist?

"Just so you know," he says. "If you're trying to win me back, don't bother. I'm not that man any longer. I'm not into Nate's sloppy seconds. I'm more into loyalty and staying power rather than a pretty face and shapely ass these days."

God, that hurts like a slap across the face. Somehow, I manage not to flinch, but a part of me wants to curl into the fetal position. I honestly thought I'd meant more to him than that. I honestly thought I was more than those things. I knew I'd hurt him when I left, but he'd left me long before we physically split.

"You never used to be so mean," I mutter dully, trying to appear unaffected when my insides twist like alpha helices.

"Circumstances change people, Hildy. You should know that."

Another dig at something I'd said to him the day I left our apartment. He'd asked why suddenly I objected to his long hours when I'd always known how intense his job could be. My response had been circumstances change people and the things that they're willing to put up with. He was certainly holding on to a lot of hurt and bitterness, more than I'd ever considered.

Sam returns to his papers, and I go to my desk to continue the charade that I'm interested in the data results. Any other time I would be. I'm good at my job and generally enjoy trawling through trial results. It's kind of like being a scientific detective, searching for the whys and why nots. But I want to prove Sam isn't the mole. My ex is not making my job easier.

I stare at my screen, trying to focus on the data in front of me.

The intercom on Sam's desk buzzes.

I glance his way.

He presses a button. "Sam Grant."

"Hey, are you ready for me?" a woman asks.

Sam grins, something I haven't seen him do since I arrived, and buzzes her in.

The door whooshes open, and a woman enters. She's in an all-in-one leather suit that motorcyclists wear.

I do a double take. *God, she must be sweltering in that.* And then I take a closer look. *Holy shit! She looks damn sexy in that thing.*

The petite woman holds a helmet under her arm and an envelope in her hand. Her long blonde hair hangs in beach waves down her back, the ends almost touching her leather-clad pert and round ass. She's stunning and young, really young. My stomach sinks to my feet.

Who the hell is she, and how does she know Sam?

She winks at Sam, who gives her a genuine, warm smile.

My blood turns green, and my fingernails dig into my palms.

Sam used to be a boob guy, so maybe he has changed a little. He seems to be a sucker for a pretty face and a shapely ass. But what's his relationship to this young woman? I hate that I need to know.

I have no reason to be jealous. I mean, he's my ex, right? But I am ... curious. Yes, that's all I am.

She goes to his desk. "Hey, Sammy, how are you doing?"

Sammy? Fucking Sammy?

My mouth hangs open, and I close it.

"Hey, Geraldine." His smooth voice is as rich as hot fudge sauce. "How are you, honey?"

Honey? Fucking honey?

My skin prickles. Who is this person? Again, curious minds—that would be mine—want to know.

"I'm so good, handsome." She winks and then glances at me and startles. "Oh, jeez, sorry, I didn't see you there."

I flash a quick smile and fight the urge to tell her if she hadn't been ogling my ex-husband, she might have seen me. I don't, of course, because I don't care. She can call him handsome, and he can call her honey all the damn time, and I don't fucking care. It means nothing to me. Nope, nothing at all.

I plaster on a smile. "I'm Sam's wife."

She flinches, her eyes going wide.

Ha, *take that, Geraldine!*

"Oh, okay." Her gaze bounces from me to Sam back to me again. "Lovely to meet you."

"Ex," Sam says, and Geraldine spins around to look at him. "Hildy is my ex-wife."

Geraldine shrugs as if to say to me *you win some, you lose some,* and it pisses me off.

"Sam, *honey.*" I'm ready to slap someone who shall be known going forward as Little Biker Girl. "What would you like me to do for you today?" I admit I ask with more than a hint of innuendo. I had sex with this man in a gazebo at our wedding reception. Who was she to come in being all sexy and cute with him?

It's just annoying. That's what it is. I'm annoyed.

He shrugs. "Just do what you did yesterday."

He turns to Little Biker Girl and flashes her another gorgeous smile. "You have it?"

She holds out the envelope in her hand. Just like the one Sam removed from the drawer, it has tamper tape across the flap. I watch for any lingering touches as he takes it, but thankfully, there are none.

"Do you have a return?" she asks, too perky for her own good.

"I sure do." Sam's voice is bright and cheery, and I realize he's just grumpy with me.

"Thanks. See you soon." As she turns to leave, she gives me a single nod.

"Sure will," Sam calls out.

Sure will, I mock him in my head. Little Biker Girl is way too young for him, like twenty or more years too young. That's just wrong.

As she leaves, she wiggles her ass more than necessary, and when I turn to see Sam watching her go, I'm about to burst with green goo jiggling around inside my chest. I shouldn't feel this way about him. It makes no sense. And then it hits me ...

I'm focusing on the wrong thing.

Even though I want to know more about Little Biker Girl, the new envelope Sam slips into his bag is the most important thing. Is it an invitation to a party or a rare comic book or maybe something from a scientific journalist? Whatever he's got, I've got to see it. "What did she give you?"

He shoots me a strange look, one that says I have no right

to ask him anything. Maybe not, but I already did.

Sam lifts his chin. "What it is, Hildy, is none of your concern."

"It's all very secretive. Tamper tape and all."

He nods once. "And still, none of your concern."

God, he's infuriating, and I must get away from him before I say something stupid, something I'll regret horribly. "I'm going to see Nate."

Sam sits at his desk and doesn't glance my way. "Yeah, of course you are. He is *your* fiancé."

Ugh. Sam's back to being grumpy and ignoring me.

By the time I arrive on the twenty-second floor, I'm fuming. My frustration grows at a fast rate over Little Biker Girl and her role in whatever Sam is doing. Because he's doing something. I just don't know whether it's nefarious.

And that pisses me off.

Sam Grant and the word *nefarious* should never be used in the same conversation, let alone sentence.

Zelda's door is open. I really am not in the mood to deal with her. I peer in from the side of the doorway closest to me. Her chair is empty so I run to Nate's door. My badge doesn't open the door, and I press the intercom button.

"Is that you, love? Forget your badge?" he asks.

From his warm and loving tone, I know he thinks I'm Zelda, and a yearning swells inside me. Given my track record, I shouldn't want a relationship, and I don't, but I still wish some man would talk to me like that and mean it. I clear my dry throat. "It's your fiancée."

As I wait for the door to open, I tap my foot on the carpet.

I'm angry with myself as well as Sam. For the same reason—my stupid jealousy. Oh, I might have pretended it was everything but that in Sam's office, but the reality of what I feel hits me hard. I'm angry with Sam for making me feel territorial over him, and I'm angry with myself for acting that way around him. I shouldn't feel anything toward him. I'd been the one to end our marriage so why the hell did I want to chase after Little Biker Girl and tell her to stay away from him?

"Nate," I snap after being let into his office. "I really can't spend more time with Sam."

"And good morning to you too." He relaxes in his chair and grins at me. "Why not?"

"I went in this morning and searched his office. He's got it locked down so tight I can't find anything, but then someone came by this morning. She gave him an envelope, and he handed her another. Both had tamper tape on the flaps. That's the proof you need. Now I can go. You'll save money on my accommodations and per diem. You can thank me by paying the rest of what you owe me and ripping up my contract."

My need to get away from Sam makes me not care that I'm throwing him under the bus. He has Little Biker Girl to soothe him, so why should I give a fuck?

Nate goes to his desk, opens a drawer, and pulls out a folder. "Is this the courier?"

I like my name for Little Biker Girl better, but I examine the photo. "Yes."

Nate pulls out a printout. "This person has been to Sam's office twice a week for months now."

"If you knew this, why did you ask me to spy on him?"

"Because we never knew what was being exchanged."

"I don't know what's inside the envelope." As soon as the words are out, I want to take them back. I get the feeling Nate will want me to do more digging to find out what's being exchanged. But I just want to get the hell out of Seattle. Being around Sam Grant isn't good for my mental health.

"It's him, Hildy. This confirms what I've felt in my gut." Nate straightens. "I'm sure Sam's the one who's been talking to that reporter."

I blow out my cheeks and pace in front of his desk. All the evidence points that way. Still, I hate that this is what's happening. "Are those visitor logs and photos enough proof?"

Nate shrugs. "Maybe, but it would help if you could get ahold of one of those envelopes."

"I can't." I sound like a petulant child.

"Can't or won't?"

Despite us being friends, Nate won't let me off the hook. I've signed a contract. "You don't understand. It's so hard being around him."

"I understand more than you realize." He points at the door. "I work with Zelda. We're often together seven days a week. I just want to go back to how things were before we divorced. So I know how badly you want to leave and go to New Zealand. But I need your help. Please, Hildy."

Ugh. "Fine." I huff. "But there's no guarantee I can get one of the envelopes."

"All I ask is that you try." Nate smirks. "And just think. The sooner you get ahold of the proof I need, the less time you have to spend with Sam."

Any amount of time would be too long. I sigh. "One more question."

"Shoot."

"Why does Sam hate you so much?"

Nate crosses his arms over his chest. "Get me what I need, and I'll tell you."

Sometimes I think Nate sees everyone around him as pawns in a game and we're all rolling a pair of loaded dice. But I still need to do all I can to find the mole, and I will. I just hope Nate will take care of the rest.

CHAPTER 8

SAM

Day two of working with Hildy sucks almost as much as yesterday, and I haven't even been here long. I stare at the empty desk—she's still upstairs with Nate, and I wonder if he's got her on her knees in his office—and now I try desperately to erase that image from my head.

Fuck. Why did I let my mind go there?

So many things are wrong with this situation. I know she's up to something beyond her being engaged to Nate. No way did she just decide to organize the storage cabinet and beat me to the office to do it. She would have to intentionally wake up early to do this. That's not her. Hildy grew up with a live-in housekeeper, so cleaning isn't something she does by choice. It's strictly by necessity and that had been a point of contention when we moved in together. She wanted to hire someone to come in weekly, and I thought that was a waste of money. I made a chore chart, which only upset her more.

It's not her pulling everything out of the cabinet that bothers me. She shouldn't have touched anything of mine, but I keep thinking about how my gum was moved. Was she really looking for a pen or something else?

The *something else* worries me. I glance around, trying to see anything that might be out of the ordinary for an office. My mind goes blank trying to think of what she might be interested in looking for or finding.

We haven't communicated in years. I hadn't blocked her, but it didn't matter. After her email tomes, she never reached out to me again. Neither did I. There'd been no reason. We had no shared property, and we each had our own cars. It was a clean break, even though the splitting up of our household items was tense given the circumstance but free from drama overall.

That's why I can't imagine what she's trying to find in my office. I mean, I'm as boring as a person gets. I've always been a what-you-see-is-what-you-get kind of guy. I don't play games, literally or figuratively, which is why WYSIWYG describes me to a T. I'm a bookworm who spends his free time reading science fiction novels. I often fall asleep with a book. At least that way I don't wake up alone.

The only thing outside of the geeky scientist stereotype is my suits. I glance at the brown jacket hanging up and remember Mr. Beauregard, my high school science teacher. He had a thing for old movies. Once I graduated and turned eighteen, he told me he would have sex with every male actor, even at their current age, who starred in them if given the opportunity. He's the one adult who recognized my potential and pushed me to take AP science and math courses, worked with me on my college applications, and showed me how science fair projects could help me win scholarships. Those Golden Age actors inspired his style, and he gave me a similar suit when I graduated from college. For weddings, funerals, and interviews, he'd said. I ended up wearing it to his funeral, and during the reading of his will, I learned he'd left his entire collection of suits to me. That inspired me to embrace the same style over the years.

I may be well dressed, but beneath the surface, nothing sets me apart.

The door whooshes open, and Hildy enters. She's not smiling, but none of her clothing appears to have been put back on in a rush, and her stockings look undamaged.

"Working hard?" she asks.

Hardly working, but I'll die before I admit that to her. "Yes."

She heads to her desk, and her sexy librarian attire makes it nearly impossible for me to look away. Her hair is pulled back in a tight bun, like Sophie wore when she worked as Max's assistant. Hildy's replaced her contacts with black glasses, and she wears a white blouse and a black skirt that almost looks like a dress. Her outfit is so tight, I can see her voluptuous ass moving seductively underneath. Each ass cheek bounces like it's moving in time to a drumbeat.

The worst part?

Memories of her ass naked and soft in my bed surface. Fuck, I don't need that in my head. This woman drives me crazy.

Focus, Grant.

I pride myself on being professional, but Hildy makes me consider jacking off in the executive bathroom. That would get me out of my workspace, which has its own bathroom, but she's here.

The only reason I don't is because I'm trying to avoid Nate.

Rumor has it, he's showing people around this floor to drum up interest in a new sunscreen Zentello's developing, so I've remained holed up in my office. The last thing I want to do is bump into him and have to play nice in front of strangers.

Sleeping with my ex-wife was one thing. He'd also taken Hildy's side in the divorce, not that I'd ever consider him a friend again after what he did, and I'd heard from Bradley that Nate was always there for her if she needed anything. Strange when he'd been my friend first and the best man at our wedding, and I'd been his when he married Zelda. Though maybe not so strange now that he's engaged to Hildy.

It's a fucking soap opera.

I want no part of it.

I never want to talk to the man again, even if he is my boss. I'm not sure how achieving that goal will work in the future, but I'm going to try.

Hildy stares at me with an unreadable expression.

"What?" I ask.

"You didn't put on your lab coat."

"I'm not going into the lab today."

As I sort through the profiling groups, I catch Hildy watching me from the corner of her eye. I get the feeling she's checking me out, and pride rushes through me.

Take that, Lowe.

I might not play games, but I can be petty as hell. I loosen my tie and undo the top buttons of my dress shirt to reveal the bottom of my throat and a little bit of chest.

Hildy used to say the bottom of my throat was one of her favorite parts to kiss because it was soft and smooth and the start of the path to my abs, which were ridged and hard and, of course, led to her favorite part of me.

I narrow my gaze on my screen. "Something in your eye, Hildy?"

"No," she replies a little too quickly. "Don't know why you'd ask that."

"I was a little worried since you're wearing glasses and not your contacts today."

She releases a heavy, frustrated breath.

Good. I'm getting to her. If she has to work here, I won't make it easy for her.

As I reach for my bottle of water, I notice she's leaning back in her chair and has also undone a couple of buttons on her blouse. She's pulling apart the collar and fanning herself with a piece of paper. The breeze causes her hair to flutter, and her magnificent breasts rise and fall, straining the white fabric. I'd put money on her bra underneath being white satin since red or black would show.

"Damn." I roll my chair closer to the desk to hide my burgeoning hard-on.

"You okay?"

"Mm-hmm. Fine."

She clears her throat, and I stupidly look at her. She crosses her legs, causing her skirt to ride up, and fuck it, I get a glimpse of the top of her thigh-highs and the black lacy garter belt holding them up.

As she moves in her seat, my gaze travels upward from her legs, and I groan. She's also stretching and pushing out her chest.

"Dammit, Hildy."

She seductively licks her top lip. "What?"

"Seriously." I quirk a brow at her. "You want to do this? Really?"

"Come on, Sam, you're really telling me that you haven't thought about it?"

"What about Nate?"

Her teeth drag across her bottom lip. "We have an open relationship."

Open relationship? Nate seems too selfish to share, but that would explain him and Zelda. Bradley was involved with a couple who practice ethical non-monogamy before he met Christina, so I'm familiar with the concept of polyamory. It's not something I'd want in a serious relationship ...

Hildy's finger traces a pattern on the swell of her breasts, and all I can think about is doing that with my tongue. "We were always good at sex. No matter if we'd argued, we managed to fuck away all our troubles. You always could make me scream."

Fuck it. I jump up, rush over there, pull her out of the chair, and have her in my arms before either of us can second-guess whether this is a good idea. Teeth clash, hands grab, and my dick goes rock hard as we grind against each other.

I lose myself in her kiss. I always knew we were good together, but this is better than I remember. She tastes minty, and I can't get enough of her. Reality wants to slide in, but I don't want to let it intrude. I've missed this—her—too much.

I cup her breast, and she arches against me. "God, I forgot..."

I kiss her neck and nibble on her earlobe.

She moans. "So good."

It's better than good, and I want to keep going. I pull her closer, unable to get enough of her.

Her fingers pluck at my belt buckle. "Sam …"

Her scent intoxicates me. Who am I kidding? Everything does. "You drive me fucking crazy."

"I know."

A tingle starts in my lower back as I pull her blouse from her skirt. I feel like I'm about to explode. I can't remember the last time I came in my pants, but …

Something clicks in my brain. I have no idea what or why, but clarity hits.

What the fuck am I doing?

I jerk away.

Hildy's shirt hangs out of her skirt. Strands of hair have come loose from her bun. Her lipstick is a mess, and I'm assuming some of it is on my face. The ends of my belt buckle dangle, and my dick strains behind my pants.

I want her. Yet …

I can't do it. It doesn't matter whether she and Nate have an open relationship. That doesn't matter. I do.

I can't put myself out there for her to crush my fucking heart again.

Hildy puts her hands on my waist. "Sam, what?"

I take another step away from her and shake my head. "I can't do this."

"Why? You want this as much as I do." She stares at my pants, where my fucking dick refuses to settle down. "I can feel it. See it."

I shake my head, unsure where this willpower originates from when all I want to do is take her hard and fast, but ... "Sex isn't the answer. Sex won't repair the mistakes we've made and the pain we've caused each other."

"Is the thought of having sex with me that bad?"

I half laugh even though there's nothing funny about the situation. "Yes. What we almost did just now proves I'm out of my mind."

"I'm sorry." She moves farther away from me. "You're right, we shouldn't have done that. I just ... I guess I miss you like that, and being here with you brought back some good memories."

She flops onto her chair, and I take the opportunity to tuck in my shirt and fasten my belt. The time gives my breath and pulse a chance to steady. I don't want to look at her because my resolve will shatter.

I'm a masochist, though, and foolishly move my gaze to her. She's beautiful with swollen lips and eyes bright with the excitement of what we'd been about to do. If I was a man who hadn't already had his heart shredded by her, I'd have fucked her, but I'm not him. I'm the man whose heart *has* been shredded by her.

"Sam," she says quietly.

"No." My voice is harsh, but I don't care. I can't care. "I can't do this. I can't have sex with you, and I can't work with you. It's too damn hard. I'll tell Nate or you can."

Regret flashes on her face. "I need this job."

Not my problem.

"Mathilda is a single mom. She has a son, not quite three

years old, and he needs treatments she can't afford."

Mathilda is Hildy's younger sister. She'd been a gregarious young woman who seemed a bit directionless when I met her. While Hildy focused on her education, Mathilda preferred to party and acted out to get her parents' attention. She always seemed to be in some trouble, and Hildy constantly bailed her out. It looks like nothing has changed.

But Mathilda not being able to afford something makes no sense, given how wealthy the Bauer family is. "Your dad—"

"Disowned Mathilda. He went so far as hiring the jerk of a sperm donor, setting the douche daddy up with another woman, and getting him a shark attorney to make sure he pays minimal child support and doesn't have to see the kid."

"So you ...?"

Hildy blows out a breath. "I'm helping her. She lives in my apartment, doing her best, and is a really great mom, but it's been ... rough. The money I'll earn working here will pay for Flynn's therapy."

Of course she's doing that for her younger sister. I'm not surprised. Hildy always stepped up for Mathilda. She had no choice when they were younger. Her parents might have provided whatever money could buy, but that's all their children got from them. Nothing Hildy did or accomplished ever pleased Werner. I imagine Mathilda had it even worse. Hell, Werner hated me.

But there has to be some other way ... "Have Nate help Mathilda and Flynn."

"He gave me this job."

Huh? Nate comes from a wealthy family and has money of

his own. He always gives to those in need, so why isn't he helping his future sister-in-law himself rather than making Hildy work for it?

"Please, Sam." Hildy's eyes implore me. "If you won't do it for me, do it for my sister and nephew. I'll do my analysis in the lab so you can have the office to yourself. Just tell me how to make this work for you."

I consider her offer. There's a desktop in the lab she could use.

"You won't find someone more qualified than me to help you with that data," she adds, the words rushing out.

Unfortunately, that's true. With Hildy's help, I'll get through the data quicker and be able to leave Zentello sooner. Of course that means working with her. A real-life catch-22.

But fuck.

I'm not some evil villain who wants to make Mathilda's son suffer. I might hate Hildy, and I can be a big dick as well as petty, but I won't hurt some innocent kid. Especially one without a dad.

I take a breath and then another. She'll only be here for thirteen more days, counting the rest of today, and not all of those are workdays. I know I'll regret this, but … "Let's just stick to what we agreed upon yesterday. We'll be professional. No more touching."

The tension in her face lessens. "Or kissing."

I'm not sure if she's asking a question or stating a fact, but I nod. The kissing nearly pushed me over the edge. There can't be more of that.

"No personal stuff and we'll only concentrate on work."

She swallows. The corners of her mouth tip up. "Thank you."

"You're welcome." That's the professional thing to say, right? "Let's get to work and forget that we almost ..."

My cheeks warm. Fuck, am I blushing?

"Forget what?" she asks. "I have no idea what you mean. I've simply been sitting here doing my work."

I know Hildy's only doing what we agreed upon, but fuck, I wish things could be different. I wish ...

Shut up, Grant.

I know better than to waste time wishing for anything. I spent my entire crappy childhood making wishes, and none of them came true. And when one finally did as an adult—marrying Hildy—it imploded in the worst possible way, leaving me alone again but with a broken heart that nothing, including time, can mend.

Wishes are for suckers.

CHAPTER 9

SAM

Somehow, I manage to get some work done, but I take my two breaks and eat my lunch elsewhere. The less time I spend with Hildy, the better, but we're finally making real progress with the data, so I suppose I should call her being here a sort of win. Or maybe boon is a more apt description. We don't even argue the rest of the day. But if we aren't comparing notes on various subsets of data, she's playing twenty questions with me to the point I want to call her Ms. Nosy McNosy.

Do I still prefer using graph paper composite notebooks to notepads? What do I think about Zentello? Would I ever do an exposé on a company I work for?

Random questions, but couple them with her "pen" search, and I have a feeling why she's so damn nosy. She wants to pry into my business. I don't know the divorce statute, but I'll bet her lawyer wants her to see if there are any assets she can claim, given she left our marriage with nothing but her car. Not that I had anything to give her then. I hadn't saved much, choosing instead to pay off our debts. I'd also loved lavishing my wife with designer purses, clothes, and shoes. I'd wanted to prove to Werner Bauer I was good enough for his daughter, even if Hildy said she didn't care what he thought and didn't need any of those things. Now, I'm a well-respected scientist who earns a ridiculous amount of money working at Zentello, and maybe Hildy wants a piece of that.

Who knows? I certainly don't, but perhaps her concern over Mathilda is playing into this.

My cell phone buzzes.

I glance at the screen.

Bradley: *Just a reminder. Seven p.m. tonight at our place.*

Oh, right. I have a date tonight. I'd rather go home and read more of the book that's taking me forever to finish, but I told Bradley yes, which means I'll follow through whether I want to or not. I type a reply.

Sam: *I remember. I'll be there. Red or white?*
Bradley: *Either works. We're having surf and turf.*
Sam: *I'll bring one of each.*
Bradley: *Perfect. See you soon.*

Soon being a relative term. Bradley, like me, is always on time or early. Christina is perpetually late. He tells me they're working on it, but he doesn't seem to mind. The man is head over heels for her in the best possible way.

I hope tonight goes well. It isn't my first pseudo-blind date. I've had so many setups organized by the wives, fiancées, and girlfriends of people I work with or know that they all seem to blur into one. Everyone sees me as a fixer-upper project—the hopeless workaholic who has no clue how to find himself a woman.

I glance at Hildy bent over her keyboard again. She'll ruin her back if she keeps that up.

Those people are right to a point. I am a hopeless workaholic, always have been ever since my first job at a fast-food restaurant after I graduated from high school, apart from a brief respite when Hildy and I first met. That period of putting someone before my work lasted longer than I would've expected, but I adored her and wanted her to be happy. The fact that as soon as I started working long hours, she quickly became unhappy proved work and relationships don't mix for me, which means there's been no one special since Hildy. I've had a series of coffee and dinner dates with a few one-night stands off the back of them, but I haven't met anyone I wanted to get seriously involved with.

The alarm on my phone goes off.

Hildy jumps to her feet. "What's that?"

"My alarm telling me it's time to get out of here."

"I guess we worked past quitting time."

I nod, putting my things into my bag.

"Where are you off to anyway?" she asks. "Leaving early to go drinking again?"

"It's hardly early." I slip on my jacket. "And no, I'm not going to a bar."

She doesn't respond at first, but then she takes a deep breath. "Do you want to have dinner so we can talk?"

I almost fall backward with the shock. We are barely on

speaking terms, never mind sharing a meal.

"As much as I'd love to spend a couple of hours bantering with you over dinner, I can't." I flash her a smile. "I'm on my way to a date."

Hildy's eyes widen, and she appears to be trying to stop herself from gasping, but I hear the tiny intake of air. "Two dates in a row?"

I shrug since I didn't actually have one last night. I only led her to believe I did.

"Sure, you have another date," she finally says once she regains her composure.

"Yes, I do. Tonight's is courtesy of Bradley and Christina. They're fixing me up with her best friend."

"Name?"

Ruby, but ... "None of your business."

"You don't even know." She laughs. "Want to meet up later, then?"

"I just told you. I have a date."

"A date is a few hours. It's not all night, Sam."

"It might be, Hildy." I raise a brow, trying to imply I'm going to get laid later. That might not be the truth, but she'll never know.

"You don't have sex on a first date."

"I didn't say it was a first date." I glance at her to see if I've swayed her, but she doesn't appear convinced. Well, I know what I can say that might do it. "And I slept with you on our first date."

She grins. "What does that tell you?"

"That maybe you're a little too easy." I move past her to leave.

"Sam," she calls out.

I turn. "What?"

She smirks. "I'll see you later once you've taken your date home. I was given the list of Orchid team members and their contact info. I know where you live."

As she wiggles away in that too damn tight, too damn sexy outfit, my pants get tight, and all I want to do is blow off the date and go home. But they're expecting me, so I'll do what it takes even though I'd give anything to cancel if I could.

The evening is turning out to be much more pleasant than I imagined it being. I'm glad I didn't beg off. As I take a sip from my wineglass and sit on the couch, Christina and her friend Ruby go into the kitchen.

"What do you think?" Bradley asks. He sits across from me in a chair with a blue throw artfully arranged on the back. I don't have blankets or pillows or anything that would count as decor. The only thing I have are bookshelves full of books. My bedding came in a bag, so it all matches. And I bought an extra set of sheets. Low maintenance all the way.

"She seems great," I reply honestly. Ruby is pretty and curvy, just my type, and we've enjoyed each other's company. She's easy to talk to and more than once had me belly laughing.

Bradley tilts his head to one side. "But?"

I watch him over the rim of my wineglass. "Who said there's a 'but?'"

"I've known you for a long time, Sam. I know there's a

'but.'" He leans forward and lowers his voice. "Is it because she isn't Hildy?"

"What?" The word bursts out. "She's my ex. I haven't even mentioned her tonight."

"You didn't have to, buddy. Ruby's intelligent and beautiful, but your tie is still in place."

I laugh. "What in the hell does that mean?"

"When you're hot and bothered, you loosen your tie. Your tie was always loose when you were dating Hildy and then married her."

I shake my head, knowing he's dead wrong. "You're bullshitting."

Bradley laughs along with me, and some of the tension I've been feeling since Hildy dropped into my office lessens. I really need to make more of an effort. Ruby is a lovely woman, but she's just not ...

Nope. Not going to say it or even think it.

"So Ruby's helping Christina with her perfume business?" I ask, wanting to change the subject.

"Yeah. Jules was a big help for the initial marketing, but she has her own business to run. Ruby has a business background and has a keen sense when it comes to product strategy."

I know Jules Harrison from her work with the original Happy Pill that evolved into the Orchid project. She's Sophie's best friend, so she spends a lot of time with Max, too. Jules dated Bradley two summers ago. It was an interesting relationship since Jules has a longtime boyfriend named Reid. I was surprised when Bradley gave polyamory a shot, but he realized he didn't like sharing. They've all stayed friends, which is more than I can say about ... Nope. I don't want to think about her. "I'm glad Christina found some help."

Bradley grins. He's so proud of his fiancée. "Remind me to give you a bottle of Christina's fragrance. It's called Joyous and is unbelievable. You can give it to whomever the next lady in your life is."

I raise a brow. "Who says I'll have a lady in my life?"

"I'm an optimist." Bradley grins.

He is, but in this instance, the guy is dead wrong. Still, he means well. That's why everyone likes Bradley Zimmer.

Christina and Ruby bring out four bowls of chocolate mousse topped with whipped cream and raspberries.

Ruby smiles seductively at me. "There are leftover raspberries and whipped cream if you want more. Here or ... to have at home."

Her innuendo is clear. I won't have to be alone tonight if I don't want to be. My chest puffs, and I search for something pithy to say. "Such a tantalizing blend of sweetness always leaves me craving more."

That sounded better in my head, but the way Ruby beams suggests she likes what I said.

We dig in. The dessert is as delicious as the dinner. The conversation is lively, and despite enjoying my time with Ruby, I can't help but think something's missing. Not something, but someone. Hildy. She should be here with me, and I hate myself for thinking that.

When it comes time to leave, Ruby waits expectantly for an invitation to come home with me. I open my mouth, but the words don't come. I clear my throat. "It was great to meet you. I had fun tonight."

She nods. "Same."

"It's getting late." I feel like a jerk for leading her on. Not sure I truly did, but her smile falters for a nanosecond or two before she recovers.

"Yes, it is. I'm sure you have to be at work early."

Ruby's not a woman in STEM like Christina, but she's intelligent and kind. I should want to take her home, but I just don't feel a spark. That can't be forced. Still, I feel like an idiot for not taking this beautiful woman home and fucking her into my mattress. Work be damned. "I do."

Bradley gives a shake of his head and a silly smile. I hate he knows the reason I'm turning Ruby down.

"I need to run to the restroom." With that, Ruby retreats.

Christina comes up and kisses my cheek. "I have another friend," she whispers as soon as she hears the bathroom door close. "She even works in the marketing department at Zentello. Her name is Amelie, and she'll be better suited to you."

I can't help but laugh. Anyone who is part of a happy couple wants all their single friends to pair up. Max and Sophie are the same way. "Thanks, but we'll see."

I'm at home a little later, swirling the whiskey around in my glass, thinking about my night. Instead of alone, I could be naked in bed with a beautiful and eager woman.

Ugh. What the fuck is wrong with me?

Hildy's voice streams through my head as I sit on my couch. Even she knew I wouldn't be bringing my date home, but she'd been so confident it was borderline arrogant. I'd always liked that about her. When we met, she'd been the one who came over with a bottle of beer and asked if I wanted to find a quiet place to talk. She'd been the one to suggest I take her home with me, and we made out in the back of a cab on the way there. And she'd started undressing on my apartment doorstep. Yes, she was confident, even brash at times, and crazy, too, but I'd loved that about her.

It's not yet eleven. I'm not ready for bed, so I grab my book off the coffee table, even if that sentient being makes me think of black matter, which reminds me of Hildy.

The doorbell rings.

Who could it be at this hour?

And then I remember what Hildy said at the office. My stomach drops. She wouldn't come over here, would she?

The resounding answer, unfortunately, is yes.

But why the hell isn't she with her fiancé? This makes no sense.

I take my time going to the door and opening it.

Hildy stands there with a bottle of wine in her hand. Yep, she's crazy.

I clutch the door handle. "Hildegard."

"Samuel." She takes a step forward, but I block her way.

"What are you doing here?" I ask.

"You're alone."

I hate how she says it as a statement, not a question. "What does it matter?"

"I told you I'd be over."

"It's late."

"I know, but ..." She motions to my clothing. "You're still dressed, and my guess is your mind is spinning as you analyze how tonight went."

Fuck. I drag a hand through my hair. How does she still know me so well? "Shouldn't you be fucking your fiancé about now?"

Hildy pushes past me with a hand against my chest. "Just go with the flow, Sam. You know I'm not leaving."

I know that damn tone, so I know she's not going away. I don't want to cause a disturbance. It's a quiet neighborhood, so someone will notice her standing on the porch all night and call the cops. The last thing I need is to have to explain the situation to the Seattle police. Which means I'm stuck with her. Again.

Fuck my life and my ex-wife.

She struts inside, heading toward the living room, but poking her head into each room or closet she passes. "Nice bathroom."

I follow her, my back stiffening at the thought of her riding public transport at this hour. Maybe she used one of the rideshare apps. "How did you get here?"

"Cool your jets, Sam. I drove and parked in your driveway. There was space behind your car. Though I would've thought by now you'd have traded that old thing in and bought a newer model."

She never liked my car, but now it's paid off, and I don't drive that much. I can walk to the Link station and take that to work or anywhere else I want to go. "It runs fine."

She drops onto the couch, kicks off her shoes, and sits crisscross.

I step back, feeling as though I've been punched in the gut. The pose is a familiar one. What isn't the same is how she looks perfect sitting like she belongs here.

Hildy hands me the wine. "How did the date go?"

I take the bottle and head to the kitchen. It's an open floor plan so I can still see her as I stand at the counter. "Good, but I told you she wouldn't be coming back here."

"I believe I told you that."

I know better than to respond. As I open the wine and grab two glasses, I can't believe she used an internal document at Zentello to get my address. This isn't where we'd lived together. I couldn't stand to be at that apartment because of all the memories. This place was a foreclosure, and mine was the winning bid. For once, something went right for me, and I'm grateful to this day. But the reason for her visit is suspect. I have to uncover what she's plotting. It doesn't take my doctorate degree to know she's not here to reminisce over a bottle of wine.

I hand her a glass and sit in the chair, hoping the distance will give me some advantage.

She stares at me. "Your date wasn't worthy of a nightcap back at your bachelor pad, then?"

I set my empty glass on a coaster on the coffee table and hold on to the bottle. I've drunk enough wine during dinner, and my whiskey remains almost full. I don't need more alcohol to dull my brain around her. "Your green-eyed witch is showing."

She holds out her glass for me to fill. "You mean monster."

"You're a lot of things." I fill her glass and mine to about a quarter full. "But you're not a monster."

Hildy rolls her eyes. "And a witch is so much better."

She settles back onto the couch like she did every night we were married and takes a sip of wine. I'm tempted to down both the whiskey and wineglass, but I pick up neither.

But fuck. She looks far too comfortable here, and I kind of like it. She didn't want to be married to me, though, so I'm not sure why she's here. No matter what she and Nate do in the privacy of their relationship, she chose to be with me tonight.

Does she still want me?

After the incident in the office earlier, I might be tempted to say yes. But why now? It makes no sense.

I'm not the sort of guy who wants to be with a woman who isn't interested in me. Yet I can't deny how much I wanted her earlier until common sense reigned supreme.

"Anyway." She stares at me over the rim of her glass. "I'm not jealous of your date. I've had plenty of dates with you, and meh, they're not that special."

I burst out laughing. I should be more offended, but she's just too much.

Hildy winks at me and then takes another sip.

Fuck it. I pick up my whiskey and down the entire glass. The wine will be next.

It's been more than five years ... I blow out a frustrated breath. Will I ever get over this woman?

CHAPTER 10

HILDY

Sam's right. I really am a jealous witch, though he was most likely being polite and really meant to call me a bitch. I don't know why I showed up at his house at this hour. Okay, I do. My skin is probably green enough for me to play Elphaba in *Wicked.*

But it's not like I want to feel this way.

"I'll be back in a minute." Sam rises from the chair and goes into the bathroom I'd checked out on my way in.

I take another sip of wine, wondering if I should sneak out before he returns. That would probably be the smartest thing to do. But I'd likely keep thinking about him—the way I have all night long.

I'd stayed at work and searched both Sam's office and the lab for any proof I could turn over to Nate. I came up empty-handed again, though I couldn't break into his locked desk drawer. Then I grabbed takeout, went to my temporary apartment, and ate while watching TV. Well, I tried to watch something. I had no appetite for the cardboard food after getting myself worked up thinking about Sam on his date. Though I wondered if he hadn't lied to me about having one last night, too.

I hold my glass, but I really don't feel like drinking any more. The only reason? I might not stop.

The idea of Sam out with another woman has been filling every spare space of my brain for hours. I hate it. I shouldn't care that he had a date.

But I did, so much. And I'm pissed at myself for feeling that way.

At one point earlier tonight, I'd fought the urge to trawl the bars and restaurants Nate told me were popular with employees. What I'd have done if I had found him and her together, I had no idea. But I needed to see him out for myself. I needed to watch him engaging with her and see if they had a solid connection.

Thankfully, logic shut down that stupid idea.

Who in their right mind would do that?

Not me, that's for sure. Yet I find myself inside his house now.

Probably another stupid idea I also should have said no to. Over the years, I haven't thought about him dating. He honestly hasn't entered my mind much other than a fleeting thought. But now that I'm in proximity to him, the thought of him with another woman makes me want to go nuclear. Talk about nonsensical.

Do I want what I can't have?

That's a distinct possibility. I have no clue.

I'm just relieved he's alone now. Well, not counting me. I swirl the wine in my glass.

Being around him again brings back a lot of the old feelings I thought I'd gotten over. I'm surprised to feel as much as I do or that the thought of him dating someone makes me nauseous.

The door to the bathroom opens. I take a tiny sip of wine to give myself something to do while he approaches. Well, something other than staring at him, which I've been doing since I arrived.

So not subtle.

But what can I say? I've been shooting from the hip since yesterday. First with him and Little Biker Girl. Then Nate showing me the visitor logs with her on them. And now, his date with some unknown woman.

Earlier, I'd so confidently said he didn't sleep with women on the first date, but that was the old Sam—the guy I fell in love with and married. I have no clue whether that's still the case. He might've changed during the time we've been apart. I mean, I know he's changed because he's turned into an even bigger grouchy asshole, but I don't know about any of the other changes. For all I know, he's exactly the man Nate claims he is—a mole and spy who's desperate to destroy Zentello.

A part of me doesn't want to believe that, but I can see why Nate thinks so.

Sam sits in the chair and rubs his hands against his pants. He eyes his wineglass, but he doesn't pick it up.

"Did the date go well?" I ask.

He shrugs. "She's nice. Pretty, interesting, smart, and funny."

The way he might as well be reading a grocery list makes me exhale the breath I've been holding. "But?"

"But I don't think I'll be seeing her again. She'd be a good friend but nothing romantic."

My relief is immediate and immense, but I can't be so obvious to Sam. He doesn't need to know I've been obsessing about his date all night. I give him a small smile. "That's a shame."

Sam shrugs. "Not really. Dates are to see how compatible you are. Otherwise, you might go straight into a relationship that could turn out bad."

"A bit like we did." I wink so he knows I'm joking.

"We were a whirlwind." Sam takes a sip of his wine. "Do you regret that?"

Emotion swirls like a cyclone in my chest. I take a breath, hoping things will die down within me. "I don't regret anything about us except the end."

Sam doesn't nod. He presses his lips together, remaining so quiet I wonder if I've offended him.

"What about you?" I finally ask to break the uncomfortable silence. "Do you regret us?"

As Sam smiles, his eyes crinkle at the sides. Those crinkles weren't there five years ago, but as far as I'm concerned, they add to his looks. He's like a bottle of red wine that gets better with age.

"I could never regret you, Hildy." His Adam's apple bobs. "I do regret a lot of things about our relationship but never you. *Never* you."

My eyes sting. I don't want to cry, though. That would ruin everything. But it's hard. I swallow around the lump burning in my throat. We both did so many things wrong in our marriage, and now I'm in the awful position of proving he is sabotaging the company where we both work.

I sip my wine, trying to think of a way to steer the topic of discussion away from us before I say something I shouldn't. The problem? All I can think about is us. Before I know it, my glass is empty, and I'm refilling it.

"What are you looking for in a relationship?" Somehow, I manage not to cringe or grimace after saying those words. I have no idea why I'm putting myself through such torment. I'm not fooling anyone by pretending not to care, including Sam.

He puts his sock-covered feet up on the coffee table. "Why are you so interested?"

"I just am." Saying I'm borderline obsessed with my ex wouldn't be a good look.

"That makes no sense." His intense gaze pins me, and I try not to squirm under the scrutiny. "You've been out of my life for more than five years. Your numerous emails after you left made it clear what you thought about me, yet here you are acting like our split was amicable and we still vacation together or something."

Everything he says is the truth. But watching him watch me, I'm not sure I have the nerve to say the words on the tip of my tongue. I'm interested because I still have feelings for him. Yet how could I when I've been tasked to catch him in a lie? To prove he's selling out the company that trusts him with their most prestigious project to date—their future.

"Well?" He sounds harsher than usual. "What game are you playing?"

"None," I say in a rush. My face feels warm, and I hope I'm not blushing. That happens when I get flustered, and no one can make me feel that way more than Sam. "None at all, but we do need to talk."

"About?"

I take a deep breath. One isn't enough, so I take another to compose myself. I may appear calm and collected on the outside—nothing rattles Hildy Russell—but I'm quivering on the inside, trying not to hunch my shoulders and hide the way I used to when Dad told me I'd never amount to anything just because I was a girl.

This conversation with Sam should happen and could be a good thing. I need to find out whether I have feelings for him and if he's the mole. Knowing the answers to both of these things would make my life so much easier ... and better.

"Us." I lift my chin. "We need to talk about us."

SAM

As Hildy's words sink in, my heart clatters in my chest. She wants to talk about us.

Does that mean she wants to discuss how things ended or ... does she want to talk about the possibility of *us* getting back together?

I'm not sure how I feel about that second option. Of course, I'm attracted to her, and yes, I'm probably still a bit in love with her. But for all I know, that's not what she wants to discuss, and this is about her and Nate. She might tell me what happened at work can never happen again as we agreed, but she wants to shut down everything and make it clear we won't be having any near misses in the sex department. That must be it, because her emails made it sound like she would never get back together with me. And I'm not sure how I feel about that, either.

There's only one way to find out what she wants to say ...

"Okay," I say, keeping my voice steady. "Go ahead."

"The thing is ..." She looks everywhere but at me. Her second glass of wine goes down faster than her first one did. "I'm concerned about us."

"But why?" I'm trying to make sense of this because there's no us. But there's one thing ... "Because of our chemistry?"

"Yes, exactly." She slaps the arm of the couch. The upholstery mutes the sound, but it echoes in my soul. "That's why it's important for us to have this conversation."

"We just started it."

She's stalling, and that's okay with me since it means she'll be on my couch for a while longer. I'm enjoying the view and not having to spend another evening sitting alone. I also enjoy our conversations. I've missed them, which I hate. I hate that I miss them, if I'm being honest with myself.

"It's work," Hildy finally responds. "Because we work together, I wouldn't want there to be any issues with HR. You need to be covered."

"I do? That's pretty gallant of you."

"Can't a woman be gallant?" she asks, repositioning herself so I get an even better view of her ass in her yoga pants. "Is there a female version of that?"

Man, she's got some nice curves, but given what we're discussing, I need to focus on her eyes. "No idea, but please elaborate on why I need to be *covered*, as you put it."

She tilts her head to one side, contemplating what she

plans to say. "We almost had sex in your office today. What if I decide to put a complaint in about you?"

"I could put one in about you." I tip my glass at her. "You ripped at my belt buckle, desperate to get my pants off."

"Well, you had an enormous erection rubbing up against me." She talks faster than usual and refills her wineglass even though it isn't fully empty. "I admit I had something to do with all that rubbing and grinding, but it wasn't all my fault."

"No, it wasn't. We were both involved and need to accept responsibility, which is why neither of us should have to worry about a sexual harassment claim. And we both agreed it should never happen again. I'd never force myself on a woman."

"Come on. You'd never need to force yourself on anyone." She holds her hand in the air and moves it up and down like a game show hostess showing off the grand prize. "Look at you."

My chest swells because the beautiful woman sitting in front of me still finds me attractive. There's never been any doubt I think she's gorgeous, sexy, funny, and kind, so when she used to tell me how "damn hot and amazing" I was, I grew ten feet taller, figuratively.

I let my gaze take her in. "I'm the one who lucked out there, baby."

Her lips draw into a thin line. "Oh, please don't disrespect me, Samuel. I am so much more than my body."

I burst out laughing. Hildy joins in with me, and I love the hearty sound of her laughter.

"Seriously, though." She licks her lips, not in a quick my-mouth-is-dry swipe of the tongue way. Her tongue is slow and purposeful, seductive even. "What are we going to do about work to make sure it doesn't happen again?"

She's correct. Us agreeing might not be enough. My temperature keeps rising. "We could have a chaperone."

She takes another drink of her wine. "That might work. We already have rules, so a chaperone might help."

"Or we just stick to our word." This conversation makes no sense to me. I hope I don't appear as confused as I feel, but I'm trying to rein it in so she doesn't think even less of me than she already does. "I'm not the type to normally have sex on my desk. I can behave."

"I'm the one who needs the rules." She bites a knuckle.

Seeing her finger in her mouth just about does me in. What the fuck is she doing?

I'm confused about her relationship with Nate and why her *fiancé* seems to have no issue with her sleeping with an ex. It's weird, and her explanation of an open relationship doesn't make sense, knowing what I know about her and Nate.

"Tell me, what exactly am I getting into at Zentello anyway?" she asks.

Huh? She's making even less sense now. "I'm not sure I get where you're coming from."

"Zentello. What sort of place am I working at?"

The conversation has quickly veered off in a different direction, and I have no idea why, especially when she probably knows more about the place, given her relationship with Nate. But it's a question I've often asked myself. It's why I've been doing my own internal audit of sorts as part of my job to certify the Orchid project. I'd heard rumors of misogyny among the board members. Bradley and Max said it had been rife when they presented the initial Orchid project proposal. That got me wondering about the actual board members and how they'd gotten their seats. I also wanted to investigate product safety and find out if Zentello cuts any corners.

The funny thing is I'm not doing it because I hate Nate, my once friend. I simply want to know if the drug going to women, and possibly millions of them in the future, is safe. I may have worked on the government side of pharmaceuticals, but I know companies will put profit ahead of anything. I don't want any future customer to suffer because all Zentello cared about was the bottom line.

Maybe not everyone feels that way, but I do. It's the kind of person I am. Everything must be right, proper, and equal. Hildy operates the same way. At least she used to. I'm sure she'd be on board with everything I'm doing.

"Zentello has its issues …" I pause. Should I tell her what I really think? Can I trust her? I'm about to spill my plans until I remember Nate. She's engaged to him. Of course she'll tell him whatever I say. "But ultimately, it's a great place to work."

Nope. I shouldn't tell her, and I can't trust her.

I spot her fast blink. She's noticed my change in direction. She can read me so easily I might as well be a *New York Times* bestselling novel. I can't say anything, though, not until I have proof and not until I'm certain she won't run to Nate with the information.

"That isn't what you were going to say."

Yes, she knows me far too well.

I frown as if I have no idea what she's talking about. "Yes, it was."

"Tell me," she demands, her lower lip sticking out in an adorable pout.

"It's late, and you're imagining things." I reach into my pocket for my phone. "Let me call you a ride. You've been drinking. You can get your car tomorrow."

She appears bemused as she finishes what remains in her wineglass, drops her feet to the floor, and slips them into her shoes. I could easily stay up all night talking and bantering with her, but a bitter taste of regret and betrayal still swills in my gut when I think of her and Nate being together. I just can't get past that. And to be fair, I shouldn't have to. She's my ex for a reason.

We don't speak while we wait for her ride.

Hildy sits at my kitchen island, drinking the glass of ice water I gave her. Three glasses of wine in the time she's been here is more than enough.

A drop of condensation falls from the glass, landing on her collarbone. It slowly slides down, down along her cleavage.

Fuck. I want to know where it ends up.

Feeling my temperature rise, I head to the living room window to distract myself. A sedan pulls up in front of the house, and I receive a text from the driver.

I lead her to the front door. "Text me when you get home."

She nods and stands on her tiptoes to kiss my cheek. When she drops back down, I place a hand behind her head and dip my mouth to hers. At the last moment, I kiss her cheek, scared I'll flout those rules we've discussed.

As the door clicks closed behind her, I wonder if I'll ever get rid of the bitterness where Hildy is concerned, or will I forever regret I couldn't be the man she wanted?

CHAPTER 11

SAM

As the cab's taillights fade down the street, I can't shake the feeling that Hurricane Hildy just whirled through my life once again. The only difference? Tonight, she wasn't wearing high heels.

Talk about a strange evening. I still can't believe Hildy showed up here this late. Worse, she'll be back tomorrow to pick up her car.

Shit. That calls for another drink.

Some wine remains, so I snatch the bottle off the coffee table and fill my glass with a generous amount. I don't drink all that much, but now I've drunk two nights in a row.

This is what Hildy does to me and my poor liver.

Yes, I'm blaming her.

I take a long drink, gulping it down as though it's the antidote to the confusion coursing through my veins. Science can't do much for matters of the heart, but alcohol has its uses. I remember drinking a helluva lot more post-divorce until a mix of common sense and self-preservation took over.

Don't fail me now.

The house is so quiet—too quiet—and once again I blame

her. This place feels wrong without her voice or the clink of her wineglass echoing off the walls.

How can someone so infuriatingly magnetic waltz right back into my life when I never wanted to see them again? And why do I want her to come back and not just to pick up her car?

"I'm losing my goddamn mind."

That has to be the reason.

"Fuck it." I toss back the rest of my wine. It leaves a warmth that almost makes me want the chaos that is Hildy in my life. Almost.

I refill my glass. Maybe I've been alone too long. Maybe I've forgotten how to share my space with someone who isn't a lab rat. An unsettling thought creeps into my mind.

Maybe something more than the chemistry we acknowledge still exists between us.

I take another sip.

"Nope. There's nothing there."

Are you sure? The little devil on my shoulder mocks me. *What if she's the missing variable in your life's equation? The one that balances everything out and makes it all make sense?*

"She had her chance and sucked my happiness and my life into a black hole."

Fuck. I'm talking to myself.

I drink more. No matter what's happening, I can't be distracted by this ... *this* ... whatever the hell it is. I need to finish the project so I can move on from Zentello to bigger and better things, including a much larger paycheck with more benefits and stock options.

I need to stop the thoughts in my head. I'm a well-respected scientist, not a lovesick teenager.

But as I raise my wineglass to my lips, my fingers curl around the stem and my hand trembles with uncertainty.

Fine. I take a long swig. I'll admit her presence intrigues me. And dammit if my heart doesn't race at the thought of her here. "Just intrigued."

I plop down on the couch next to the spot where she sat. It's strange how easily Hildy fits in here. My usually cold and sterile house had felt like a home. And that scares the shit out of me.

I glance around the room. Everything looks the same, yet it all feels different. I glance at the empty spot next to me. I can almost picture her here in the future, animatedly talking about Gödel's incompleteness theorems, her fingers tracing patterns in the air as if she's painting the very fabric of the universe and breathing life into the dead space.

Into me.

"Get a grip, Grant." This isn't some damn rom-com where the full-of-gumption leading lady sweeps in and changes everything with her wit and charm. This is real life—*mine*—and I need to keep my head in the game.

My gaze falls onto the pillow next to me, still indented from where she'd sat earlier. I reach for it, unable to resist the urge to hold something that had been close to her. I hesitate for a second before bringing it to my face and inhaling her scent deeply.

My heart lurches in my chest. Her perfume is sweet and intoxicating, like honey mixed with wildflowers. The scent of her lingers in the air like a ghost, teasing me, tormenting me.

My body reacts. My heart races, and my palms go slick with sweat.

Something stirs deep within me—an unspoken longing I haven't allowed myself to feel in more than five years.

"You goddamn idiot." I toss the pillow onto the floor. "She's your ex-wife, not some siren luring you to your doom."

But even as I try to convince myself, I know I'm only lying to one person: me.

I finish the rest of the wine.

What about Hildy makes her so damn irresistible? Is it her intelligence, her beauty, or something more?

Whatever it is, Hildy left her mark on me—and my house—and I can't help but crave her, and I hate myself for wanting more of her. I need to get away from this spot.

I stand, swaying slightly. The buzz isn't the only thing that makes me off-balance. It's Hildy, and the way she's managed to get under my skin after all this time.

"Shit." I rub my face in frustration. "I need to clear my head."

I stumble toward the window, forcing it open, and take a deep breath. The temperature has cooled now that the sun has gone down, but the night air does little to tamp down the fire burning within me.

"Sammy boy, you're in deep shit." I lean against the windowsill. "You're letting her get to you, and that's exactly what she wants."

"Who are you talking to?" a female voice calls from the sidewalk.

I look out to see Mrs. Muldoon holding on to her

chihuahua's leash and staring at me curiously.

"Uh, just myself," I reply sheepishly, trying to regain some semblance of composure. "Got a lot on my mind."

"Sounds like someone needs to lay off the sauce," she says with a knowing grin, shaking her head.

"Thanks for the advice."

"Come on, Pedro," she says with a wave to me. "You need to do your business so we can go home."

I close the window. As much as I hate to admit it, Mrs. Muldoon is right. Alcohol won't solve my problems, and neither will wallowing in self-pity. What will help clear my jumbled thoughts, make my skin feel less clammy, and maybe lessen the buzz is a shower.

As I head to the bathroom, I peel off my clothes with a mix of urgency and frustration and toss them onto the floor. I place my glasses on the counter.

As I twist the faucet, the water streams out. Steam fills the bathroom, fogging up the mirror and surrounding me in a hazy cocoon of heat.

Already I feel better.

Stepping under the spray, I let the hot water cascade over my body, seeking solace in its warmth and hoping it will wash away my turmoil. I let the water rinse my face, turning the cheek that Hildy had kissed when she left toward the stream to wash off that spot. I need every trace of her gone.

Damn her. Damn me. Damn this whole fucked-up situation.

I grab the body wash and lather the soap in my hands, working it into a frothy foam. The mundane task soothes me, even as my body thrums with tension.

As I close my eyes against the spray, my thoughts drift back to Hildy. The curve of her lips, the swell of her breasts beneath her shirt. Unbidden, my hand drifts lower, fingers wrapping around rigid flesh.

Thinking of her on my couch, smiling and fitting in so perfectly, haunts me. I rest my forehead against the cold tiles. As much as I hate to admit it, I can't shake the physical attraction that seems to grow stronger by the minute.

Stop, Grant.

She's engaged to Nate. His ring is on her finger. They are probably fucking right now.

All those are reasons I shouldn't do this, shouldn't give in to base urges like some hormone-addled teenager. But the more I fight it, the more my traitorous body rebels.

I let go of myself. I need to focus on something other than her scent and the way my pulse picks up at the thought of her. I consider one of the test groups, and what the data suggests ...

Shit. It's no use. I can't stop thinking about her.

The shy way she averted her eyes when we first met, only to boldly hold my gaze later on. The quick flash of laughter that lit up her face. The curve of her neck that begged to be tasted.

Not even listing the effects of oral birth control with Orchid can stop me from getting harder. I can't deny what needs to be done.

The image of Hildy's smirking face is seared into my mind, her eyes dark and challenging as she dares me to want her.

I wrap my fingers around my dick once again and move my hand up and down.

Unwanted images flash through my mind—tangled limbs, hungry mouths, fingers twisted in dark curls. I imagine the sounds she might make, my name a throaty cry on her lips.

The hot water cascades along my body, intensifying the pleasure coursing through me. Droplets of water trace paths along the lines and contours of my body. I find a rhythm that intensifies the sensations making me lose control.

I picture her glossy hair that curls on the ends, her quick wit, the way she commands a room, and her lips. Those lips wrapped around my hard cock, smearing lipstick all over me.

"Goddammit, Hildy." My breath comes in ragged gasps. A twinge of guilt gnaws at me, but it's quickly swallowed by the overwhelming desire pulsing through my veins.

I imagine peeling off each piece of her clothing to reveal supple curves and silken skin. My lips trace every inch, finding all the spots that make her gasp and arch into me. Her nails rake down my back as our bodies join again and again.

My hand moves faster, fueled by the relentless current of desire swirling around me like a whirlpool. Every stroke brings me closer to the edge, teetering on the brink of an abyss that both terrifies and exhilarates me. And as much as I want to pull back, to regain control over my own reckless thoughts and desires, I can't help but plunge headfirst into the void.

"Fuck," I hiss, my hand moving even faster as the pressure builds inside me.

I groan, feeling the coil inside me tighten with every passing second. The tension builds until it's almost unbearable, my body trembling with the effort of holding back the inevitable. And then, suddenly, everything snaps into place. My body shakes violently as a powerful climax tears through me, ripping away any last shred of resistance I might have. My breath catches in my throat, coming out in ragged gasps as waves of pleasure crash over me in a relentless torrent. My knees threaten to buckle under the weight of the sensation. It's too much, too intense—yet, at the same time, not nearly enough.

"Fuck," I whisper this time, leaning against the shower wall as the water rains down on me. Somehow, I knew that this wouldn't be the last time I'd find myself at odds with my feelings for Hildy—but for now, it's all I can do to try to keep my head above water.

As the aftershocks of my release slowly fade, I lean once again against the tiles, trying to catch my breath. My heart hammers against my rib cage in a rapid staccato beat. Ribbons of cum drip down the tile. Relief and disgust wash over me. I know full well I can't escape the hold she has on me, even if it's only in my mind.

I stare at my trembling hand, the one that sought solace in memories of Hildy, and clench it into a tight fist. Hot and wild like the water cascading down my back.

I wince at what I've just done. I might be able to control myself around her, but I wouldn't call jerking off to her a victory. I need to get a fucking grip. "She's my goddamn ex-wife and engaged to my fucking boss, not some ... some fantasy."

But even as I try to convince myself this was nothing more than a momentary lapse, a single indiscretion brought on by too much alcohol and too little self-control, I know deep down that isn't true. Hildy has gotten under my skin, wormed her way into my thoughts, and made herself right at home. No matter how much I might try to deny it, even now I want her more than I've ever wanted anyone else. "This is bad. This is really, really bad."

I want her still. I always have, and I fear I always will.

But I can't have her.

"Son of a bitch." I close my eyes, letting the water wash away the last vestiges of my guilt and desire. But despite my best efforts, one thing remains clear: Hildy is a force to be reckoned with, and resisting her will be the greatest challenge I've ever faced.

And God help me, I can't wait to see how it all plays out.

Walking into my office, I'm surprised to see Hildy at my computer, given her car remains parked behind mine. It's a good thing I take public transit to work. I thought she'd swing by first thing this morning to pick it up. "You never picked up your car."

"I don't need it to get here."

Did she take the Link, or did Nate give her a ride?

I ball my hands. Maybe I deserve the reminder of her engagement when she haunted my dreams last night after I jerked off. But fuck it. This isn't how I wanted to start my day—walking into *my* office and seeing her on *my* computer.

We've been through her using my computer. At least I changed the password. She's smart, but no way could she guess the new one.

"What are you doing?" I ask as I come closer. "Didn't we discuss this?"

I know damn well we did, but I'm trying to be professional. *Professional.*

I say the word mentally to remind myself.

She twirls the chair around to face me. "I'm missing the file on the trial group."

"I emailed it to you." I take off my jacket and hang it. "Now if you don't mind, please don't use my desk again."

She stares at me with a quizzical expression, and when I motion at the chair, she jumps to her feet.

"Oh yes, sorry." As she goes to her desk, I stand away from her to avoid any unnecessary touching. I don't wholly trust myself with her. I get the feeling from what she said last night that she has the same problem, so the best thing would be for us to avoid touching or getting within kissing range of each other.

"Maybe if you gave me access to the primary files, it wouldn't be an issue." Her tone is haughty, something she does so well. "I wouldn't have to keep asking for the secondary ones."

I shake my head. "Only lead scientists have access to the primary files."

That's a lie, but I'm not in the mood to follow a clear and open policy yet. My gut tells me that file isn't what she really wants. Why? Because I have no doubt I sent it to her, and she saved it on the desktop of her laptop.

The gears in my brain spin. She's up to something, and I get the feeling it has to do with the question she asked me last night about Zentello.

"So tell me, handsome," she says as I take my seat. "Did you dream about me last night after I left?"

Fuck her. I won't give Hildy the satisfaction of the truth. "No."

"Not a little bit?"

"No," I say a little harsher.

She shrugs. "Okay then. I guess we're not playing today."

My face heats. "No, we're not. You wanted rules, so we've got them."

She sucks in a breath, but I don't bother looking at her. I won't and can't be compromised just because she looks damn gorgeous again. Yes, I notice her tight pants that accentuate the curve of her hips and the sleeveless shirt that hugs her fantastic boobs.

Man, it's going to be another long day. But on the bright side, only twelve more to go before she's out of my life forever. I hope I can survive.

I sit at my desk and answer emails.

Hildy gives a bored sigh.

I keep my gaze on the task at hand. "What now?"

"I need a tour. Maybe visit the labs connected to the project to get a feel for the place."

I turn my chair to face her. "Why?"

"I feel disconnected from the project."

"This is only your third day; I wouldn't expect you to be fully connected yet. I *would* expect you to be professional and do your work to the best of your ability. I would also expect you to understand the vision and therefore be excited about what we're doing with the data, but as for being connected and knowing the team, that will come with time."

"I'm not here for *that* long. I need to meet as many people as I can in person." She crosses her legs, showing off sky-high shoes with the thinnest of heels, pointiest of toes, and red soles.

Damn her. "Have Nate give you a tour."

"He's the CEO. He doesn't have time for that."

Of course not, which means I have to waste *my* time, which in her eyes isn't as valuable as Nate's. Fuck it.

But it'll be safer for both of us to be in another area with others around. "Okay. Let's go. Put your lab coat on."

She feigns disappointment. "But you can't watch my ass, then."

"Rules, Hildegard. Get your lab coat." I shrug on mine.

Halfway through the tour, I'm seriously annoyed. She acts like an excited puppy. Like she's never seen a working laboratory. Because of her exuberance, everyone thinks she's marvelous, and several research assistants check her out even though they're much younger than her.

She wants to know about the network, which raises the hair at the back of my neck since she was at my computer again. I need to lock it down with more than just the screen password. Each file should have one. At least until I discover what she's up to.

"She's asking a lot of questions," Max says in his clipped British accent as Hildy pulls her chair closer to Macie, one of the research assistants. "Is she doing a thesis or something?"

He grins because he's joking, but he kind of has a point.

"I know," I say quietly. "She's been like this in every lab."

"Maybe she's the mole." Max slaps my back and laughs.

When I don't join in, his brows rise in question behind his glasses. "You can't be serious, mate."

"No. Shit. I don't know." My mind reels as I try to piece together what I've seen since she's been here. "I caught her trying to get on my computer this morning. She wanted a file, but I know for a fact I already sent it to her."

"Maybe she didn't save it," he offers.

"I watched her save it. No, she's up to something."

"I doubt she's the mole, though, mate." He adjusts his glasses. "She's only been here a few days."

True. Jennings was fired a year and a half ago. That's a long time without anyone on the inside. "Unless she's a replacement."

Max and I glance at Hildy as she makes notes in a spiral pad, and then we look at each other.

"Nah." Max shakes his head. "She's too obvious."

"Hiding in plain sight?"

"I doubt it. Now, I've been ordered to ask if you're free on Friday night. Sophie has a victim lined up for you. I think she and Christina are tag teaming on finding you a woman."

I roll my eyes. Another date is the last thing I need. "Tell your wife I appreciate her efforts, but I'm good."

He laughs. "As if that'll get you off the hook. Prepare yourself for a text onslaught, my friend, because you know it's going to happen."

Max walks away, and I decide it's time I take Hildy back to the office. "Ready to get to work?"

She nods, so we head to my office. "That was so interesting. I learned so much."

Max asking if she might be the mole set off a warning in my head. It's been bugging me ever since. "Why all the questions?"

"No reason." She turns away from me and drops her notepad into her purse.

I grab her arm and make her face me.

Her forehead creases. "Sam, what are you doing?"

"I asked you a question." My voice is firm but not harsh. "Tell me why you're so interested, and don't give me any bullshit about wanting to connect with the project."

She flinches. "I like to know my work, that's all."

Her cheeks turn a dark shade of pink. She shifts her weight between her fuck-me heels. I have zero doubt she's hiding something. And this project is too important to me and my future to let it drop.

"Bullshit, Hildy." I pull her closer. "I want the truth, and I want it now."

PHARMA LAB NOTES #270

BY JAMES AUSTEN

An insider at one of the X, Y, or Z pharmaceutical companies claims unethical treatment of lab animals has been ongoing and a source of contention since the company was founded. This has led to disagreements that could explain why one of the executives acts as a silent partner. How regulatory agencies will address these accusations remains to be seen, but this puts their current products in development, including one using an all-female cohort of trial participants, in limbo should the government decide to crack down and investigate the allegations.

One of those products includes some of the top researchers in pharmaceutical science, including Drs. G, Z, and G. Scientists of that caliber could find their prospects limited if the claims prove true. If that's the case, we will publish the names of the lead scientist as well as their support team of research assistants and lab technicians. Our inquiries to the company have yet to be answered.

CHAPTER 12

HILDY

Sam looks so determined with his shoulders back and his teeth clenched. Not to mention the telltale pulse right on his jawline. He knows something is going on, but how in the hell do I tell him I'm trying to figure out if he's a mole?

Well, that isn't strictly true.

Nate asked me to, and yes, he has his reasons, even if I don't want to believe it. Which is why I'm also trying to prove it's not Sam. I thought by asking the team questions about Orchid I could see who knew what and who might trip up and give me a clue they were the mole—mission unsuccessful. All I did was tip Sam off that I'm up to something.

Not smart, Hildy.

I plaster on my best smile, the one I'd used when Dad and Mom wanted to show all their wealthy friends what a perfect family we were. "I was just being friendly. I want to connect with the project, but I'm embarrassed to say I need some friends as well."

Sam's eyebrows scrunch together. "I've never heard such BS in all my life. You have plenty of friends."

Dammit. I forgot he knew that. "Well, they're always busy."

"Tell me the truth, Hildy. Now."

"You can't tell me what to do, Sam. We're not married, and we've talked about this many times. I can talk to whomever I like."

He winces, and I'm not sure whether it's the "not married" comment or the "talk to whomever I like" that did it. Me talking to other people, specifically other men, had caused one of our biggest ever arguments when we'd been married. So big I'd stormed out and not come home for five hours. By the time I got home, Sam had been frantic, particularly because a woman had been hit by a car on First Avenue. My favorite coffee shop happened to be on First Avenue, and I often went there when I needed thinking time. I also wouldn't answer his calls or texts. Admittedly, the make-up sex had been awesome, and we were both sorry—I may have been a little too flirty, and he may have been a little too jealous—but we both wanted to forget that argument. Until we broke up, and I mentioned it in every single one of my awful emails I now regret writing and sending.

"Glad you remember we're not married," Sam snaps, still staring at me. "But for your information, I don't care who you talk to. I care about why because I know you're up to something."

While I can easily wriggle free of his hand on my arm, I can't get out of this situation. We still have to work together. Plus, I don't want to believe he's the mole. Little Biker Girl and her courier services aside, Sam is extremely professional and loyal. Okay, he and Nate lost their way as friends, but what about everyone who works at Zentello? Sam wouldn't risk their jobs and his own by causing problems for the company.

I sigh, realizing I have no way out of the mess I've gotten myself into. "Okay. I'm doing a favor for Nate."

Sam lets go of me. The disgust on his face tells me I said the wrong thing.

"Of course you fucking are." He growls and jerks his hand away. "Why am I not surprised? Sent you out to spy on his minions, has he?"

"Kind of."

"Wow." Sam throws his hands in the air. "Nice work, Mr. Lowe."

I pull out my phone from the pocket of my lab coat, flick through some emails, open one, and thrust it in Sam's face. "This is why."

It's a new article about Zentello and whether their treatment of lab animals is ethical. The piece suggests what's happening could influence Orchid's chances of getting past the Food & Drug Administration's final review process.

Sam reads the article and then shakes his head.

"It's all speculation. The FDA can investigate, but they won't find any unethical treatment of animals. Everyone knows that. This is just a cheap rag pretending to be a scientific magazine. They never back up their sources. If that's what's got Nate's boxers in a twist, then he's wasting energy and should ignore it."

I watch his face carefully. "You don't think there's any substance to the accusations?"

"No. I wouldn't work here if I thought Zentello were taking shortcuts, never mind testing on animals in the way that piece of crap says we do."

The anger he feels toward the article is evident in his voice and stiff posture. My relief is almost palpable. It's not him. I believe him when he says he wouldn't work here if those allegations were true, but someone is feeding the reporter information.

"The article claims to have a list of team members and has the key leads' initials, including yours, Bradley's, and Max's. Whoever wrote this knows the clinical research is using all-female participants. They're getting that information from somewhere."

Sam takes my phone and rereads the article. "You've got a point, but it took a while to find the last informant. How would you find this one?"

He hands me back my phone, and I rest it against my chin as I consider my options. Nate wants to know who the mole is, so that gives me an idea.

"I have a plan."

"You do?" Sam sounds wary, and I honestly don't blame him. "What is it?"

Grinning, I tap him on the chest with my phone. "I'll tell you, and you, my friend, will help me."

He doesn't even blink. "Since when have we ever been friends, Hildegard?"

This man ... "There's always a first for everything, Samuel. Just hear me out."

The only problem?

I don't have a plan. Not at all. I have no clue how to find out the mole's identity, but Sam will help me put my non-plan into action.

He cocks a brow. "How am I going to help you?"

Dammit. He knows I have no plan. "I don't know," I admit. "But I dare you to do it."

He always enjoyed a challenge in the past. Maybe he still does.

Sam rubs his face and then grins—that beautiful one that crinkles his eyes at the edges. "Double dare you."

Just like old times. God knows what the double dare will be now, but I've never been one to shirk the chance to do something I probably shouldn't. When I see Sam's shoulders shaking, I join in the laughter. Yes, just like old times, and my chest tightens.

"What do we do, then?" Sam asks.

Might as well come clean since he can read me as easily as a pH meter. "You know that I have no plan, right?"

"I know."

"Do you even have a dare for me?"

His smile doesn't waver, and he shakes his head. "It appears we're both unprepared."

That would be a first for him.

"I'm sure I can come up with something for the dare." I wink at him, and when he surreptitiously adjusts the crotch on his pants, a deep sense of satisfaction flows through me.

This is us at our best and why we were so damn good together until work and stubbornness got in our way.

"Nate really asked you to do this?" Sam says, clearly changing the subject. "He must think I'm a suspect."

I don't want to fuel the flames between them, so I'll be vague about what Nate believes. "He wants to know who's been selling information to some journalists who keep using false names."

Sam nods. "Yeah, I've heard about them. Bradley had a run-in with them last year. Christina, too."

"Nate told me."

Sam's face hardens. It happens whenever I mention Nate. I have no idea what the hell happened between the once-close friends, but if I hand over evidence, Nate will tell me. I want to know.

"Seems like he told you a lot of things," Sam mutters.

I choose to ignore him. "Seems like we really need to stop this mole and quickly before Salinger or Hemingway, or whatever their name is, publishes any more crap."

"Maybe we should read all the articles first to see if we can find a common thread or theme."

"Yes, yes." I hold my hand up for a high five, but he leaves me hanging. "Okay, I forgot that you don't high-five. We have data to look at now, but after work, let's get all the articles and cross-reference them to see if anything sticks out that only certain people would know."

"Sounds like we have a plan now." In the office, Sam walks over to his desk and pulls out his chair. "And can I just say, I knew you were up to something. Let it be noted in the minutes I was right."

"For once."

"If you remember correctly, I was right quite often during our marriage."

I sit at my desk. "Hmm, only because I let you think that."

After we spend a full day verifying trial data, we get to work on the various articles I'd printed off. For the next three hours, we review each piece with a fine-tooth comb. For once, I'm glad of Sam's precision and attention to detail. He even creates a spreadsheet.

"Look at this quote." Sam points at one of the articles. "It's the same phrasing as another." He then points at the spreadsheet and a quote from two months earlier.

"Wow, you should be a detective." I smile at him, wondering, not for the first time, how the hell we managed to lose our way.

"You know me. I like to be thorough."

And didn't that send little shivers to my lady parts. Sam is the best lover I've ever had. I don't know whether it's the scientist in him or the fact he's a true gentleman, but he was, as he said, extremely thorough. I often wondered while lying in bed whether he'd actually licked, kissed, and nipped every inch of my skin to ensure nothing felt neglected.

"You read me the salient points in that article." Sam turns back to study his screen. "I'll cross-reference them and add them to the sheet."

Here we are, working together, and it brings back memories of when we were married. During the best of times, we'd been a team who helped each other. If I did something and it didn't work, Sam always came up with an alternative plan. If Sam tried something and didn't get the result he required, he'd talk it through with me, and we'd discuss what needed to be changed. It was the way we worked.

Now, we're working together professionally, and it's like we've done it for years. I think outside the box while Sam follows procedure and ensures we don't miss anything. Our process even worked with chores like cleaning the apartment or doing the laundry. I hated doing both of those things, which he knew, so he handled those things, and I cooked.

We were so great together, yet I never told him. All I ever did at the end was tell him all the things that pissed me off about him and our marriage. I lost sight of all the good things. I didn't mention how he'd go out and buy me mac and cheese from Beecher's and passionfruit yogurt from Ellenos at Pike Place Market when I had my period.

Not once did I note in those massive emails how grateful I was for the time he drove me to Sacramento when my friend from college Eliza ended up in the hospital because her piece-of-shit boyfriend knocked her around. Sam even went to their apartment, knocked the guy out, and collected all of Eliza's stuff. To top it all off, he drove us to Eliza's mom's house in Bend. Needless to say, when Sam and I broke up, Eliza thought I was crazy and gave me shit for weeks. She's okay now, but she still writes Sam's name in the Christmas card she sends me each year.

"Why are you doing this?" I ask him.

As I tap my pen against my chin, I study him. It's an honest question because I've been nothing but a bitch to him since the divorce.

"Doing what? Helping to find the mole?"

"Yes. Because you don't have to," I admit. "You could have told me to do it by myself."

"The way I see it, snooping around and helping you means if I find out things are going to shit, I can get out before it ruins my reputation. I can then tell Nate he's an even lower-rent douche than he already is for involving me and wasting my time."

The vitriol in his tone drips from each word. "You really don't like Nate, do you?"

"Nope."

"So why stay at Zentello, or even work here at all?" As I wait for him to answer, I swirl my chair a full three-sixty. He doesn't respond. "Well, why stay here?"

He finally shrugs, but his posture is too stiff for him to be indifferent. "It's a job."

"With a man you supposedly hate—"

"There's no supposedly about it." Sam's eyes blaze with anger and something I haven't seen before. "And you know why."

"I don't know. Please tell me why you hate him."

Sam springs out of his chair and cages me in mine with his hands gripping the arms. Before I can speak, his mouth lands on mine, and he kisses me, slowly and softly. He silently urges my lips to open. They do, and he slips his tongue inside and caresses mine with it.

Our mouths move together like they've never been apart. As the sound of my heartbeat thuds in my ears, I desperately want to push my hands into Sam's hair, but the kiss has left me frozen because it's everything. Everything I've missed. Everything I've loved about kissing him. A little moan escapes my mouth, and Sam pulls back, leaving me bereft.

Sam smooths my hair with his hand. "That's why I hate him."

"W-what?" I ask, putting my fingers to my swollen lips.

Sam doesn't reply. Instead, he gives me a sad smile and returns to his computer, making it clear that's the end of the conversation. But he didn't answer my question, and now I'm even more confused than I was before.

CHAPTER 13

SAM

As I sit at my desk, I rub my fingertips across my mouth desperately trying to erase the lingering feeling of Hildy's lips on mine. Kissing her had been a huge lapse of judgment. In other words, a mistake. Mostly because now I want to do it again, even though I'm pissed at the thought of Nate's lips having been in the same places mine have been, and not just on her mouth.

Nope. I'm not thinking about it any longer.

Dammit. Now that I'm not thinking about Nate's lips on Hildy's body, I'm thinking about my own.

"You want to expand on that?" Hildy asks.

I raise my eyebrows without looking at her. "The kiss? You know what expanding on that would mean, honey."

She huffs a breath, which makes me smile. In the past, a similar huff had led to wild abandon sex because that's where we were most compatible—in bed. Although, to be honest, we'd been a pretty good team all around until everything fell apart.

Hildy continues to huff and puff for at least two minutes. "Expanding on the kiss ... Would it be so bad?"

"I'm not ready for this conversation. Plus, we have work to

do." I pick up the bottle of water on my desk and point at her. "This flirting has to stop."

"You started it by kissing me."

She actually huffs again, and fuck, it shoots straight to my dick. I pull my chair closer to my desk and hope my erection deflates soon. The woman is a damn curse.

Not that I've ever had reason to believe curses exist, but it's the most plausible explanation at the moment.

"Are you actually going to answer?" she asks.

I swing my chair around to face her. "Answer what, Hildy?"

"Well, there are two things, to be precise. First, would it be so bad to expand on our kiss, and second, what the hell does you kissing me have to do with you hating Nate?"

"Third, I don't want to discuss either of the above." I open the bottle and take a long swig, hoping it'll distract me from the dick in my pants.

"God, you're so annoying."

"I know. You told me that in the many emails you sent me." I roll my eyes and turn back to my desk. "Now, let's get on with the task at hand, shall we?"

The silence lasts four minutes and thirty seconds before she taps her pen on the desk.

"Hildy," I groan. "What is it now?"

"I'm just curious. You and Nate were close. He was the best man at our wedding, for goodness' sake. And you were his when he married Zelda."

"I told you I don't want to discuss it." I pinch the bridge of my nose. "Listen, why don't I go work in the lab or at home and give you some space?"

I stand, ready to shut everything down and leave. She shoves her chair back and jumps to her feet, stopping me.

She places her hands on her hips. "Speak to me, dammit."

Two can play this game. I mirror her stance. "You want me to speak?"

She huffs again. I go from half-mast to the damn king-in-residence-at-the-palace within seconds.

In two strides, I stand in front of her and have her in my arms. Before I can worry about asking for her consent, her fingers are at my belt buckle. Mine go to the button on her pants, and as soon as it's open and the zipper is down, I pull her shirt up. At the first sight of bare skin, I lean down and kiss her soft skin, which smells of coconut.

I don't want to lick my lips, but I do. "Fuck, you taste exactly the same."

"Oh, baby." She moans. "I've missed your mouth on me."

That's all I need to hear. I push her shirt up higher and pull down the white lace of her bra. Sucking her nipple into my mouth, I feel the deep throb of ecstasy running through my body.

"Knock, knock, you in, Sammy?"

"Fuck." I pull Hildy's bra up and her shirt down. "It's Geraldine."

Hildy frowns and scrambles to dress as I try to make myself look presentable. My hard-on rages, so I opt to leave my shirt untucked at the front, like I've had a hard day rather than I'd been about to have sex with my ex-wife.

"Geraldine," I call out a few octaves higher than usual. "How are you?"

HILDY

Ugh.

You in, Sammy?

That woman's voice winds me up. *She* winds me up, and I hate her and her cute little ass in her tight leather riding pants. Coming in here calling my ex-husband *Sammy* like she has a right to. Like she knows that he loves Reese's Peanut Butter Cups on a Sunday with his first cup of coffee, that he prefers a bath to a shower, or that when he's tired but trying not to fall asleep so he can watch a movie with me, he sneaks into the bedroom and jogs for three minutes to wake himself up.

No, she can't possibly know those things, but I do because I was married to him. He was my husband, and I loved him. Well, Little Biker Girl isn't going to have him. I'll make sure of it.

As Sam makes small talk with her and tries to hide his erection, I reapply my red lipstick. A quick glance at my hair in my mirror shows me it's still intact, a little ruffled maybe, but generally, I don't look like I was about to be ruined on top of my desk.

"I need to go visit the lab, honey," I say in the sweetest voice I can muster. "See you in a little while."

Call me irrational or a bitch, but I kiss him. Full on the mouth. Hard and quick. I then wipe the lipstick off his lips.

"Later, honey," I say, emphasizing the last word.

With that, I shimmy out of the office, making sure I wiggle

my ass more than usual—the way I always exited the room when I knew Sam was watching me.

And I have no doubt he's watching me now.

Take that, Little Biker Girl.

Sam Grant might not be mine, but he'll never be yours. Never.

SAM

"Is she okay?" Geraldine thumbs over her shoulder toward Hildy's disappearing ass that is doing some strange walking-twerk action. "She looks at me like she hates me."

She kind of did, but that has nothing to do with Geraldine and everything to do with my ex-wife. And yes, I'm partially to blame for the way she's reacting.

"Oh, she's fine." I keep my voice lighthearted. "Hildy's just Hildy. Now, tell me about your college search. Which have you decided on applying to?"

Geraldine lifts her shoulders in a shrug and sighs heavily. "I have no idea. It's like the worst decision in the world to make. I narrowed my list down to my top three, and each one has great childcare facilities for my little boy."

"Well, I guess that's as important as a major for you." I perch on the edge of my desk. Thankfully, my dick has fully deflated. "Still thinking business with a major in accounting?"

"Yes, that's right."

"From my point of view, Pennsylvania is the best fit. Solid program and excellent reputation."

"You think?"

I nod.

"Good. Because I think so too, and my boyfriend's company has an office in Philadelphia, so that would work. They also have an apartment we can rent that's close to campus, so if I have to go to class early, Ben can take Louis to daycare, and I can pick him up." She leans in and hugs me. "Thanks, Sammy. I think you made my mind up for me."

"No problem, kiddo. Now, do you have my package?"

"Oh God, yes. I almost forgot." She reaches into her messenger bag and pulls out a brown envelope with tamper tape across the flap. "Here you go."

I take it from her and open it. This contains the information I sent to "my guy" to be coded and returned. All a little James Bond, I admit, but I don't want to risk anyone finding my notes. That's why I send them over to Toby, and he puts them into an encrypted report that no one without the code can read.

I trust him implicitly.

I've not only paid him a lot of money, but he's only fourteen and has no clue what he's working on. I found him when a former non-Zentello coworker invited me to a barbecue, and I got talking to his kid, Toby, who's into Secret Service and NSA stuff. After the science reporter wrote about Zentello, I had to do something. I had a whole stack of notes and didn't feel safe putting them on my desktop or laptop. I also didn't want to save them on a hard drive that could be stolen or lost. A coded report was the best option, so we struck a deal, and I hired Toby.

The kid's a fuckin' genius.

Anyone looking at the report would simply see a list of letters and numbers. On the other hand, I know exactly what it says—everything I've noted during my tenure at Zentello. And I mean everything.

It's not the sort of crap the journalist—or should I say journalists—reports on, which are rumor and gossip. Everything in my notes is based on facts. It matters that things are being done correctly and rules are being followed because I care about my work and that it's accomplished ethically. I want to be proud of the company I work for, but ...

The report isn't something I want Hildy to see. She's too close to Nate, both professionally and personally. I doubt he'd be down with me probing and detailing the running of his company. I'm mindful of my NDA, but this is a necessary action I must take.

Geraldine opens the flap of her messenger bag. "Anything to go back?"

I do have something. I unlock and open the drawer and remove an envelope with tape across the flap. Thankfully, I'd gotten it ready before Hildy distracted me with her plan and then us almost having sex.

I hand it to Geraldine and smile. "See you next time?"

"Sure. Will your ex-wife throw me shade again?" Geraldine laughs and pokes me in the shoulder. "Though, is she still the ex, or are you back on?"

I clear my throat. "What gives you that idea?"

Geraldine lets her head drop back and laughs raucously. "Give me a break, Sammy. I caught you with your pants down, almost. I'm pretty sure if I'd arrived two seconds later, I might have witnessed the conception of your first child."

I shake my head. "You've got it all wrong."

"Like hell I have," she counters. "I can practically smell the sexual tension in here."

To be perfectly honest, it's a wonder she can't smell the actual sex. I half laugh.

"You really should tell her how you feel, you know," she says.

I flinch. "Hildy?"

"Yes, your ex-wife. She should know you want to give it another shot." Geraldine zips up her bag with my envelope tucked safely inside. "It's clear it's more than a quick roll on the desk. I've only seen you twice since she's been working here, but you look perkier, Sammy."

"Perkier?"

"Yep, perkier."

"Geraldine, I've never, ever seen myself as perky, never mind perkier."

She rolls her eyes. "You're totally perky. You clearly have big feelings for her and should tell her that."

I can't believe how easily Geraldine has cut through the years of crap. I've only known her for three years. Back then, she worked at the coffee shop I used to go to almost daily. When I would give my name for my order, I always said Sam and she wrote Sammy. It was the start of our strange friendship, though I'm not sure what you'd call us.

But one summer day, not unlike today, I found her outside on the sidewalk in tears. She'd been fired after getting sick. She was pregnant, and I'm the one who called her boyfriend to come get her because she was too scared.

Hell, I'm old enough to be her dad, but I feel more like a mentor of sorts. I did and continue to do what I can for the young couple who only want the best for their little boy. Her son's middle name is Samuel, and yes, that's in honor of me. When she decided to become a courier, I told her the risks of riding a motorcycle, and she laughed in my face. She used to race motocross, and her boyfriend fully supports the job. I never mentioned my concerns again, though I did suggest a term life insurance policy since she has a dependent. Once again, she laughed.

"Come on, Sammy boy, tell me everything." She might be young in age, but she has an old soul. I can see it in her eyes.

"You really want to know?"

"I can't believe you haven't told me already."

That makes me laugh. "Okay."

"Wait." She settles herself into Hildy's chair. Like a leather-clad pixie, she pulls her legs up, crosses them, and steeples her fingers under her chin. "Now spill the tea. I want every last drop."

And I do.

When I finish, she stares at me with a what-a-pair-of-idiots look.

"What a pair of idiots." Geraldine sighs. "It's obvious you still love each other. She was trying to make a point when she left you, and you, like a fool, didn't realize it. This is your second chance. You need to make her realize what happened was a stupid misunderstanding and you'll never put work before her again. If you get back together, you'll cherish her and put her on the pedestal she deserves to be on."

I freeze, thinking about what Geraldine's just said. She kind of nailed it.

Geraldine claps her hands and drops her feet to the floor. "Okay, I'm out. I still have three more drops to make. When I see you next, I hope you'll have gotten your wife back."

"Geraldine," I warn.

She giggles and waves me away. "Don't let me down, Sammy."

As the door slides closed behind Geraldine, her words echo through my head. Could she be right?

CHAPTER 14

HILDY

As I make my way toward Nate's office, the high-tech glass walls shimmer under the soft glow of the overhead lights. I stride down the hallway, my heels clicking against the sleek twenty-second floor. The rhythm matches the beat of my heart. My lips still tingle from Sam's kiss, but I'm pissed the Little Biker Girl showed up again.

I need to get to the bottom of whatever she's doing with Sam and those envelopes. My heart tells me Sam isn't the mole, but I need to confirm that feeling with hard data. But that's not why I'm a woman on a mission right now.

I need answers to get to the bottom of his hatred toward Nate. There has to be a reason.

Sam won't tell me anything—at least nothing I can make sense of—so Nate will have to tell me the truth.

Evidence be damned.

I quicken my pace, passing Zelda's doorway, and hurry to Nate's office.

"Looking for Nate?" Zelda's voice stops me in my tracks. I turn, and she stands outside the doorway to her office, her eyes narrowed.

I put on my best fake smile. "Hey, Zelda. What's up?"

"Just letting you know your fiancé has left for the day." Her voice is ice cold.

"Thanks," I say, trying to hide my irritation.

Her eyes practically bore into my engagement ring. "I'm surprised he didn't tell you, or have you been so caught up in wedding planning you forgot?"

"Oh, maybe I did forget." Anger surges within me like a tidal wave, threatening to drown my reason. How could Nate not have told her our engagement wasn't real? He told me he would handle it. My fingers curl into fists at my sides, nails biting into my palms.

I want to scream, to shake Nate until some sense rattles loose inside his thick skull. But he isn't here, so I'm left with Zelda, who doesn't deserve any of this. As much as I'd love to spill the truth—and I should after I told Nate I would—I need to see him first and find out exactly what's going on.

But no wonder her voice drips with disdain. She thinks I'm stealing her ex-husband. I want to tell her the engagement is all fake. Damn him for not talking to her yet and leaving me standing here, playing his pretend fiancée.

Zelda adjusts her glasses and studies me. "Is everything okay?"

No, nothing is okay. I'm still gritting my teeth but force myself to unclench my fists. "I'm fine, but ..." I might as well take the opportunity to probe her a bit. "Have you noticed anything ... off ... off between Sam and Nate?"

Zelda raises an eyebrow, her gaze narrowing. "What do you mean?"

"Like ... is there some sort of history between them I should know about?" I try to keep my voice light, but my curiosity is getting the better of me.

"Ha! You could say that." She crosses her arms. "But I'm sure your dear fiancé will fill you in on the details. Enjoy your time with Nate while it lasts, Hildy. He's married to his work, and he'll only ever truly love whatever company he's working for."

A bitter laugh escapes me. "You don't say? That sounds familiar. Like a certain ex-husband of mine."

Zelda smirks. "I guess you have a type, huh?"

"Apparently," I grumble, thinking back to the long nights Sam spent hunched over his lab bench, leaving me home alone. It was one of the many reasons our relationship imploded.

"Then you won't be caught off guard the way I was. But even so, watch your back."

Zelda's words hit close to home. Not that I'm doomed to repeat history since I'm not really engaged to Nate, but that begs a question. "Would you ever get back together with Nate?"

"That's an odd question for you to ask since you're marrying him." Her tone is wary.

I shrug. "Well, you work together. I guess I want to know if there's still something between you."

Because Nate seems to think there is, but I leave that part out.

Zelda rolls her eyes. "No, there's nothing between us. We're friends. Best friends, even, but I'd never get back together with him. Not in a million years," she says firmly, her voice ice cold. "I'd rather work with Bitter Belinda and the lab rats in the basement than marry Nate again."

Ouch. That's harsh, but she's piqued my curiosity. "Who's Bitter Belinda?"

"Someone you need to keep your distance from. She's bad news. Always complaining about everything, like she's the only one with problems, while taking pleasure in the misfortunes of others."

With that cryptic warning, Zelda turns on her heels and returns to her office.

I guess if Nate's gone and Sam is busy entertaining the Little Biker Girl, there's nothing left for me to do except leave and make a note to avoid Bitter Belinda in the future.

By the time I get home, Sam's kiss still has me hot and bothered. Okay, I'm horny. I need to get my vibrator out. Sam has me wound up like a coiled spring, and I need to release the pent-up tension.

To be fair, masturbating usually gets me off just fine. Today, it's totally unsatisfying. My head is still in the office with Sam and the Little Biker Girl, wondering what they were doing. Peter, what I named my vibrator, doesn't talk dirty, he certainly doesn't believe in foreplay, and he doesn't smell like Sam, so it's a total bust.

Flicking on the TV, I watch some guy wooing and giving roses to women who gush and giggle and act like they're eternally grateful for being involved in such a misogynistic, backward-thinking reality show.

"Oh my God," I say to one of the women on the show who tells the guy she has real feelings for him after two damn days. She's in her early twenties, but that's no excuse. "Get a grip on your life."

Bed's the best option; however, it's only ten and I'm not that tired. I could try to find a movie or ...

A knock sounds at my door.

That's strange. Only a couple of people know where I'm staying. Nate being one of them. I wonder if it's him. I hope so because I'm ready to rip into him for not talking to Zelda yet.

I get off the couch and pad my way across the living room, my pink furry slippers slapping against the floor. My eye goes to the peephole, and I gasp.

Nate isn't standing on the other side of the door. It's Sam.

I fling open the door. "Hey. Something wrong?"

"No, just returning the favor." Sam holds up a bottle of my favorite Empress 1908 gin in one hand. He's got tonic water and a lime in the other. "It's not wine, and I can't sing, but you know that I'm a wine, women, and song kind of guy rather than sex, drugs, and rock 'n' roll."

Laughing, I take the gin from him. "What the hell are you talking about?"

He shrugs. "I have no idea."

I'm confused, but that's my normal state around Sam. "You have no idea why you're here?"

"I do. I just have no idea what I'm talking about."

Hugging the bottle to my chest, I lean against the doorjamb. This is so unlike him. Something must be up. "So why are you here?"

"To catch up." He smooths his shirt, though it's neatly tucked and unwrinkled after a long day's work.

He's tieless and jacketless, but he still looks like a tall drink of water on this hot summer evening. His gray dress pants rest on slim hips, and his crisp white shirt hugs his broad chest, and when I see his forearms, I rub my thighs together. For whatever reason, this man does something to me sexually. And yes, I wish he didn't.

Sam sighs. "We need to work out what's going on here."

"Going on here?" I push away from the door and straighten. This seems like a standing-up-straight kind of conversation. "Or between us?"

"Here and at Zentello. Between you and me. And, well, Nate."

I hate lying to Sam about the engagement. I need to ask Nate if we can just drop the charade. His concerns about not opening a req for the position seem to have been a non-issue. No one has challenged my working at Zentello. "Trust me, Nate doesn't play into any of this."

Sam's jaw tenses. "Open relationship, right?"

As I sort of nod, my gut twists. It's not only the lie about the fake engagement. I'm all for people doing whatever they choose to do as consenting adults, but I could never be in a non-monogamous relationship. Sharing the person I *love* is *not* for me. "Is this a booty call?"

"No." His gaze drops to my chest for a moment before he looks me in the eye.

Too bad, but it's probably for the best. Sam's right, we need to discuss what's going on between us, particularly after we almost had sex in his office. Add to that, as I said, he looks hot and sexy and dammit, I miss him more than I realize.

I move to one side. "You'd better come in."

When Sam enters the apartment, he goes exactly where I think he'll go—to the full bookcase. Which, I should point out, freaked me out when I arrived with my two suitcases. Who the hell leaves a stack of books to the mercy of a renter? I wouldn't. I packed up my books even though Mathilda is staying in my apartment. I would have loved to take them with me, but I couldn't ship them all to New Zealand.

"How did I know you'd home in on the books?" I ask.

Sam grins over his shoulder. "You know I'm a sucker for a sci-fi book, and whoever owns this apartment has some good ones."

"Is reading still your favorite hobby?"

"It's my only hobby, though I've toyed with the idea of writing a book myself. Even have an outline I scribbled one weekend."

My jaw drops. He looks like the same Sam Grant who I married and divorced, but that man was all work and no play. Reading was his relaxation back then, but writing his own story ... I have no words.

He pulls out a book and studies the back cover. "You think I can borrow this one?"

"I guess so, but I'm not here for long, so you'll need to read it quickly."

He laughs, and then I laugh because we both know he would devour the book in a couple of days—hours, if he didn't work so damn hard.

"Remind me to take it when I leave." Sam puts back the book and faces me. "Are we having a drink or not?"

I look at the bottle. "I'll get glasses."

I place the gin on the coffee table and go to the kitchen, where I fill two glasses with ice. I also grab a knife for the lime.

When I return, Sam has opened the gin and the tonic bottles. He sits on the couch, his hands linked behind his head, and his feet on the coffee table, legs crossed at the ankle.

I smirk at how he's made himself at home, but then again, I did the same thing at his place last night. We're quite the pair.

Well, we used to be.

I place the glasses on the table. "Are you comfortable?"

"Yes." He drops his feet to the floor to reach the glasses. "I believe this is pretty good on its own without tonic, but I brought some and the lime in case you drink it differently now."

My heart thuds. "You remembered."

"I remember everything about you, Hildy." He takes a deep breath and drops his head to study the gin bottle.

I sit on the other end of the couch, facing him, and put my feet up. Sam pours a good measure and passes a glass to me.

My hand trembles as I take it. My urge is to gulp down the drink to put myself more at ease, but that would be stupid. If I get even a little buzzed, I'll probably throw myself at him. But I know something I can do ... say ... that used to make him happy. "What's up, Gus?"

Sam flashes me a gorgeous smile. "I used to love it when you'd say that."

"One of the only things I can thank my mom for," I quip. "Her silly little sayings."

"You're still having problems with your parents?"

I try not to frown and shrug instead. "Do bears take a poop in the woods, Sam? That'd be a yes. We barely speak these days."

"It's gotten worse, then?"

"You could say that. I did some therapy only to be told I was raised by a misogynistic father and codependent mother, who both used conditional love to try to control me. She's so weak where Dad is concerned, and when I told her I was taking a job in New Zealand, she called me a selfish little bitch for leaving Mathilda and Flynn alone even though she's not doing anything to help them because Dad won't let her."

Sam's eyebrows arch almost to his hairline. "You're the least selfish person I know."

Okay, that makes me laugh. "What? You're not shocked at the little bitch part?"

Sam picks up his glass, and his smile widens from behind the rim. I know he's smiling because his eyes wrinkle at the edges.

We're silent for a few moments, and then Sam takes a deep breath.

"Do you ever wish we'd had kids?" he asks.

I blink. That isn't where I expected him to go, especially when discussing having kids invariably led to a fight. "Where's this coming from?"

He shrugs. "It's something I've thought of a few times over the years. I just wondered if you had too."

Had I? Only like a thousand times since the divorce. I want a child, but having a baby together would have given me a connection to Sam. We wouldn't have lost touch over the last five years if we'd had to share custody, and maybe ...

No going back, Hildy. I know that, but sometimes my heart forgets. "Yes, I'd have liked for us to have a child, but you said it wasn't the right time."

I'd been ready, so ready that I couldn't even hit snooze on my biological clock. Sam was the one who kept pushing off me getting pregnant.

His lips narrow. "I wanted to be further ahead in my career and make more money first."

Familiar frustration coils at my tailbone and makes its way up my spine, vertebra by vertebra. "You were doing great at your job. You made more than enough, kept getting promoted, and worked way more hours than needed."

He snickers. "Oh, believe me, baby, I know what you thought about my work hours. It used to infuriate you. 'You make me so mad, Sam. Why do you have to work so much, Sam? Why don't you ever want to spend time at home, Sam?'"

As he scrubs a hand down his face, his shoulders sag in defeat.

Had I sounded so whiny and judgmental when we were married?

Dammit, yes, I had. The reason? Him. That's how he made me feel working all the time. I hadn't been enough for my dad. I wasn't enough for my husband. Looking back, it still pisses me off.

"So why didn't you, Sam?" I should shut up, but I can't. I don't know why things are escalating so quickly. I haven't drunk enough to blame the gin, but my blood is boiling, and I have to get this out. "Was I so damn awful to be married to that spending hours working in your lab was preferable to being home with your loving wife?"

"I was working on an important breakthrough. You know that." He throws his hands into the air. A gesture he hasn't appeared to have outgrown. "I also wanted us to have a good life. Have anything we wanted."

"Except for kids and a dog," I mutter, reliving the empty feeling in my heart that marriage had brought me.

"I didn't say no!" His voice sharpens. "I told you that. I told you that in time we could have those things. Well, the kids anyway. But I didn't want to be an absent father and—"

"So you decided to be an absent husband instead."

"To give us a solid foundation to build the rest of our lives on. I had a plan for our future. It would have worked if you hadn't been so impatient and needy."

"Needy?" My voice rises an octave. I place my glass on the table so I don't spill anything. "Wanting to be loved isn't needy. It's part of a marriage."

"I was loving you. Each hour I worked was for you."

"No." I shake my head to emphasize my point. "You ignored us for some blueprint you imagined. Only we weren't bricks and mortar. We were a couple. Two people in love who should've spent time together, grown together. All I wanted was you and me, a couple of kids, and a big dog. I didn't want a big house, a walk-in closet, or a swimming pool. I just wanted the simple things. The things we talked about when we first fell in love."

I blink to keep the tears at bay. I don't want to cry in front of him, not after all the times I've sobbed over him in the past when he hurt me so deeply, demolished my self-worth, and broke my heart knowing I wasn't enough to make him happy.

"You only say the simple things because you grew up with money," he says.

"I would have exchanged two loving parents for everything. The same for a devoted husband."

"I was devoted." A vein twitches on his jaw. "You had everything you ever wanted while growing up."

"Except unconditional love," I say so softly I'm not sure he hears me.

"I ..." His voice trails off. His expression appears almost haunted, a way I've never seen him look.

I lean toward him. "What?"

"I didn't have the same things you did. Not even close." His words are laced with pain, and they make my heart squeeze tightly. "I did what I thought was best for us."

I hear that in his voice, but ... "It wasn't for the best, Sam. I told you so many times it wasn't. I begged you. I pleaded with you to listen to what I wanted, but your damn pride thought I was only trying to spare your feelings."

"Your dad told me I'd never be good enough for you." Sam springs to his feet. "He said Todd Brewster earned more in a month's bonuses than I did in three months' salary. I had to work hard to make a name for myself, to get noticed in the pharmaceutical world so I could get jobs like this and be considered successful. So I could earn more fucking money than Todd fucking Brewster did."

Todd Brewster had been my boyfriend through high school

and college, and Sam was right. My dad thought he had golden balls. My dad is a dick. Todd Brewster is also a dick. Sam didn't need to try to live up to either of their expectations.

"You know I hated Todd by the time I ended things with him. You also know my dad and I didn't have a good relationship back then either." I take a deep breath to keep my temper from ramping up. "In fact, not good is putting it mildly. You knew all that and how I didn't listen to anything my father had to say. Still don't."

"I wasn't sure ..."

"My dad and I are no contact. We have no relationship." We barely did when Sam and I were married, but things are even worse now. I try not to care, and therapy has helped with that. "Things got so bad between us that I chose never to be a Bauer again. That's why I took Russell, my mom's maiden name, after our divorce. Dad never wanted me or Mathilda. He only wanted sons to carry on his company's name. Now he has Todd and Mathilda's baby daddy to do that for him."

I'd dated Todd to fight back. He had a car, he partied hard, and he lived in a two-bedroom apartment on the wrong side of town with his mom and three brothers. I thought he was everything my parents would hate, so of course I wanted to be Todd's girlfriend.

Who knew Dad would freaking love him? Who knew when Todd went to college, Dad would pay his tuition, and when Todd graduated, Dad would give him a job at his investment company? Who knew Todd would turn out to be brilliant at it? And who in the hell knew Todd would model himself on Werner Bauer and become just like him?

I couldn't have foreseen any of it.

The final straw was when Todd told me I couldn't wear a short skirt out to dinner. I was done. D-O-N-E after that.

Three weeks later, I bumped into Sam at a party and fell head over heels. It should have been my happy ending, and it was until I couldn't stand feeling lonely in my marriage any longer.

"It was never a competition between you and Todd," I say to keep the topic on track.

Sam's mouth twists. "I still had your father in my ear all the time."

"You hardly saw him!"

"It didn't matter. Werner's words imprinted here." Sam taps the side of his head with two fingertips. "It's like I was programmed to believe it, and no matter what I did, I had to make sure that I got you everything you deserved."

"Yeah, well," I grumble. "You should have listened to me instead of him."

"Maybe I should have." Sam downs his drink. "Maybe then I wouldn't be so fucking miserable."

"You're miserable?"

"Was miserable," he clarifies, but I don't believe him. His pink ears are a dead giveaway.

"I hope you can be happy now." I eye my drink and decide I've had enough. Still, there's more I need to say. "Despite our divorce and how much you hurt me, I've only ever wanted what was best for you. I just thought at the time it was me. If it's that Little Biker Girl—"

"Who?"

"Geraldine."

He chuckles. "She's just a kid I met when she was in high school who ended up pregnant and needed a friend and mentor."

"You're not—"

"Never. She has a boyfriend. I help them when I can. College info and job applications. Stuff like that."

"Oh." That isn't what I expected to hear, but I'm so fucking relieved. "And the packages ..."

"Something I'm doing on my own. I'm not the mole, if that's what you're asking."

"I'm not." *At least not at this moment.* "But thank you for telling me that. We've always been honest with each other."

His ears turn beet red, and my stomach drops. "Sam?"

"There is something I haven't told you."

My heart thuds in my chest like a bass drum. Sam said he wasn't the mole, so what could it be? Oh my God. Does he have a girlfriend or a fiancée? I swallow around the lump in my throat. "You know you can tell me anything. I was your wife."

He shakes his head. "You would've seen me differently."

Past tense. Except I feel no relief, just an all-consuming gnawing in my gut. "Please, Sam. Tell me."

He takes a drink and wipes his mouth with the back of his hand. "You want to know the real reason I worked so hard, the reason I wanted to be more secure before we had a family ...?"

I nod, unable to even breathe.

Silence envelops the room. I have no idea what he's going to say, and a chill creeps down my spine. Whatever it is, I know it's important, and I know whatever it is I can't get upset at him.

At least not until I hear him out.

He takes a breath and then another. "You know how I never talked about my family."

Sam would tell me a random story about his childhood here, another there. We never visited them. No one came to our wedding. When I asked, he didn't want to talk about it. I assumed they were estranged, and given my parents, I understood.

I nod.

"My parents died. A house fire. Lost everything, including our two dogs and three cats. I don't remember much about them since no photographs survived, but I know my dad worked hard to give my mom the house she wanted. I know this because they fought about money all the time, including the night of the fire. That's something I'll never forget. The arguing and the blaming each other. I didn't want to be like them."

What? I stare at him in disbelief. I truly am speechless.

"I grew up in foster homes. I moved around a lot and had nothing except what would fit in a garbage bag. Never came close to being adopted. The only thing that saved me was spending all four years in the same high school. Once I aged out, I was on my own, and it was ... hard."

My mouth gapes. I still don't know what to say.

"You grew up with everything you could want," he continues. "Your dad was only looking out for you. I don't blame him for that. And I wanted to make sure I could give you and our children the same thing he gave you."

A part of me is pissed at him for not telling me his past. Would it have made a difference? I don't know, but at least I would have understood him better. Now I feel as if I never really knew the man I married, the one I thought I'd loved.

It's my turn to take a breath or two. I might need a third one.

"Thank you for telling me." That's about all I can come up with when I imagine a younger Sam stuck in the system and then aging out with literally nothing. That had to have sucked. "For trusting me with that piece of your past."

A huge piece, but at least it was out there.

"I thought you had become a Werner Bauer clone, and that's why you wanted to work so much and not spend any time with me. Our marriage turned into me reliving my childhood since my dad was never around, or if he was, he didn't want to spend any time with me. He never wanted a daughter at all, and he ended up with two of them. But that made me feel like I wasn't enough for him. And I thought you ..."

"You were always enough for me, Hildy. I always wanted you. I just thought you deserved ... everything. I wanted to give you everything my dad tried to give my mom. But I never wanted things to end in a fiery death trap of our making. Seems like it did anyway in a figurative sense."

Memories of our divorce rush back. My chest tightens. "All I wanted was to be loved. I didn't need everything. I only needed ... you." My voice cracks.

Tears stream down my cheeks, and I swipe at the wetness. I force myself to breathe slowly before I hyperventilate. We should've had this conversation a long time ago.

All Sam had been trying to do was prove himself. I knew that then, but all I wanted was for me to be enough for him.

Pride on both sides caused the disintegration of our marriage, not lack of love.

"I'm sorry," we say at the same time and then laugh.

I reach for my drink and hold up my glass. "To communicating better."

"For two intelligent people, we failed there." He taps his glass against mine, and we both drink. "But now we get a second chance."

A second chance at what? Communication? Being friends? Something more?

My mind is so full of what he's told me tonight, I don't know what to say.

He glances at the time. "It's getting late. I should go."

A part of me wants to invite him to stay, but I'm not sure that's the right thing to do. Not after everything we've discussed and with our emotions running so high. At least mine. But I do want to spend time with him and not just in the office. "Can we do this again?"

"Spill our secrets and bare our souls?"

I can't help but smile. "Yes, or maybe dinner."

"Tomorrow night. Seven o'clock. My place."

That was easy, even if I worry that being with him again won't be. I raise my chin. "I'll be there."

CHAPTER 15

SAM

The following day, I arrive at the office before Hildy and focus on the task at hand—data analysis. Somehow, I make progress. I'm excited to see the Orchid project delivering as promised. The few anomalies can easily be confirmed with additional testing. And I must admit Hildy has a sharp eye for patterns and numbers, as evidenced by her breast surgery observation.

I make the most of my time alone until the door whooshes open. She acknowledges me with a tilt of her head but says nothing. I barely glance her way. I ... can't. Instead, I concentrate on the data, but I'm aware of her putting on her lab coat and going to her desk.

Focus.

I do and try not to watch the clock.

My knee bounces, something abnormal for me, but Hildy has frayed my nerves. She hasn't even opened her mouth, but the tension is practically viscous.

As she works at her desk, I try to ignore it—her. I've managed not to make a fool of myself yet. But each minute that ticks by, memories about last night at her place swirl in my mind.

Fuck.

I still can't believe I told her about my past. I suppose it's something I should have mentioned before saying *"I do,"* but I never wanted her to see me as less than—the way I'd been seen every day since my parents died. I went from being lower middle class with two parents to an orphan to a foster kid to an at-risk student on financial aid with nowhere to spend holidays. No one except Mr. Beauregard expected me to amount to anything. People made assumptions about my parents' deaths. They thought I'd use my love of science to make meth as if my parents were druggies and blew up our house with a drug lab or something.

I hated being seen that way. Still do. I wanted to be more than those labels—so much more. Werner Bauer didn't know I had nothing, but he sensed it. The slant of his mouth and the better-than-you gleam in his eyes told me he knew something was off with what I did say about my background. I feared if he knew the truth, he'd color Hildy's view of me, even though I knew I would make something of myself someday.

Hell, even coming from nothing, I'd earned a PhD and gotten accepted into a prestigious postdoc position. I'd come so far from the skinny college student washing dishes or serving food at the dining hall. And that guy was a world away from the even skinnier foster kid who kept his head down and tried to get by without causing any problems.

But what I'd been doing in that postdoc lab wasn't enough. Nor was the government job, despite the many promotions. Hell, even this position isn't enough.

I want more.

And I *will* make something more of myself and reach the success I've dreamed about.

I'll show each person who made fun of or bullied me growing up what I can do and be. Nothing will stop me, including Nate Lowe, Mr. Z, or even Hildy herself.

Hildy stretches. She's wearing her hair loose today, and man, does she look sexy. I know I shouldn't think of her in those terms, especially at work, but it's hard not to when she is so beautiful. Even her sighs sound sensual.

Her smart-girl glasses are back on her face. That only adds to her appeal. Her black blouse shows off her breasts, and the black-and-white plaid skirt accentuates her hips and makes her legs look even longer.

I reach for my water bottle. A couple of sips of this will keep me from overheating.

Hildy glances my way, catching me staring at her, but she says nothing. "The BRCA gene group's data will be uploaded on Friday. The team asked each woman to do additional lab work. We'll get the results once Bradley and Max review it."

"Thank you for suggesting that."

"You're welcome."

My phone alarm sounds, and I turn it off. "Break time."

"Reading the new book?"

I'd taken that book from her place last night. "I'm finishing another one first, then I'll start that one."

"I'll be quiet."

"No need." We've acted one hundred percent professional and been productive, but I need some distance if only for a few minutes. "I'm going to head out for a few minutes."

"Twenty, right?" She shakes her head and laughs. "Enjoy your break."

"Plan on it."

A few minutes later, I have a cappuccino in hand, my book tucked under my arm, and a seat in the cafeteria. I set everything on the table and take a sip. The coffee goes down warm and smooth.

A young, thin guy pushes a bin full of envelopes and catalogs. A lanyard hangs around his neck, only he has more than just his badge on it. He must have special key cards or something due to making deliveries.

He wears dark sunglasses, making me wonder if he's trying to be cool or has something going on with his eyes. When I take a closer look, I notice a gauze pad covering one of his eyes like a makeshift bandage or patch.

Poor guy. I hope it's nothing serious.

He hands a stack of items to the cafeteria manager, who gives him a cookie. "See you tomorrow, Ryan."

"Looking forward to it." Ryan takes a bite of it and rolls his cart toward the exit.

For such a high-tech company that claims to be on the cutting edge, it cracks me up they still have a mailroom, but I guess not everything can be automated, or the USPS wouldn't exist.

I open my book, ready to dive into the "all is lost moment" of the novel. The sentient being can't decide whether to destroy the human it's befriended or not. I must admit the author has reeled me in.

"Sam."

Fuck. I'd recognize that voice anywhere.

Ignore him. I concentrate on my book.

"Sam," Nate repeats.

Nate is like an annoying pimple that shows up right before a big event. He won't leave me alone, so I might as well acknowledge him, or else I won't be able to get back to my book. I glance up at him. "What do you want, Lowe?"

"How's everything working out with Hildy?"

"I'm sure your fiancée has told you."

He sits across from me. "I'd rather hear it from you."

"Hildy has been a big help with the data analysis. Satisfied?"

"Very." Nate stretches his legs out in front of him. "How are you two getting along?"

"We're working together fine."

He frowns. "Nothing else?"

"She's your fiancée, not mine."

Nate straightens. "Right. I just wondered since the two of you have ..."

A past. Chemistry. Sparks. "Things are coming along well with the project."

"Glad to hear it."

Is he really? I have my doubts. "So are you going to do long distance while Hildy's in New Zealand?"

Fuck. I hadn't meant to ask, but I can't stop thinking about their engagement. Maybe the answer to the question will rid Hildy from my mind once and for all.

"Something like that." Nate's vague answer doesn't satisfy me one bit.

A sense of protectiveness surges inside me. Hildy might be my ex-wife, but she doesn't need the golden boy of the pharmaceutical industry to use and discard her like a lab sample gone bad. "You'd better treat Hildy the way she deserves. If you're an asshole and break her heart ..."

A wide grin spreads across Nate's face. He brightens like the Space Needle whenever one of the Seattle sports teams wins big. "You still care about her."

"I'm a human being with empathy. Something you know nothing about."

"You care." Nate's double-downing, and I have no idea why. "Does she know?"

"Stop asking me about your fiancée. You talk to her more than I do."

Forget reading. There's too much stench in the air, all coming from Nate.

A smug expression crosses his face. "I don't mind if you talk to her more."

All of his brain synapses aren't firing properly. If I were engaged to Hildy, I wouldn't share her. Hell, I'd want to know who she was talking to and when. She's too much of a catch, which Nate should know. I'm tempted to tell him about her coming to dinner at my house tonight, but he doesn't deserve the warning.

"Shut up, Lowe." I grab my book and coffee and stand. "If there's any justice in this world, Hildy will realize she's better off alone than with an egotistical asshole like you."

I don't wait for a reply and rush out of the cafeteria to the elevator.

Nate Lowe will never be able to satisfy Hildy, especially if he's sleeping around with other women and letting her do the same with other men. Their relationship is nothing but a giant red flag waving in the wind for all to see. I can't wait to watch the two of them fall apart.

And if I can make that happen a little faster, so be it.

I can't believe I'm doing this. Cooking dinner for Hildy, my ex-wife, in my own goddamn kitchen. But here I am, sautéing like some kind of domesticated superhero.

I blame Geraldine, who dropped off the ingredients for what I'm making. It came from the meal box she ordered for this week. She's done the same before when she felt I was on the verge of scurvy or malnutrition from eating out so much. But this time, it's all about her being Team Sam's Happily Ever After, even if Hildy was rude to Geraldine.

As I toss in a handful of diced onions, the pounding of my heart almost drowns out the sizzle of oil in the pan. They crackle and spit, filling the air with their sharp, sweet aroma.

I don't have to glance over at the island where Hildy sits on a stool to know she's watching me. I can feel her gaze on me.

Will she enjoy this meal? I'm giving it my all even though the recipe is simple and all the instructions are on a glossy, full-color recipe card. But something about cooking for her feels intimate, like a secret shared between old lovers.

"Wow, Sam. It smells amazing in here." Her dark hair bounces around her pretty face as she tilts her head. "You never cooked for me when we were married. I didn't know you had it in you."

"Neither did I. I guess I wasn't quite the domestic type back then." I focus on the pan, stirring. I throw in some garlic and let the fragrance mix with the onions. My hands shake a little. Nerves or excitement, I can't really tell. "But people change, right?"

"Right," she agrees, though there's a hint of skepticism in her voice.

It stings a little, but I can't blame her since I used to leave the food to her. I did most of the cleaning when I could. That seemed like a fair trade—no housekeeper necessary. "I started cooking after our divorce. Figured it was time to level up my life skills."

"Level up, huh?" She smirks, crossing her arms over the hot pink dress that hugs her curves so perfectly I find it hard to breathe. Yes, she'd changed into something different for our dinner, a sexy dress that kept drawing my gaze. "Is this the part where I find out you've also learned how to fold fitted sheets?"

"Fuck no." I flip a piece of chicken with more force than necessary. "There are limits to my personal growth."

"Good to know."

She laughs, and the sound is like music to my ears. God, I've missed her laughter.

"So what's on the menu tonight, Chef Grant?"

"Chicken piccata," I say, trying to match her casual tone. "With a side of roasted vegetables and garlic mashed potatoes. And, um, tiramisu for dessert."

The dessert isn't part of the meal kit, but something

Geraldine decided to toss in as a bonus.

"Damn, Sam," Hildy says as if genuinely impressed. "You really went all out."

"Only the best for you." My cheeks heat.

Focus, Grant. Just concentrate on the damn food.

"Thank you for going to so much trouble." Her eyes lock on mine.

There's something in her gaze, something I haven't seen in a long time.

It makes my heart race, and my chest tighten. I clear my throat. "Why don't you grab a seat at the table? Dinner's almost ready."

"Sure thing." She walks over to the table and sits, crossing her legs with that same grace as always—like a goddamn movie star from the Golden Age of Hollywood. She swirls the wine in her glass. "I have to admit, I didn't expect all of this."

Hildy's gaze darts around, taking everything in. It feels strange, having her here like this, but a part of me revels in the discomfort. It's proof we're both still breathing, still changing— even if it's not always for the better.

I plate the food. "Sometimes, you've got to learn to do things differently just to survive."

"Is that what you've been doing? Surviving?" Her voice has no malice, but the question stings all the same.

"Maybe," I admit, trying to keep my voice steady. "Or maybe I'm trying to find some much-needed balance in my life. You know, between work and ... everything else."

I carry the plates to the table, setting one in front of Hildy and taking my own seat across from her. The tension in the air is palpable, but I do my best to ignore it as I dig into my dinner.

"This is amazing." She holds her fork mid-air. "Seriously, I'm impressed."

"Thanks." I try to focus on my food and not the way her lips curve around her fork or the faint hint of cleavage peeking out from her dress.

Fucking hell. Get a grip.

The delicious aroma and the clink of cutlery on plates creates an atmosphere that reminds me of a warm embrace. I can almost forget our history and allow myself to believe we're just two people sharing a meal, nothing more and nothing less.

"Is there anything else you've learned since ... since we split up?" she asks before diving back into her chicken.

"Nothing quite as impressive as cooking," I admit, swallowing hard. "But I've been working on some things like fiction writing. And trying to be better. For myself."

"That's important, Sam." She looks me in the eye again. "I'm glad to hear it."

"Are you?" The question slips out before I can stop it. A weight presses down on my chest. "Because sometimes I wonder if you ever really cared about me. If any of it mattered after I read your emails."

The atmosphere shifts instantly, tension crackling in the air like static electricity. Hildy sets her fork down and fixes her gaze on me, dark, glossy curls framing her face. "Of course it mattered. And I'm sorry I sent those, especially now that you told me about your past. I can only imagine how much they hurt you."

"Not as much as you walking out on me and our marriage."

Her eyes gleam with tears. "In case you're wondering, it still matters, goddammit. So much. I apologize if I never made you feel like it did. And that you had to hide being a foster child from me. But I understand why you didn't tell me after what my dad had said to you and ... me."

I let her words sink in. They are more than I hoped for. I take a breath, but it doesn't calm me.

"To be honest, I wasn't sure you'd even read what I sent," she adds. "As time passed, I hoped you hadn't."

My pulse races. "Well, I did. And I've got to say, they hit me harder than I expected."

"Sam, I—"

"Let me finish," I say, my voice firm. "I know we both made mistakes in our marriage. But those letters ... They showed me how you saw me and told me why you left. And there were things about myself I'd never considered before. They forced me to confront parts of myself I didn't even know existed. And it hurt like hell."

She bites her lip, clearly affected by my words. We sit in silence, the tension between us palpable and heavy.

I take a deep breath, trying to find the right words, a surge of emotion welling up inside me.

"Those letters ... They stirred up some old demons for me. I grew up feeling like I didn't belong anywhere. Like I wasn't good enough." My hands grip the edge of the table, knuckles turning white. "When I read what you wrote, it brought all that shit back to the surface. It was like a goddamn punch to the gut."

Her eyes shimmer. "Sam, I'm sorry. If I'd known ..."

"But you didn't know." My voice cracks. "I felt like such a failure as a husband, as a partner, as a man. But instead of wallowing in self-pity, I decided to do something about it. I made a list, Hildy. Of every single point you raised in those letters, and how I could address them. How I could be better." I pause, searching her face for any hint of understanding. "Because I didn't want to be that person anymore. That guy who couldn't live up to your expectations, or mine."

Her mouth hangs open in surprise. "I had no idea, Sam. I never meant to hurt you like that. I just ... I wanted you to see me, really see me, and understand what I needed from you. But I guess I went about it the wrong way."

"Damn right, you did," I snap, then immediately regret it. I sigh and rub my temples. "But maybe it's what we both needed. To see the ugly truth and make some hard choices. I still put in a lot of hours on the job, but I've been working on my shit, and I hope you can see that."

"I can, Sam. I really can. And I'm sorry. I didn't realize how much my words could hurt you, but I promise, I'll do better too."

"Maybe we both will," I say softly, reaching across the table to take her hand. It's a small step, but it feels like the start of something new. It's about hope and the possibility of redemption.

As our fingers intertwine, we stare at each other, the space between us seeming to narrow as if we're drawn together by a force beyond our control. Slowly, I reach out with my other hand and brush a stray strand of hair from her face, my fingers lingering on her cheek.

She glances down. "I want …"

"Come here, baby." I pull her to her feet and lead her to my side of the table until she's sitting on my lap. She wraps her arms around my neck and presses close, her body fitting against mine like a missing puzzle piece. Our lips meet in a tender, unhurried kiss that speaks of forgiveness and healing.

As our mouths move together, the desire that's always been an undeniable part of our relationship flares to life. It's not the desperate, all-consuming need that defined our past encounters. It's slower, more deliberate, as if we're taking the time to truly explore each other again.

"Sam," she whispers against my lips, her breath warm and sweet. "I want you. Now."

"Are you sure?" I ask, my voice low and gravelly.

"Please," she begs, her voice a throaty purr.

My heart pounds in my chest. I scoop her up in my arms, our lips never parting.

CHAPTER 16

HILDY

Sam carries me out of the kitchen. I have no idea where we're going, but I hope it's to the couch or his bed. Hell, the floor would be fine. I'm not picky. I just want him—badly. He seems to want me too.

His lips haven't left mine, and I hope they don't. I'm already wet, and a need keeps building deep inside me. This man ...

He's sexy and swoony and ...

Sam lifts his lips from mine.

What the fuck? I open my eyes. "You're no longer kissing me," I say, no doubt sounding pouty. I don't care. He should still be kissing me. We have lots of time to make up for tonight.

"I need to put you where you belong."

"Where's that?"

"My bed." He sets me in the center of the mattress with such care I almost want to cry.

"Okay." I sound breathless. This is what he does to me. It isn't fair. "You're forgiven."

"I'm going to make you feel so good."

"Promises, promises," I tease, but I haven't forgotten just

how hot sex with him was. I'm ready to spontaneously combust as it is.

"You'll see, but you still have your shoes on." His fingers touch my leg, and the feel of his skin on mine reignites the heat between my legs.

I suck in a breath. "That feels so good."

"We're only getting started." His hands run along my calves until he reaches the straps of my favorite shoes that I wore just for him tonight. "I can't believe the height of these heels, but they make your legs go on forever."

That was the reason I wore them. I had no idea what tonight would turn into, but I wanted to look my best for him. "Thank you."

Sam removes my right shoe, caressing my ankle as if it's a rare element, and then he takes off the left one. He tosses my red-soled shoes onto the floor. "That's step one."

"You have a plan?"

"Always." His fingers travel back up my legs, to my thighs, and he rolls down my stockings until they are off my feet. He carefully places them on the nightstand. "Your legs are so amazing, even better than I remember."

His smooth, seductive tone makes my nipples go hard. Yes, I want him, but this feels different from yesterday in the office. Sex then would have been nothing more than a quickie with someone I found attractive. Here, now, it's more … intimate.

I don't know if it's what we've discussed the past two nights or if we just need to fuck quickly and get it over with. Oh, I still want to fuck him, but this slower pace feels … right.

Though I still need him. "Sam."

His eyes soften as his fingers whisper up and down my skin. "I've got you, baby."

He drops to his knees on the mattress and gets between my legs, pushing my dress up around my hips. The way he looks at me, like he wants to devour me, makes me even wetter.

"I'm going to ruin you," he says in a growly voice.

"I'm ready." *So, so ready.*

"You're not even close to being ready." His gaze rakes over my lace panties. "But you are stunning. And tonight, you're mine."

My pulse skitters. A part of me wants to ask if it's just for tonight, but I don't want to ruin anything. One night is more than I ever thought I'd get again. I want to make the most of it. "Go ahead."

Laughing, he kisses my right thigh and then my left, getting closer and closer to where I want his mouth. Assuming what he intends to do—what I will beg him to do if it comes down to it—I squirm.

Sam glances up at me. Wicked laughter lights his eyes. "Patience."

I shake my head. I don't want to wait. I want …

He licks my panties, a long brush of his tongue that has me writhing, and then he sucks through the lace.

Oh my God. I arch off the mattress. "You're so fucking good at this."

"Like that?" Sam puts his head back down to me and inhales so deeply I can feel the intake of air. "Fuck. I forgot how good you smell. Delicious. You'll taste even better."

Each word turns me on more. I can't wait. I know he wants me to wait, but … "Do I have to beg?"

Because I will. I'll do whatever he asks me to do.

He slips a finger underneath my panties and teases me with featherlight touches. I wiggle my hips trying to get him closer to where I want him.

"Be my good girl."

His voice rumbles over me, and I must be dripping by now. "Trying."

Not really because I'm already on edge.

Fuck it. I thread my fingers through his hair, pulling him closer to me. He can't have any doubt about what I want ... need ... now.

Sam pushes aside my panties. "Hello, pretty pussy. I've missed you."

Gah. I don't know how much more I can take. I lift my hips, hoping he'll take the hint.

He pulls my panties down and sits up so he can remove them. The next thing I know, my legs are on his shoulders, and he's licking me like he can't get enough.

His tongue flicks over my clit, and sensations pulse through me. He goes to town licking and sucking me until I'm moaning.

Has it always been this good with him?

Because this is the definition of amazing.

His finger joins in on the onslaught. We're no longer at war, but his plan is a well-thought-out strategy that's left me wanting to surrender. Between his tongue and his finger, I'm a hot mess. He's breaking me down lick by lick, touch by touch. I should care more than I do that he's destroying my control, but I'm lost.

"Don't stop." I can barely talk, but I manage to say those two words.

His finger rubs my clit in a rapid circular motion. "I wouldn't dream of doing that to you. I can't wait to make you fall apart."

I'm getting closer. "So close."

I barely recognize my voice.

He pushes his finger inside me while his tongue darts between my folds and my clit. My breathing becomes more shallow and rapid. The pressure inside me builds and then ... "Sam!"

The sensations push me over the edge, and I'm falling. Falling so fast and hard and ...

"So beautiful." He kisses my pussy. "And sexy. And mine."

His? Oh my God. I can barely breathe, let alone move. Does he mean it for real, or is he caught up in the heat of the moment? The funny thing ... I'm not sure which I want it to be right now.

I open my eyes to see him looking at me. He has steam on his glasses. "Thank you."

He laughs. "So polite."

"Fuck you."

"I plan to fuck you. But we're overdressed."

I realize my dress is still around my hips, and he's fully clothed. "We must remedy that quickly."

Sam places his glasses on the nightstand and then kisses my stomach. "Oh, I plan to, baby. Just giving you a minute to recover before I make you come apart again."

I take a breath and move my legs off his shoulders. I sit up enough to untuck his shirt from his pants.

He grins wryly and lowers his lips to mine. "So that's how you want it."

It isn't a question, but I still nod, fumbling with his belt. His kissing my neck doesn't help me do this with any more finesse, but I manage to unbuckle it. I work the button open, the zipper down, and slip my hand into his boxer briefs. I wrap my hand around his long, smooth, hard dick.

"Oh God," he cries out. "I've missed you."

"I've missed you too. You have no idea."

"We need to be naked," he rasps.

Within seconds, my dress is over my head. He cups my breasts, sucking on each nipple through the lace, and then unclasps my bra and frees them.

He stares in awe at me. "Gorgeous."

"Not yet. I need your clothes off so I can see you. I need to see you." Between the two of us, we get him out of his shirt, boxer briefs, pants, socks, and shoes. I stare at him in awe, my mouth watering. He's older but just as handsome. "Hello, lovely."

Sam positions me to straddle him, bare skin on bare skin. Writhing on him, I love how his hard shaft rubs against me, sending my eyes rolling into the back of my head. The sensation is amazing, but I want more.

"Sam, I need you inside me. Now."

"I need to be inside you."

Dammit. I just got wetter. He nips me with his teeth and reaches up to one of my breasts and squeezes gently. It's all too much but not enough. I shift my hips.

Sam groans. "Now, Hildy, now. Do you have condoms?"

Do I have condoms? I'm a single woman. And then I remember I cleaned out my purse before coming to Seattle. I didn't think I'd need any because I would only be here for two weeks and working the entire time.

I drop my head. "Shit, no. You?"

"No." Sam drops his chin to my breasts and looks up at me.

"*Sam.*"

"What? I haven't dated for a while. I don't have any."

There's no way we aren't having sex. "Sam, have you ever had sex without a condom?"

He inhales. "What are you saying?"

"Have you?"

"Only with you. What about you?"

"The same. I had a full physical for the job I'm taking and asked for a full panel, so I know I'm healthy. I also take birth control."

A boyish grin breaks out on Sam's face, and he wiggles his eyebrows. "You mean ...?"

I wiggle my eyebrows in reply. "Yes, I mean."

He touches me, rubbing my wetness all over me. "Now you're ready."

"Told you so."

Grinning, Sam flips me so I'm on my back. He opens my legs so they're spread apart, pushes my hands above my head, and then drills into me with such force I'm pushed toward the headboard.

Every thrust sends my senses overboard. Each push brings me closer to the edge.

He gets on his knees again and lifts my hips to change the angle. One thrust, two ... He adds his fingers to the mix, focusing on my clit.

Oh shit. This feels so good.

I'm floating above my body. Goose bumps erupt over my skin, and another wave of pleasure starts in my stomach. The sensations are amazing, and I feel like I'm back where I belong. I've missed this man, even though seeing him and having sex with him again isn't in my plan.

Don't think about that now.

We are so in tune with each other our rhythm seems to follow the beat of my heart and his—our hearts. They seem as happy as we are that we found each other again.

Each time he drills into me, he hits that spot inside, emanating tingles outward. It's as if we were made for each other. Maybe that's why he's my perfect lover, the same one who comes to me in my dreams and is now with me in real life. His muscles tense, and he speeds up, driving me even crazier.

"Sam ..."

"I know."

Sweat coats his skin, and the air smells like sex. I never want this to end.

As he continues to send my body to places I forgot existed, my fingers dig into his flesh. I want to hold him forever, but then ...

The waves roll through my body, and my breathing becomes heavier as I get closer and closer to the precipice. I moan and arch, and even though he's taking me there, I want to help get myself to the edge.

"I'm going to come," Sam gasps. "Dammit, Hildy."

This is it, and with one more thrust, I fall and fall and fall. I come even harder than the first time a few minutes ago, coming like I haven't come in years. Not since the last time I had sex with Sam before our divorce.

As I cry out, I feel Sam's release inside me, and as we cling to each other, both groaning out our pleasure, I wouldn't change anything. Except ...

I get the feeling I've just done something stupid. And I really hope that isn't the case.

ZENTELLO STAFF TREATED LIKE THE LAB ANIMALS THEY USE FOR TESTING

BY SCIENCE STAFF WRITER
KING COUNTY TIMES

Taken from an article in the Lab Notes column of BioTech Beacon, a local science magazine that focuses on the pharmaceutical industry. Recent claims suggest a company with the initials of X, Y, or Z has been abusing their lab animals. This is a serious accusation which requires follow-up. But we have been told that the abuse isn't only of lab animals. Staff have been treated so poorly that there's been a constant stream of resignations, and most project teams are thoroughly understaffed and overworked.

Sources claim the co-CEOs are to blame for the mistreatment, and no solution has been offered by the management team. Our attempts to speak with executives went unanswered, but we hope to hear from someone soon.

CHAPTER 17

SAM

The sun filters into my bedroom through the edges of the blinds. I blink open my eyes to find Hildy wrapped around me. My heart seizes and then stumbles in my chest. I'm relieved I'm horizontal or I'd be flat on my ass—no, my back—remembering what we did.

If I died right now, I would leave this planet feeling the happiest I've been in years. I snuggle closer to her, soaking up her warmth and her scent. Two things I could easily become addicted to, never mind the mind-blowing sex.

At least that hasn't changed.

I twirl the ends of her hair, the silky strands curling around my finger as if they're meant to do that. Satisfaction flows through me. Having her with me in bed is something I never thought would happen again. I brush my lips over her head and relish being together again.

Two point seven seconds for reality to kick in.

My gut clenches as the surreal dream I've been living dissipates. It's as if the fog has lifted and someone opened the curtain. The view shocks me even though, logically, everything has been in the back of my mind. I just haven't wanted to acknowledge the truth.

Shit.

I've dreamed of having Hildy back in my life for years, ever since the day she left, and I've missed her even when I told myself I hated her. I cup her head, wanting to hold on to this moment and her a little while longer.

But I forgot something, something important. What I've come to realize after thinking about our marriage for the past five years is that in some ways Hildy's like a beautiful butterfly who needs to fly free. Being with me stopped her from doing that. Oh, she wanted to be married to me back then, but that wasn't the only thing she wanted.

Even though I've learned and improved myself after reading and rereading her emails, can we really make this work? Despite Geraldine's advice, I'm still not that perfect guy Hildy dreams about. Can I be him?

I ... don't know.

I work many hours. I spend more time at Zentello than at home. My goal is to be successful. I need to be that. Nothing will change my drive and ambition.

So how would this be different from five years ago?

I glance down at Hildy. Her eyelashes form half-moons, and her lips are slightly parted.

I'd let her down in so many ways ...

My working every hour possible meant we didn't get to do the things she wanted us to do. We didn't go on vacations to Europe. We didn't walk in the park on Saturdays, drinking take-out coffee while we watched kids play baseball. We didn't swim in the ocean or go to see a show at The Paramount. We didn't ever visit the pyramids or walk across London Bridge or view Paris from the top of the Eiffel Tower. We didn't do any of the things she'd said she wanted us to do together because I was always working. On top of all that, she'd turned down jobs out of town she'd been recruited for because of *my* career.

I'd held her back, and I don't want to do it again. Yes, I have more balance than I did when we were together, but ...

She needs someone who will put her first. I'm still not there since I have goals of my own—a level of success I need to reach for a multitude of reasons.

Last night was beyond amazing. Our bodies fell back together, working in unison like they'd never been apart. We made love twice, and I almost said *I love you* to her, but I knew that wouldn't help matters. I knew the words wouldn't change the fact that today we'll have to go back to how things had been before we had mind-blowing sex.

It is for the best.

The best, I repeat to myself.

"Morning." Hildy gives me a sleepy smile and stretches her arms. "Did you sleep okay?"

"Yes, thank you." I had slept well. The best night's sleep I'd had since she left me.

She turns on her side to face me and tucks her hands under her cheek. Fuck, she's adorable. "What now?"

What now? Well, I want to have sex with her again, but that won't resolve anything. "We need to talk about what last night meant."

"Wow." She grins at me. "We're going straight there."

"It's important."

"I know. We should talk." She nestles farther under the

duvet. "Okay, let's go."

I guess that means I go first. Given I'm the one who brought it up, that makes sense. "We work well together in bed."

"We do," she agrees with no hesitation. "Last night was a testament to how compatible we are, and I should say, Dr. Grant, you haven't lost any of your stamina or expertise."

I roll my eyes and laugh. "Thank you, but we need to be serious."

She blows out a breath. "I know, I'm sorry. Continue."

"We're good in bed, but not so much out of it. Wouldn't you agree?"

"I totally agree." She doesn't even pause like I expect or blink. "We're terrible out of bed. We make an awful couple."

I lie on my back and stare at the ceiling. My heart must be still beating, or I'd not be able to form a conscious thought. But I'm stunned she so readily agreed with me. I thought I'd have to fight to convince her because a part of me doesn't think that. Not at all. And I don't want her to see I'm lying. Somehow, she always knows when I'm lying.

I focus on a small dot on the ceiling, something I've never noticed before, but it keeps my mind from wandering and my gaze from traveling to her.

The hot lump in my throat grows bigger, and I swallow around it. I glance her way. "We should quit while we're ahead. I know you have an agreement with Nate, but I'm monogamous. Hookups are one thing, but I need to be exclusive if I see someone more than once."

"Understood."

"And you'll be leaving for another job soon."

She nods as if I'd told her to be sure to lower the toilet seat. "In New Zealand with EnergyMed. I'll be leading a research team of six for a new product in development. It's a dream position."

"You always wanted to go to New Zealand and hike the Milford Sound."

She nods. "I plan to do that once I earn vacation time. I'm not sure if it's called PTO down there."

The fact she's already making plans for her first vacation tells me what I should say next. "We need to go back to simply being colleagues and put last night down as a one-time thing for old times' sake."

I hold my breath, hating every word that has just left my mouth. A part of me wants her to say no and declare her undying love for me. For a man who's considered to have high intelligence, I feel really stupid right now.

"That's fine," Hildy says brightly. "I agree. That's the most sensible thing to do. I should get home so I can shower before we go to work."

I can see she's smiling. A part of me wishes I'd kept staring at that dot. Her acquiescence pisses me off. But it's exactly what I want, isn't it?

"Okay, great." The idea of sharing a morning shower appeals to me more than it should, so I kiss the tip of her nose to act like I'm A-OK with walking away as if she means nothing to me. "I should hop in the shower too."

"Well, you do kinda smell like me." Hildy throws off the duvet and gets out of bed, her breasts jiggling.

Trying not to look at her pert, naked ass walking to my bathroom, I close my eyes. Why does it suck that she agrees with everything I said?

Because I still want her.

Fuck. I want her even more than I did. And I get the feeling what happened between us might make things worse, not better.

When I enter the lab, I see Hildy talking to Macie, one of Bradley's research assistants. I hadn't expected Hildy to beat me to work, but I took a long shower and didn't rush to get ready. Unfortunately, that gave me more time to think about last night and this morning in bed. I'm at a loss. Why do I still feel so unsatisfied with how things turned out when it was what I told her we should do?

"Morning," Hildy chirps, bright as a songbird. She's dressed in sleek black pants and a purple shirt. "Do you need me, or do I have time to finish up here?"

Macie gives me a little wave. "I have everything I need."

I walk closer and see Hildy's been given the latest results from the trial. Those will come in handy. The sooner I finish verifying the data, the sooner I can leave Zentello for a better position. I've had feelers out for a month. A new job won't double my salary, but it'll get me closer to my goal.

I smile at both of them and then look at Hildy. "I'm wondering whether you received the report on the results from the menopausal participants. I want to see it."

Hildy gives me a closed-mouth smile like she hadn't had her legs over my shoulders while my tongue was inside her the night before. Her polite and professional expression is the way it should be. So why do I hate it?

"I do," she replies in a business-courteous tone. "I must have forgotten to email it to you. I'll go do it now."

"Thank you," I say, smiling at Macie who hands papers to Hildy. "Great job, Macie. Keep up the good work."

I follow Hildy to the office and wonder, for the millionth time that day, what sort of idiot I am for what I'd said that morning. I can't do anything about it now. It's done, and we're both moving on.

Separately.

"So what do you really want to talk about? The mole?" Hildy enters the office, and the door slides closed. "Because I know I sent you that email yesterday morning."

"I know, and yes, you're right. Another article about Zentello has been published."

Her eyes widen. "No way. What's this one about?"

I tap on my phone and bring up the article; this one is a bunch of crap about staff conditions. The headline reads "Zentello Staff Treated Like the Lab Animals They Use for Testing." This article has a bigger issue associated with it: the story has been published by the largest newspaper in King County, not just some crappy pharmaceutical rag that no one outside of the industry would even know about. Someone is playing hardball.

Hildy gasps. "This is crap. That headline is nothing more than clickbait."

"I know." I perch on the edge of my desk. "Most people will see that and make assumptions without reading the article, and those who do read it will have no clue this is a pile of crap."

"There's just enough reality to make it sound like the truth."

"Do you have any more ideas on who is giving this information?" I stare through the glass to the lab wondering whether it's someone on the Orchid team. If it is, I'll not only be disappointed but hurt too.

"No idea." Hildy's gaze follows mine. "I haven't seen any reason to suspect someone on the team." She gives me a soft smile, and my heart expands. She knows how to make me feel better.

"The idiot needs to be stopped." I pinch the bridge of my nose. "A reporter used to call me all the time."

"They did?" Hildy sits and rests her chin on her hand, giving me her full attention. "What happened?"

"I must've told him to fuck off enough times because he stopped calling."

"He sounds like a dick."

"From my brief conversations with him, yes, he is. Christina met with him and confirmed he is."

"Okay," Hildy says. "Let's figure out who this douchebag is."

HILDY

As Sam and I read through the latest article to look for clues, our conversation in his bed keeps playing in my mind. I hate that he wants us to be just colleagues. That's even worse than just friends. After spending the night together, I thought we'd moved on to something different. That we might get back to how we used to be.

That was a big fat no.

Deep down, I know he's right, but it still hurts. He brought up Nate, which is a non-issue, and now, all I want is to finish the data verification, find the damn mole, and then get the hell out of Dodge. New Zealand will be such a respite after this. I need to focus on having my own team and running the lab. It's everything I hoped to find. I should be happy, not sad.

When we come up empty from analyzing the article, I sit back in my chair. "Nate's going to be upset over this latest article."

"Of course you're worried about Nate," Sam mutters.

"Zentello is important to him." I frown, wondering once again what the hell went on between those two. "He's worked hard to build this company from something small into an independent and powerful business that's done a lot of good for people. From customers to employees, including you."

Sam's face hardens. "Nate's all about the profit. Don't let him fool you."

"We all want profit. Some more than others, but we do."

"Yeah, and he wants more than profit." He sounds like a naughty schoolkid talking back to his mom.

"What the hell went on between you two?"

He presses his lips together, resembling a toddler about to throw a tantrum.

"This is ridiculous. How did two best friends of more than a decade manage to end up hating each other? Actually ..." I realize I'm wrong. "It's not two friends. It's just you who's being an idiot and hating on Nate. Why?"

Sam grunts and turns his back to me.

"Samuel! Do not turn your back on me." My voice sharpens, but he's pissing me off. "Tell me—why the hell do you hate Nate?"

Sam turns around in his chair so fast the wheels nearly spin off. "I told you if you're so damn interested in knowing, talk to him yourself. I have work to do."

He goes into the lab and sits at the far bench.

I don't understand why most times I mention Nate it sends Sam from zero to sixty in a flash. But I'm determined to find out what the hell's going on. I call ahead to make sure Nate's in his office. Zelda assures me that he is.

When I arrive on the twenty-second floor, Zelda simply smiles from the doorway of her office. The door to Nate's office is open. He waves me inside.

"Hildy. Great to see you." Nate greets me with a huge smile from behind his desk. "What can I do for you? Or have you found proof that Sam's my mole?"

"I'm working on it, but I want to know what's going on with you and Sam. Why the hell does he hate you?"

Nate shrugs. "I don't know what you mean. Friends just grow apart sometimes."

My hands fly to my hips. "Don't bullshit me. I know you better than that."

Nate takes a breath and exhales slowly.

The way his eyes darken worries me. "What is it?"

He rubs his chin. "You're not going to like it."

"Tell me," I snap. "Now."

"After you and Sam divorced, I told him we slept together."

My heart drops to the pit of my stomach. I open my mouth to speak, but no words come out. I think I'm going to be sick.

He cocks a brow and stares at me. That jolts me from my stupor.

"You what?" I finally grind out. It's a good thing a desk separates us or I might strangle him.

"I told Sam we fucked."

I flinch. My heart beats quicker than it should. No wonder Sam hates Nate. No wonder Sam stopped asking me to reconcile. No wonder he hates me. "Why the fuck would you do that?"

"It doesn't matter," he replies in a matter-of-fact tone. "I had my reasons."

My blood heats. My anger spirals until I want to go nuclear, and I lean over his desk. "You absolute asshole! How dare you mess with my life like that? With Sam's life? Well, I'll tell you something, I quit. Find your own fucking mole, and for your information, it's not Sam."

I turn to leave.

"I wouldn't, if you want the rest of the money you're owed. You need it, right?"

Fuck. I do. For Mathilda and Flynn. I turn around. "You don't play fair."

"You signed a contract."

"I did." But one thing wasn't in that contract. I tug the

diamond engagement ring off my finger and hold it up to him. "I'll stay, but our engagement ends now."

Nate grins. The asshole appears amused by all this. "It was nice while it lasted."

He reaches for the ring, and I snatch it away.

"No, no, no." I put the ring in my pocket. "You said I get to keep it."

His smile widens, reaching all the way to his eyes. "I was hoping you'd forget."

I raise my chin and stare down my nose at him. "Not on your life."

"Had to give it my best shot."

The fucker doesn't even sound upset. What kind of game is he playing? And ... why?

CHAPTER 18

HILDY

Flared nostrils and a set jaw are not an attractive look. Yet I'm sure my face has both right now. I've had my say and should leave, but my feet remain in front of Nate's desk. Something inside me tells me this conversation isn't finished even though I wish it was. I flex my fingers hoping to lessen the tension bunching my muscles. Whereas Nate …

His smile hasn't wavered. Not once. I can't tell if that means he's happy about something or a total psychopath. I lean toward the latter.

"Find me the proof that Sam's the mole," Nate says like he's not trying to destroy a well-respected scientist and man who used to be his best friend, "and then you can be on your way to New Zealand."

Seriously? I manage not to roll my eyes. I'll be heading to New Zealand when my two weeks are up. Nothing, including Nate Lowe, will stop me. "I told you. It's not him."

"And I told you it is. My co-CEO agrees with me."

The illustrious and mysterious Mr. Z. I keep forgetting that guy exists. "Your proof is circumstantial, at best."

"I have logs of a courier coming to his office multiple times.

You were there when it happened."

I was, and she's been there twice this week already. Sam hasn't told me what he gives Geraldine or what she brings to him, but I still feel compelled to defend Sam. This has nothing to do with us having sex and everything to do with the man I know he is. That kind of guy would never sell secrets to some sleazy journalist. He hates Nate—and rightly so—but he wouldn't put his team's jobs on the line or an entire company.

"The courier's name is Geraldine." I try to remember what Sam has told me to convince Nate. "She and Sam were friends long before he started work at Zentello."

Nate scoffs. "Sam Grant doesn't have any friends."

Okay, Nate's not wrong there, but ... "Sam's not the mole."

I keep saying that without solid proof, but I'm certain he wouldn't do something like this.

"Your loyalty to your ex-husband is admirable, but it might lead to your downfall."

"Huh?"

Nate steeples his fingers. "Well, if Mr. Z and I are right about Sam, then it'll appear you're covering for your ex-husband. That won't be a good look to future employers and others in the industry."

"It's not Sam." I double down even if a twinge of unease trickles through me. It's a small world when it comes to pharmaceuticals. Even tech companies. Word travels fast, which is why Nate, and I suppose Mr. Z, wants the flow of information stopped before the articles do real damage.

So I understand what Nate is saying, but Sam's loyalty, albeit to his postdoc work and later his job, had been a big draw when we'd dated. I thought a man like him would be loyal to me and our future children. I still believe he would have been... if he hadn't been such a workaholic.

Nate studies me. He's not smiling as widely, but the corners of his mouth still tip up. "You're willing to stake your reputation on Sam?"

Am I? My heart pounds in my ears. If I'm wrong and word gets out, that could ruin me. Logically, I should protect myself and my career. I mean, that's my livelihood and future. I'm also helping to support Mathilda and Flynn, so what happens to me affects them. But my heart believes in Sam. At least where Zentello is concerned.

I square my shoulders as if preparing for battle. Nate might be charming, but I'm seeing another side to him—a shrewd one. Though I suppose someone more easygoing and laid-back might not make the best CEO in a cutthroat industry. "Yes, I am."

Something flashes in Nate's eyes. It almost appears to be relief, but that makes no sense, given all he's done to ruin ... well, everything. "Then find me proof it's not him and evidence as to who it is."

I nod, and the way Nate glances at his monitor, I can tell I'm being dismissed. But I realize I'm still standing there for another reason. I need to know more. I need to know Nate's motivation for what he did.

"Before I go, why the hell did you tell Sam we'd slept together?" I remember what Sam said about his list. My heart aches realizing how Nate's lie about us having sex messed up our lives. I also know now why Zelda had acted so cold to me on my first day here.

I wag my finger at him. That's safer than punching him in the face. "If you hadn't lied, we might have gotten back together. You do realize that, don't you?"

Nate rubs his face. "Reconciliation was never going to happen. Not with the way you two were dealing with the separation. You weren't ever going to listen to him. Not when you were so upset. You shot him down every time he turned up at your apartment or called you. I thought if I told him I fucked you, he'd get angry and jealous, he'd punch me maybe, but that it would trip something inside him so he'd act like a caveman, kick your door down, and tell you that you were going back to the place you'd shared. After that happened, I'd planned to tell him the truth."

Not believing what I'm hearing, I blink rapidly. None of Nate's plan makes any sense. "What a ludicrous idea."

Nate shrugs. "Hmm, that's subjective. I'll admit part of me wanted Sam to forget you. He was my best friend, and you were such a bitch to him. I figured if my original plan didn't work, it might be enough to make him forget you. My version of a 'kill two birds with one stone' scenario."

"Talk about a fucking ridiculous plan. It was mean and cruel. You don't do that to someone you call your best friend. You broke him."

"You broke him first, and I didn't think of the consequences to me."

"Losing the friendship?"

He nods. "I was drunk when I came up with the idea. And in my defense, he'd been talking about you for three hours nonstop. I couldn't take it anymore."

"There's no excuse for what you did." My tone is harsh, but Nate deserves it. "It's still a mean, cruel thing to do, and I'll never forgive you."

"It doesn't matter whether you forgive me. Sam hasn't, and I have to live with that every day." Nate shakes his head dismissively. "I fucked up. That's what you want me to say, right? But what's done is done. You know what you need to do."

I turn on my heels and storm toward the door.

"Get me the mole," he says. As if I could forget what he wants. "You might not appreciate what I did, but you're my friend and I care about you. Mr. Z doesn't feel the same way. He's someone you don't want to piss off."

The words sound like a threat. I haven't a fucking clue about Mr. Z, but I can't let this go.

I stop and glance over my shoulder. Nate Lowe has always been my friend, even when he was close to Sam. I looked up to Nate. He was always so kind to me. He'd been there in so many ways when I left Sam and continued to be just a text or phone call away over the years. I now realize that I'd gotten him because Sam didn't want him. All his actions are now suspect. I'll go so far to assume much of what Nate did for me stemmed from his guilt.

I now realize everything about Nate Lowe is a crafted illusion. Forget him being the golden boy. He's as tarnished and rusted on the outside as he is on the inside.

"I'll do what I can to find the mole, but I've lost all respect for you as a person, friend, and businessman. I'll never trust you again. And you can tell Mr. Z to fuck off."

Regret flickers across Nate's face. "Hil—"

"Save it for someone who cares. I don't. I have to tell you, though. I'm wondering if you're the mole. Something you decided to do when you were drunk, since that seems to be when you make really bad decisions."

The door swishes open.

"You pretend to be so nice and caring, but all you really are, Nate, is a douchebag. No wonder Zelda said she'd never get back together with you. I don't blame her."

Maybe that's a low blow, but I'm past the point of caring. I walk out, wondering what in the world I'm going to tell Sam.

SAM

In the lab, I'm able to get some work done, but it isn't easy. I can't stop thinking about Hildy. My thoughts run the gamut from annoyance to desire. I keep replaying last night, which doesn't help matters. I hate that she's such a big distraction. One I really can't afford.

Fuck. I groan. I'm doing it again.

I need to get her out of my mind. It's not like she'll be here forever. In less than two weeks, she'll be on her way to fucking New Zealand.

My cell phone buzzes, something that usually doesn't happen. I have a very small contact list, but since I sent Toby a new file to encrypt, I check to see if it's him.

It's Geraldine.

Of course it is. I never let her know how last night went.

But I feel like an idiot having to go to a young woman for dating advice. Well, not dating. It was just a dinner. And sex. Hot sex. But definitely not a date.

Geraldine: *How'd your date last night go?*
Sam: *The meal kit was a stroke of genius. Thank you. And not a date.*
Geraldine: *Semantics.*
Sam: *It's the truth.*
Geraldine: *Was the tiramisu yummy, or did you have something else for dessert?*
Sam: *I don't kiss and tell.*
Geraldine: *Your reply tells me all I need to know and I'm proud of you, Sammy. It's about time.*
Sam: *Thanks, but we've decided to only be colleagues.*
Geraldine: *WTF*
Sam: *It's for the best. She has a job opportunity elsewhere. She'll be leaving in a week and a half.*
Geraldine: *Unless you convince her to stay.*
Sam: *I can't. But last night was worth it. Thanks for your help.*

I put away my phone, not wanting to discuss Hildy any longer. Geraldine is still young and believes in happily ever after. Even if she's not a traditional student taking a conventional route for her college education after becoming a single mom, she's doing it her way. I can't wait to read her essays she'll submit for her college applications. I have no doubt she'll be successful wherever she attends.

In some ways, Geraldine reminds me of Hildy by not letting anything stand in the way of her getting what she wants.

For Hildy, that includes me.

We mesh in the bedroom. Out of it, we're a hot mess.

It's as simple as that.

That's why I need to say goodbye to her. Sex can't save a marriage. If it could, we would have never divorced. And let's face it. I work a lot, depending on the project. Yes, I had planned to cut back for her, but I still haven't reached my career goals. Ones that matter to me to prove I'm not that foster kid whose belongings fit into a single trash bag. I'll never be that scared kid again. I'll always be able to take care of myself, but I also want to make sure I thrive. So even though I had the best intentions with my mea culpa list of how I would change, perhaps not giving it to her had been a blessing in disguise.

Five years later, and it's only since I came to Zentello that I've realized how much more success I want in life. Did I enjoy the safe job at the government lab? Yes. When I was with Hildy, I thought I could have both a stable and an excellent career, so I never had to fear being unemployed and still make an acceptable salary. But now I see that stability came with a price—lower wages. Nate Lowe showed me how much I was actually worth in the private sector, and now, I want it all— higher salary, bonuses, and stock options. I don't live large— my only debt is my mortgage—but I want to make sure I'll always have enough, which is why a year's worth of salary sits in a high-yield savings account, so no matter what happens, I'll never have to go without or be homeless. According to two recruiters, I should be able to move up significantly with my next position. I just don't want to interview yet. The Orchid project means too much to me to give any sense of impropriety.

Bottom line, what I want and what she wants aren't compatible. This isn't personal. It's logical and makes sense.

Too bad that doesn't give me a sense of calm where she's concerned.

Still, I can't hide away in the lab all day.

I return to my office to find Hildy gone. The churning of my stomach worsens, reminding me of the spin cycle on my front-loading washing machine. I have no doubt I feel this way because I know where she is—with her fucking fiancé.

An image of her and him in the close confines of his office isn't a vision I want in my head.

I need to take my mind off them, so I sit at my desk and jostle my mouse.

A screen full of data pops up.

Shit. In my haste to leave, I forgot to lock my computer.

"You stupid fuck." I scoot closer to the desk. "What the ...?"

The spreadsheet on the screen isn't the same one I'd been working on, but at least my important files are encrypted, and the password is more difficult to crack than my honeymoon destination and wedding date.

I do a double take.

This spreadsheet is about the Orchid team. Their names, email addresses, and phone numbers. It's not password-protected because it's not confidential. The file is also one I haven't looked at this week.

Why is it open now?

I know what I was working on before I left. It was the file

with the menopausal participants.

Where did that data go?

With a couple of clicks, I discover that the protected file has been moved, as have others. Call me precise—or anal—but I have a specific order of how I organize things on my computer. Files aren't alphabetized or in date order. They are placed in order by the third letter of each file name. Odd, but it works.

Someone has been on my computer and searching my files, but who?

Only Hildy and Nate have access to the lab and office. Everyone else has to be let in.

I think back, trying to remember if I'd left any other files open, but I hadn't. I'm extremely conscious about security. But why would anyone care about the Orchid team? I mean, those reporters did try to blackmail Bradley into giving up info about the identity of Mr. Z, but that seems like a stretch if the mole was someone intimate with the project. They would already know the team and have access to this information.

This makes no sense.

The door slides open, bringing a rush of air. An angry-looking Hildy storms in with heavy footsteps and pushes her chair to one side.

She growls. "I'm so fucking angry right now."

"What?" I ask, a little distracted by the file security breach.

"I'm so fucking pissed." Her face is red, and her hands clench into fists.

"What's wrong?"

I glance at my computer, trying to figure out what could be so interesting about staff records. Unless ...

That has to be it.

Nothing is interesting about the staff stuff, but that isn't what they'd been looking for. That's why the other files were out of order. Whoever was snooping must've been looking for something far more interesting. Thank goodness they couldn't open anything important, but that still doesn't answer why someone would be interested in the team's personal information.

"I don't think you really care, do you?" Hildy sounds annoyed. "As usual, you're too busy with work."

"Something is bothering me. I'm trying to figure it out."

She sighs heavily. "Please don't let me stop you."

If Hildy was up with Nate, then he wasn't in here. That means she's the only one who had full access to my computer. She's new to Zentello. Maybe she wants the team's contact info to contact them outside the office, except she already used that file to get my home address, so is this just a red herring to throw me off and not suspect her? If that's the case, what is she planning to do?

Another blackmail attempt seems a likely possibility.

But honestly, I never thought she had it in her.

Though, I never thought she'd divorce me and fuck Nate, so what do I know?

Yes, it must be Hildy. Maybe this will be the one thing that makes me want to forget about her for good.

My gaze snaps to the door. "Did you lock the door when you left the office?"

"Yes," Hildy snaps. "I typed the code into the panel like I'm supposed to."

She rolls her eyes because we've had this conversation before.

"So if the door was locked ..." I glance from my computer to her and take a deep breath. "Why the fuck have you been looking at my files? And don't you dare lie."

CHAPTER 19

HILDY

After Nate, my anger ramps up to Mount St. Helens's eruption levels. I pin Sam with a hard stare. "Why in the hell would I look at your files?"

"You tell me, or maybe I should ask your reporter friend."

Are you kidding me? His pissy tone is just too much. "Oh, for goodness' sake. Didn't we cover this already?"

"Did we?" Sam pushes back from his desk and stands. "It could be a double bluff. Work with me to find out who's helping the journalist, yet you're the mole the entire time. Covering up for yourself."

He's talking absolute crap, and he knows it. Though, I just accused Nate of being the mole, so maybe I have this coming.

"I told you I'm helping out Nate." I regret taking the job, but that's beside the point. "He wouldn't ask me to do that if he thought I was the mole. Would he?"

Sam sneers. "You know what I think of him."

I do, and I feel the same way about him now. I need to tell Sam what happened too, but we need to resolve this first. "You're being silly, Sam. But I shouldn't be so surprised. You always go off on a tangent and think the most ridiculous things.

Like the time I went to those Zumba classes, and you thought I was auditioning for Juilliard."

"You bought all the gear." He throws his hands in the air. "You wore your hair in that bun thing."

"It's a hairstyle. The leggings were a neon pink and yellow zebra pattern. As if they'd let me into Juilliard wearing those!"

Sam smooths his tie. "I considered those colors to be your style and your kickback against society."

"You only thought that because you dress like you're a 1940s movie star with a stick up his ass." I wink for a little added effect. He really can go off about the stupidest things.

His jaw juts forward, and even upset, he's still handsome.

"I do not have a stick up my ass." Now his lower lip sticks out in an adorable pout. If we'd stayed together, I bet our toddler would do the same thing. "I also don't know any 40s movie stars who looked like they had a stick up their ass. You're the one being ridiculous."

"You thinking I could possibly get into Juilliard is ridiculous." I poke him in the shoulder. "I can't even walk backward in time to music, never mind do a pirouette or jetty."

Sam scratches his temple. "It's jete."

"Whatever, the point is I was not and will never ever try out or get into Juilliard. Besides, I'm too old. Hell, I already have two PhDs. I don't need a degree in dance."

He shakes his head. "Why the hell are we talking about Juilliard?"

"I'm making a point about your damn assumptions. The current being you think I'm the one handing over information to some stupid journalist who writes shit articles about the company we both work for. And don't forget, I'm only here temporarily, and the articles started long before I arrived."

God, the man is so infuriating. How dare he think I'm the one who was trying to ruin Zentello? And how dare he do it standing there looking so hot in his impeccably cut suit, white shirt, and slim blue tie? Just looking at him makes me want to jump his bones and repeat the moves he pulled last night. This is a problem I must solve quickly.

He glances at his computer. "Someone looked at the employee records while I was out, so if it wasn't you, who was it?"

"Employee records?" I push past him and lean over his desk to peer at his computer screen. "Why would I want them? I know who the members of the team are. Hasn't the reporter already published that information? Well, the initials of the lead scientists?"

"Yes." He shrugs as if to say, *so what*?

"Also, why would I wait for you to leave to go onto the computer and get a list I already have access to?"

"I have no idea why you do anything that you do."

"Well, I certainly don't sneak around stealing lists I already have in my possession."

Sam sits on the edge of his desk, but he says nothing. I can tell his brain is in overdrive by the way he bites his lip.

When he crosses his arms over his chest, I turn and perch on the spot next to him. "Who would want that information?"

"They didn't want that file." He kicks my chair back toward my desk. "They're looking for something else."

My brows arch. "What makes you think that?"

"Something to do with how the files are arranged on my computer." He sighs. "We're no closer to finding out who this mole is."

"Even with the work we've done looking through the articles, we don't have a clue."

I'm glad he believes I'm innocent because I hate fighting with him, which confuses me. We are exes, so we're expected to argue and shout and enjoy calling each other names when we see each other. No one would bat an eye.

Maybe it's the memories and the nostalgia that's drawing me in. Sparring with Sam was one of my most favorite things we used to do when we were married. It was fun, the cutting banter where neither of us held back, and I especially loved when we made up. One time we had make-up sex on the kitchen floor. I loved it.

"I'm sorry for accusing you." Sam nudges me. "I don't know what's come over me. I knew it couldn't have been you, but my brain just went there because you're the only other person besides Lowe who has access."

I nudge him. "Something bothering you?"

He smiles. "Apart from you?"

"Oh God, you know that's my life's work."

Sam laughs and shifts his position on the desk. "You do, though, Hildy. I know we can't possibly work, but I can't stop wanting you."

A lump forms in my throat. I feel the same way. I also know I must tell him what I found out. "I was up in Nate's office."

Sam stiffens, and his entire demeanor changes. "Well, you're engaged to him."

"No, I'm not." I hold out my left hand. "It's fake."

"Fake?"

"Nate asked me to pretend to be his fiancée. Something about not having a req for this position." I shrug because the reason sounds off to me now. "But who knows why Nate does anything?"

Sam's gaze bores into my ring finger as if he's trying to see if the ring was still there but invisible.

"I was never engaged." I repeat that just to get the point across, and he finally stops looking at my hand. "Nate told me a couple of other things."

"Let me guess," Sam jokes. "He thinks I'm the mole."

"He does."

Sam's face falls and pales. "That fucker. And you … All the times I caught you at my desk, when you were organizing the cabinet, you were spying on me. For him."

I know Sam will be disappointed in me, but I also knew the risks when I agreed to do this for Nate. "Yes, but I've been looking into everyone on the team. I knew it wasn't you, and I told Nate as much. I don't know why he thinks it's you."

"I do." Sam's voice cracks, and he doesn't meet my eyes.

"Why?"

"After I verify the data, I'll receive a huge bonus. It's part of my employment contract. Something I had added to make working here more palatable, given my history with Lowe."

"If it's in your contract …"

"If I'm fired for cause, the contract will be null and void."

"That fucker." My temperature spirals. "He doesn't want to pay you."

"Looks like it." Sam rubs the back of his neck. "More impetus for us to find the real perpetrator."

I nod. I don't care what it takes, we'll figure this out for Sam's sake. But one thing—the worst thing—remains to be said. "There's something else."

"Not sure how you'll top this."

I feel like I'm in one of those "hold my beer" memes. Only this isn't as funny. I wet my dry lips. My throat is equally dry, but my water bottle is on my desk. I know I'm just procrastinating.

Telling him should be easy. It'll explain so much, and maybe he won't hate me as much as he has in the past, but I'm finding it hard to get the words out.

"Tell me," he says, urging me on.

I take a breath. "Five years ago, Nate told you he'd slept with me. We didn't. We've never had sex or even kissed on the lips. We've never been anything but friends."

Sam's jaw drops. He blinks. "I don't understand. He told me—"

"He was trying to make you jealous so you would go all caveman and drag me home. A stupid plan, which obviously backfired because you cut both of us off." I shake my head. "I have no idea how someone so smart could believe that would work."

He says nothing.

I expect Sam's face to turn red, for his hands to ball into fists, and for him to yell—loudly. None of those things happen. Instead, his breathing hitches, and his eyes gleam. Pain seems to radiate through him. He covers his face with his hands. A sound erupts from his mouth that's raw and hurts my heart.

I touch his shoulder, and he tenses. His muscles bunch beneath my palm, but I keep my hand on him, drawing small circles with my fingertip. He still doesn't say anything, so I take his lead even though I want to tell him it's okay. But it isn't. Nothing is okay about the situation.

Sam's best friend had lied to him. Sure, we'd already divorced, but reconciliation was a possibility. I knew Sam wanted that. I needed to see some effort on his part before I decided whether I wanted that too. But the divorce was supposed to be a wake-up call for him and then he stopped calling—now I know it was because of Nate's lie—and I realized our marriage was truly over, so I left Seattle.

The circles I'm making become sideward, elongated eights—infinity symbols. I like that better.

We stand beside each other in silence for I don't know how long. Finally, Sam lowers his hands just enough to wipe his eyes, making me want to cry. The only other time I've seen him cry was when I left him. And it's gutting me once again, a ripping-my-heart-out-of-my-chest, squeezing-all-the-blood-from-the-organ kind of hurt.

I can't imagine what he's feeling. Sam had lost me and Nate in what must've been the ultimate betrayal when he thought we'd had sex. Sure, Sam had been a grown-ass adult, but now that I know about his past, I would assume a foster kid would have abandonment issues and a whole host of problems and traumas.

Damn Nate Lowe.

The fires of hell are too tame for him.

Sam's body shudders. He sucks in a breath, and then his shoulders relax.

I don't lift my hand off him, for his sake and for mine.

"Thank you," he says finally, his voice still jagged. "I'm sorry I assumed the worst of you."

"You have nothing to apologize for. Why wouldn't you believe your best friend?"

Sam shrugs. "I thought maybe you'd been having an affair with him."

"Never." I shiver at the thought. "And just so you know, my friendship with Nate ended today. I want nothing to do with him."

"I already keep my distance from him, but I'll put even more effort into that." Sam angles his shoulders toward me so my hand falls away from him. "Thank you for comforting me."

"Least I could do."

Our gazes meet, and something passes between us. The connection is almost palpable, even if there's nothing physically there.

He tucks my hair behind my ears and slowly lowers his mouth to mine. His kiss is soft and gentle. Tender. I wish I could say it was full of promise and possibility of what we could be again, but it isn't. Still, the kiss is what we both need after being betrayed—I think that's the right emotion—by Nate.

As Sam cradles my face, I wrap my arms around him and hold on to him tightly. He smells and feels so good, so right.

But I don't want to take advantage of his emotions, not when he must be reeling from what he just learned. That wouldn't be right, so I pull away. "We can't do this right now."

"I know." Sam strokes my cheek, lowers his hand, and then stands. "Okay, let's get back to trying to discover who our mole is."

"Oh, just so you know, I accused Nate of being the mole."

"At this point, nothing would surprise me."

"Same, but before we get started, I need coffee." I stand and grab my wallet out of my purse. "I'm going to the cafeteria. Do you want anything?"

"Coffee would be great." He gives me a sad smile and takes off his lab coat. "I'll get to work."

As I leave the office, I see Lauren, one of Bradley's assistants, hurrying down the hallway. She must be meeting with trial participants to be in such a rush. I glance over my shoulder as the door to Sam's office closes. I understand the gloom behind his smile. It seems as though we're destined to feel bound together but forced to be apart by our past ... and the douchebag best man at our wedding. But at least Sam and I have a common goal now. Both of us want to ferret out the mole. I almost feel sorry for whoever it is because we're both smart people on our own. Together, we'll be unstoppable.

CHAPTER 20

SAM

As soon as Hildy leaves and the door swooshes closed, my shoulders sag. The last time I cried was when she wanted to separate. Even after the divorce had been finalized, I still thought we would end up together. Until Nate told me about them, and I was done with her and him. Only …

It was all a lie.

I'd stopped trying to reconcile after Nate told me they'd fucked. I'd crumpled my list of how I'd change for her and let the hate consume me. And now …

All a lie.

I hadn't even thought about asking Hildy if it were true. I'd known he was over at her place—smelled his aftershave—and accepted his word as truth. Of course, I did. He was my best friend. The only person I'd ever shared my past with until Hildy. Nate knew everything about the fire that killed my parents, to bouncing from one foster family to another, to finally finding peace and love with Hildy. I'd even shared my fear of not feeling as though I was good enough for her and whether she might look for someone else. The fear of her leaving was all-consuming at times.

Nate knew fucking everything about me. He should have also known his plan would never work because I would never try to compete or outdo anyone—especially him.

I scrub my face.

My head spins with a million and one things, and I'm not even sure what to focus on. Right now, all I want to do is fucking quit. It's all I can do not to jump to my feet, take the elevator to the twenty-second floor, and tell Nate to go to hell. That action might give me immediate gratification, but then I'd leave the entire Orchid team hanging.

I pride myself on finishing what I start. I've succeeded everywhere except my marriage, but I didn't have full control. I do with Orchid, and I really don't want to let the team down. The original members spent years working on it, starting when it was known as the Happy Pill.

Also, I can't forget that if I quit, I wouldn't have the same access I have now to find the mole. Doing so from the outside would be impossible, and I'd also lose my bonus.

How dare Nate come after that money by trying to make me the mole suspect? No doubt Mr. Z is on board, because the two seem that close. Why would they want to pay a bonus if they don't have to? I'll prove Nate wrong. If it's the last thing I do, I'll find the mole.

The office phone on my desk rings. I still don't know why we have landlines other than for the intercom system.

I pick up the receiver. "Sam Grant."

"Hey, Sam." Macie's voice is chipper, as usual. She usually sounds like this when discussing anything related to her upcoming wedding. "Bradley wanted me to tell you another set of data is ready. You should have it in the database."

Shit. There goes finding the mole today. We have requirements for the data analysis in case we need to redo anything. I can't push that aside to go hunting for whoever is selling Zentello secrets. "I'll get on it today. Thank you."

"You're welcome." She hangs up the phone.

I pull up the new file, but the numbers jumble and blur.

Fuck. I need to pull myself together before Hildy gets back. I rub my eyes with my palms. Not very hygienic, but I'm past the point of caring.

Hildy cares.

That much is clear by the way she comforted me after telling me about Nate. God, I'm pretty sure I would have lost it completely if she hadn't been here with me and so fucking understanding. I'm sure she's just as upset, but the way she was there for me …

I lower my hands.

Memories play through my mind like a photo carousel. Each one hurts, but time has lessened the pain. That tells me what Nate did will eventually fade. I hope it happens quickly because I feel as if he's stuck a lightsaber into me and I'm dying in an excruciating way. But this will be the last time he hurts me.

Nate Lowe will forever be persona non grata going forward. I already hate the man. Now, I despise him with every atom of my being. He's never been my friend, just a phony with no ethics.

Which is a problem for Zentello.

A good thing Toby's been encrypting my notes. That'll

come in handy if I need to prove Nate's been sketchy, cutting corners, or doing anything illegal.

The door swooshes open, and Hildy enters. She carries two cups of coffee and a bag with her. She smiles at me. "I also got you a donut. I know you didn't ask for one, but this feels like a donut kind of day."

Something in my chest shifts. "A donut sounds great."

If only because she thought I needed one.

She gives me the coffee and the bag. "Enjoy."

I pull a maple bar—my favorite—out of the bag. "Didn't you get yourself one?"

"No. Not much of an appetite right now. But if you don't eat all of yours, I'll take what's left."

She used to do that before—whether it was donuts, muffins, bagels, or even croissants.

"I'll be sure to save you some," I say, cursing Nate to some horrible metaverse where robotic insects will eat him alive and their saliva affects human skin like acid. "More data arrived."

Hildy blows out a puff of air. "So no mole hunting."

"What if you spend a little time doing that while I take care of the data?" I suggest. "Security might have footage of who came to my lab and office today. You might want to see if they can pull the video for you."

"I can take care of that, but if you need me on the data ..."

"I'll let you know." Times like these remind me how good we'd been together. I take a bite of the donut, and it's exactly what I need. Another part of me needs Hildy.

I told her we couldn't work out, but all I want to do is try to make it happen, even if the effort will be futile. But being with her makes me happy. When we were at my house, I no longer felt a deep depression in my bones. Having her around is like finally being able to see in color after living in shades of gray. My thoughts weren't full of hatred. Without her, everything goes back to being miserable and dark.

We spend the rest of the day working, so busy we barely speak. I work through lunch and my afternoon break. By the time I glance at the clock, it's time to go home.

"Any luck?" I ask Hildy.

"Nothing yet," she says finally. "I reviewed the security footage, and your door is just out of view. I didn't see anything other than a guy pushing a mail cart and people walking in the hallway. I also spoke to every person on the Orchid team. They all had alibis for the time you weren't in your lab. There was a meeting with trial participants and all of them were there. Lauren left to get something from Bradley's lab, but she wasn't gone long, and I saw her hurrying in the hallway. I think we need to expand our search."

"Do you know how many employees Zentello has? Not to mention the hundreds of participants in the various trials running right now."

"I know, but we can't keep thinking it's someone on the Orchid team."

"But only someone on the team would know the information that's been passed on to the reporter. It has to be one of them."

Hildy yawns. "Maybe we need to sleep on it."

We hadn't slept that much last night, and today has been emotional and long. I have more work to do, but she needs rest.

"Go home. We can start fresh on Monday morning."

"Only if you go home too."

She knows me well. "I just have to finish up a few things here."

"I can wait until you finish."

Dammit. She needs to listen to me and go home. "Hildegard."

She tilts her head. "Samuel."

Stalemate. I've been here too many times and know how this will end. Hildy isn't the type to give in.

"Fine." I shut down my computer and pack up my bag with what I'll need to work at home. "I'll leave, too."

A satisfied smile spreads across her lips, and suddenly, my dick presses against my pants.

Dammit. It doesn't take much for her to turn me on.

She wets her lips, and seeing her tongue slip out and wanting it on my mouth and my dick pushes me to full mast. "Thank you," she says.

No way am I saying you're welcome. I need to figure out how to get my jacket on so I can hide my hard-on before she notices.

Her nose scrunches. "You okay?"

Nope, but that doesn't stop me from nodding. "Long day."

"If you need anything ..."

"I know." But what I need she can't give me. At least not for long since she leaves for New Zealand in a week and a half. Will that be enough?

I don't know.

Two hours later, the mess in my head is still there, and I find myself standing in front of Hildy's apartment. I'd worked a little at home, but she never left my mind for more than a few seconds. I can't explain why, but I need to see her.

Logically I know coming here is a really bad idea after what I told Hildy this morning, but that doesn't stop me from knocking on her door anyway.

I wait.

No answer, so I knock again.

The door swings open. Hildy's silky kimono-type robe shows a nice amount of cleavage that sends my temperature climbing. Her hair hangs over her shoulders and looks ruffled as if she's been lying down.

Her mouth forms a perfect *O*. "Oh, Sam. I-I wasn't expecting you."

"Hi." My eyes graze up and down her body, and I'm already hard. "Hope you don't mind me stopping by."

"It might be inconvenient." She flips her head, tossing her hair over her shoulder. "I may have a visitor."

I raise an eyebrow. "And he let you answer the door dressed like that?"

She doesn't say a word or glance over her shoulder.

That tells me what I need to know. "I doubt it, baby."

She doesn't have a man here. I'd have seen it in her eyes; plus, the sex we'd had last night had been more than amazing, and if she wanted more, she wouldn't have gone elsewhere. Cocky, yes—so sue me. Despite what I'd told her, I'm confident if she wanted sex, she would have asked me. I push past her.

"Where are you going?" she asks, not stopping me.

"The living room, for starters."

"Sam!"

I enter the living room. It's clear from what I see that Hildy plans to spend the evening in front of her TV. A throw blanket is bunched at the end of the couch. A large glass of wine, a bottle of merlot, and a tub of Tillamook Mud Slide ice cream with a spoon stuck in it sit on the coffee table.

"Did the Duke of Bridgerton jump out of the window?" I ask.

Hildy huffs. "It's Lord Bridgerton and the Duke of Hastings. How the hell do you know about it anyway?"

"Max's wife calls him Bridgerton because of his accent. I was bored one evening, so I watched it." I turn to her. "We need to talk."

She sighs. "I'm sick of talking. We keep going over the same things. We don't work, as you keep saying. I've got it."

"That's what I said, but maybe I was wrong."

"The *great* Sam Grant wrong?" She puts her hands on her hips and her kimono gapes, which gives me a nice view of her boobs. "I didn't think you ever got anything wrong."

I shrug. "I may have had to erase an answer in the *New York Times* crossword puzzle once."

She feigns shock. "Just once? Really?"

"Actually, thinking about it, I believe it was only a couple of letters."

Hildy shakes her head. "You really are an asshole at times."

"It's one of my best qualities," I quip.

She rolls her eyes and stalks toward the kitchen. "Do you want a drink?"

"I'll have what you're having."

"Hot chocolate with marshmallows, then."

She's messing with me, and it makes me smile. Her joking around is one of the things I used to love about our relationship. I acted like I had a stick up my ass, and Hildy gave me shit for it. It got to the point I'd do stuff just so she'd give me shit because I liked it.

"Wine," I shout. "I want wine."

Hildy appears in the doorway with a long-stemmed glass. As she walks to the coffee table, I watch her ass, and my pants get even snugger.

She is so beautiful. "Nice kimono."

As she fills my glass, she glances over her shoulder at me. "How the hell did you know that's what it's called?"

"I don't live in a hole. I have a basic knowledge of fashion."

She gives me a once-over. I'm wearing a slate gray suit with a white shirt and tie. The suit is wide-shouldered and single-breasted. It reminded me of something Cary Grant might have worn in *To Catch a Thief*.

"If you say so, Samuel."

She stands but doesn't pass the glass of wine to me. Her kimono robe gapes more.

"Did I really disturb your evening?" I ask.

She chews on her lip. One hip is cocked, and she crosses her arms over her magnificent chest.

"You may not have." She tilts her head and smirks. "But you can if you want to."

As I imagine peeling off her robe and licking my way up her delicious curves, my heart rate speeds. I swallow. "How would you like me to disturb your evening?"

Hildy's hands go to the tie of her robe. "Well, not by talking, that's for sure."

She unties the knot and drops the robe to the floor. More blood rushes to my dick, making things extremely uncomfortable down there. Hildy stands before me in only a pair of black lace panties. No matching bra this time, but knowing her, she took it off after work. Her hips curve to a slim waist. I can't wait to bury my head between her ample tits and motorboat.

Fuck. She's stunning.

She cocks her hip—teasing, taunting, tantalizing me.

All I can do is stare. "You better be sure of this."

"I am," she says confidently. "I'm also sure I don't want either of us to talk about how we won't work, or that we can't work. I just want to enjoy this for what it is."

"I agree with those terms." Hell, I'd agree with anything she said for another night with her. I take a step closer and hook my finger in the waistband of her panties to remove them. "It all seems pretty agreeable."

"Good," she replies breathily.

Without any warning, she grabs my tie, pulls me against her, and kisses me sensuously. I taste a mixture of wine and chocolate. The combination only makes me want more of her. My lips move over hers, and I explore her mouth with my tongue.

Delicious. I can't get enough of her.

As we continue kissing, she works to undress me. My jacket falls to the floor, my tie follows, and then my shirt until I'm only in my pants. My hands move down her back until I cup her ass.

Hildy pulls back from the kiss. "Get the rest of your damn clothes off. Because I need you to fuck me now."

I don't need to be told twice. Within record time, my pants and boxers drop, only for me to remember my shoes. So I remove those and my socks and step out of my clothes. I also put my glasses on the coffee table.

Hildy pushes me back onto the couch and then climbs on top of me. She rubs my length against her. She's already soaking wet.

I reach my hand to her. "Let me get you ready."

"I'm so ready. You have no idea." She pushes onto my rock-hard dick.

I slide into her softness and warmth. The moment we connect, my body relaxes yet goes on high alert all at the same time. My biceps tense and my fingers grip her ass, pushing into the soft globes and pulling her closer.

It's like coming home, and my breath catches in my throat. She feels even better than last night. I piston into her.

Hildy rolls her hips and releases a satisfied moan that makes me move faster. When her tits rub against my chest, she calls out my name. I turn my attention to her nipples, pulling one of the hard buds into my mouth and sucking the way I remember her liking it.

"Sam, that's ... Oh my God."

I pull my mouth away and nip at the swell of her breasts.

They taste amazing, so I suck more and make it my mission to mark her. I want her to see it and remember I gave it to her, that my lips have been on her.

Hildy rises onto her knees before easing herself down and almost sending me into orbit. She repeats the move again and again, each time lowering herself with more force until I feel the familiar pull in the pit of my stomach.

Wanting her to come with me, I hold her hips tightly and take control, angling Hildy so her clit hits my shaft each time she drops down on it. It's not long before she tightens around me. She fucks me wildly, digging her fingers into my shoulders. I can tell she's almost there.

"Hildy, I'm going to come so fucking hard."

When I drill into her again, my cum streams inside her. I put my hand between us and use my finger to give her the final push. "Your turn, baby."

Hildy moans, then pulsates around me.

I hold on to her. "That's my good girl."

"Sam." She drops her mouth to my shoulder and groans against it as her fingertips dig into my skin.

We cling to each other as we ride the elation and let the tremors subside. Breathing heavily, I take Hildy's mouth with mine and kiss her. We share the gasps and groans as she gives lazy rolls of her hips until the final traces of our orgasms disappear.

"So ..." Hildy lays her head against my shoulder. "Did you come here to release stress after the emotional day we had?"

I smile against her neck. All I want to do is keep this renewed connection growing. "Maybe."

"I'll take that as a yes."

We both giggle. I'm still clinging to her, still inside her, not wanting to break the connection even though I know much needs to be said. But that can wait. I just want to enjoy her for now.

CHAPTER 21

HILDY

As Sam and I lie on my couch, I keep wondering when he's going to get up and leave. The more minutes that tick by and he stays, the happier it makes me. Lying in his arms as he lazily draws patterns on my skin with his fingertips fills me with warmth and tenderness, the likes I've only ever experienced from him. No one has ever made me feel like Sam does. When we work, we work to the point of awesomeness.

That's why when he came over tonight, I'd been determined to go for what I wanted. I didn't care whether he thought we worked or not, I needed him, so I made my move. Now we're in each other's arms on the couch.

"So what now?" I ask finally.

"Hmm." Sam sounds distracted. He links our fingers together and holds them in the air, studying our hands like specimens in his lab.

"Was there anything you wanted to discuss tonight before we lost our way?" God, I'm so glad we did. I'm totally satiated with a feeling of achievement after a great workout.

"I'd prefer to lose our way again, but I think I planned on

mentioning the mole." He turns my face to his and drops his mouth against mine.

My hands go to Sam's hair, my fingers combing through the soft strands. He wraps me in his arms, kissing me with long, languorous strokes of his tongue.

"I could kiss you all night," he murmurs, his lips ghosting mine. "You taste so good."

"Just kissing?"

"Maybe some sex thrown in too."

I giggle. "Works for me." But then I get curious about what he wanted to say. "So what about the mole?"

His hand runs along the curve of my waist and along my hip, finally resting on my ass. He kneads one of my cheeks. "I forgot what I was going to say."

"Hmm." I nibble on his ear. "Sex with you discombobulates me too."

"Good word."

"I know. *Mole* is another good word. Want to talk about it?"

Sam groans and pulls me closer. "Do we have to?"

I arch my back as one of his fingertips circles my nipple. The overlapping circles make me think of Moiré patterns, though what he's doing has nothing to do with physics and everything to do with making me feel so good. He's making it hard to think straight. "Well, if you came here not only for a release but you also had something to say, then say it."

Just don't stop rubbing me.

"I guess." He kisses me once more, though this is more of a peck. "Any more ideas on who it might be?"

"I haven't thought about it since I left the office."

I planned on sleeping on it and hoped I'd wake up with a better idea. To be honest, my mind has been focused on the damage Nate had done and us not working as a couple. That was why I had my favorite snacks and had turned on my favorite show. Yet here we are, working. Go figure.

I stare at him, hoping I can glimpse what he's thinking inside that handsome head of his. "How do we deal with what's happening?"

"You mean the mole?"

"That, and us supposedly not working yet continuing to have sex."

"I don't know about the latter." His voice is low and distracted. He kisses my neck, making me squirm with desire. "But the mole ..."

I reach for his dick, which is still half hard. I can work with that.

"You're distracting me."

I run my nails along his shaft.

He moans. "Fuck, Hildy. That's good."

I nip his jawline. "Do you have any more ideas?"

He lowers his hand and plays with me, his fingers concentrating on my clit. I'm getting wet again, and I'm excited at the possibility of more intimacy with him.

"I wonder ..." His voice trails off.

"Sam ..."

"If it might be two people."

I get what he's saying, but his fingers are doing incredible things down there. I wiggle to try to get him to go faster. Until...

"Oh shit, I need you to fuck me again. Now."

Sam's on his knees, and then I'm over his shoulders.

"What are you doing?" I ask, surprised and excited at the display of dominance.

"This time I'm having you in your bed." He growls and smacks my ass.

The sting sends a rush of heat through me. I'm only interested in more sex, but curiosity gets the best of me. "What about your two-mole theory?"

"We'll talk about that later. I need to fuck you again."

He places me on the bed. The next thing I know he's between my legs and hooking them over his shoulders.

I laugh. "What happened to fucking?"

"Patience."

The way his eyes devour me gives me a rush. I swear I could come just from the way he looks at me. It also makes me feel sexy. I shimmy my shoulders to make my boobs jiggle. That achieves the desired result. "Can't get enough of me?"

"Nope. Your taste is addictive."

"When do I get to taste you? Fair is fair."

"Oh, you'll get your chance."

And then he goes to town on me, licking and sucking every part of me. His tongue is everywhere, but when he flicks it back and forth across my clit, I lose it. I'm writhing and screaming and coming. "So, so good."

He reaches up and runs a finger along my jawline with such tenderness after the wicked display of passion I can barely breathe. "That's because you're my good girl."

I shouldn't like him saying those words so much, but I do.

It's as if Cupid made a direct hit on my heart. After a blow job and two more rounds of sex, I lose track of everything we do and how many orgasms we share. So many orgasms. Talk about glorious.

And it continues all weekend. He never goes home, and though we shower and eat, we don't get dressed. Having that man naked and at my disposal is a dream come true. I come so many times, I lose track. I can't remember when I've enjoyed a man as much as I enjoy Sam.

But we never talk about anything. It's all sex. I have no complaints there, but when I wake up on Monday morning, I'm alone. And that sucks. The spot where Sam slept is empty, and now I'm pissed and disappointed in equal measures.

Where the hell is he? And why did he sneak out without saying a word to me?

SAM

I suck. I arrive at the office. That isn't unusual, but leaving Hildy's bed is. I'd much rather still be wrapped up together— cozy, warm, and luxuriously tired from a weekend of great sex. I turn on my computer and get ready to start my day.

Thankfully, I remembered that Geraldine would be making a delivery this morning, and I couldn't be late. Toby texted me to say he'd finished coding the last set of notes I'd sent to him, and since Geraldine is flying to check out the college in Philadelphia today, the drop-off had to be earlier than normal.

I don't trust anyone else to deliver it but her, nor do I trust anyone else to receive it, so here I am instead of in bed with Hildy. Yes, I suck badly.

Geraldine shows up right on time. "Here you go, Sammy."

I take the envelope. "Are you all packed?"

"Yes!" She spins around, reminding me she's still so young. "My mom's taking care of the baby so that means we get a few nights away on our own. That never happens."

"Have fun."

"But not too much fun." She nudges me with her elbow. "That's how I ended up with my little boy."

She laughs, not sounding like she has any regrets, but she and her boyfriend have had to grow up fast, and she put her schooling on hold. Now, it's her turn. I hope college lives up to her expectations.

"You'll have a great time." I grab the envelope from my desk. "Here's a little something for your trip."

Her eyes widen. "You didn't have to get me anything."

"I wanted to." I motion to the envelope. "Open it."

She does, and her mouth drops. "A five-hundred-dollar gift card?"

"I don't want you to have to skimp on food or transportation." And it's the least I can do since she doesn't charge me for all the couriering she does for me. I've tried to pay, but she says I've helped her enough with all my advice, mentoring, and support.

She throws her arms around me. "Thank you, Sammy. You're the best. I hope Hildy realizes that."

I shrug, but the last thing I feel is indifference. Yesterday felt like a change in our relationship. I sure hope so. "Maybe."

"Not going to kiss and tell, right?" Geraldine laughs. "I see right through you."

I'm sure she does, but I'm not providing any more clues. "You have my number if you need anything. Text me when you get home. I'm sure I'll have another delivery for you when you're back."

She tucks the envelope into one of her leather pants pockets. "I will. And have fun with Hildy."

I plan to. As Geraldine leaves, the corners of my mouth curve more.

I sit, open the envelope to remove the coded report, and read through the pages.

The door whooshes open. Hildy enters dressed in a black skirt, red shirt, and heels. She carries two takeout cups of coffee.

Hildy places a cup on my desk, then takes a sip of her coffee. "You haven't run away to the other side of the world, then?"

I see and hear a hint of rejection. That isn't at all what I wanted her to feel when I had to leave her apartment at five that morning to get home, shower, and change.

"Sorry, baby. I had to be here early for a delivery." I reach for her free hand, but she pulls it away. Damn, I never meant to upset her. "Otherwise, I'd have been there when you woke up."

She arches a brow. "Really?"

I've never been a Boy Scout, so I know nothing about their pledges or oaths, but I can give her my word. I hope that's good enough. "I swear."

Toby's encrypted report is spread over my desk. It's only seven thirty, and I didn't expect Hildy for another half hour. My hope is I can stack all the pages before she notices.

She grabs one of the sheets with her free hand. Her gaze scans the paper and then narrows. "What's this?"

I have a stock answer at the ready—one I'd chosen when I decided to do this. "Computer coding."

Hildy eyes me warily. "Since when do you understand stuff like this? You don't even know how to set up your cell phone when you get a new one."

She's not wrong. I don't want to lie to her, but perhaps a little white lie won't hurt. "I'm helping a kid with his homework."

Hildy laughs raucously. "Liar. Now, tell me the truth."

My gaze narrows. "Why do you think I'm lying?"

Her attention returns to the paper she's holding. With her free hand, she circles her finger around her lower ear. "Your earlobes go pink."

"Never knew that."

"I know." She waves the page. "What is this? Because it's not computer coding."

"Yes, it is." I don't hesitate to answer.

She glances at the paper and then at me. "My recollection of computer science may be vague, but this is nothing that I remember. I remember a lot."

She does. I scratch my temple. "Times have changed. And like I said, the kid needed help."

Hildy sighs. "And you do that too. Scratch your temple when you're lying."

Dammit. She knows me far better than I thought.

"Tell me, Sam." She throws the paper onto my desk. "Because if you don't, then what happened last night will not happen again."

"You wouldn't."

She stares down her nose at me. "Try me."

Fuck. She probably would. "That's just mean."

"Mean and fair." She crosses her arms over her chest and glares at me. "Spill, Dr. Grant."

I have a choice to make. One involves me never seeing or touching her naked body again, which would suck. The other means trusting her—the woman who left me and broke my heart. She's also the woman making her way back into my life and turning the stone that resides where my heart used to be into something that beats again.

There's only one choice I can make. "It's the latest installment on my notes … my report … on Zentello."

Her eyes widen, and her mouth drops open. "What kind of fucking game are you playing?" Her voice sharpens. "Nate and Mr. Z will come after you if they find out."

"You don't understand."

Her mouth narrows. "Then explain it to me."

She knows I'm not the mole, but her expression and voice are full of accusation. My temperature shoots up twenty degrees. "I'm doing this to protect consumers, the patients who take our products."

Hildy studies the page in her hand as if she can decipher the unbreakable code. Not even a brilliant mind like hers will figure it out. "This isn't some personal vendetta against Nate?"

I didn't think so when I started, but now I'm not sure. I also don't want my fucking earlobes to give me away. "Don't worry," I say, feeling more pissed by the minute. My muscles harden. "I'm a fair man. And even though I despise Lowe, I won't bring down him or Mr. Z unless they deserve it."

CHAPTER 22

HILDY

What in the hell does Sam mean about bringing down Nate and Mr. Z? I've never seen Sam act like this. My hand squeezes my cup so hard coffee nearly spills out the lid. "What are you doing that can bring them down? How could a report about Zentello do that?"

"It's nothing. Just trust me."

The hair sticks up at the back of my neck. Whatever he's doing with these reports, going back and forth with Little Biker Girl, is why Nate thinks Sam is the mole. "Oh no. This is definitely something. Why are you being so blasé about this?"

"I'm not being blasé." Sam picks up the papers and slots them into an envelope with the usual red tape stuck to it.

Who is this man?

I stare in disbelief. "Yes, you are, especially when Nate knows about Geraldine's visits to you. I saw the records of the times she's been at Zentello. He knows she's a courier making deliveries and pickups. That's why he thinks you're the mole."

A vein twitches at Sam's jawline. "The notes are mine. The report contains my observations and research. I'm also taking

246

extra precautions with the information so it doesn't wind up in the wrong hands."

How can he be this dense? I take a sip of my coffee as I consider the situation, but the tension knotting my neck and shoulders doesn't lessen. If anything, it ramps up. "This report is going to get you in trouble. You signed an NDA."

"Which I haven't broken."

"In your mind, but will anyone else agree with you?" I doubt Nate will. I've never met Mr. Z, but if he's anything like his co-CEO, Mr. Z will likely respond the same way. The person who'll pay for this will be Sam.

My heart tightens. I don't want anything bad to happen to Sam. Just the thought slays me. I take a breath to calm myself.

"I'm concerned." That's a better word to use than *terrified.* "Despite your precautions, this report could get you in trouble. You could be fired and lose your bonus."

He shrugs. "Yes, I realize that could happen. And thanks to you, I know that's exactly what Lowe wants to happen."

Sam's told me he wants that bonus, so his continuing makes no sense. "So stop."

"I ... can't."

"Can't or won't?"

He says nothing.

My heart plummets to the pointy tips of my heels. Is this some sort of self-destructive action on Sam's part? If so, I might've played a part in driving him to this. The bitter taste of guilt coats my mouth, and I take another sip of coffee to wash it away. I'm only half successful.

"You have to think about the repercussions." I study Sam

with his straight tie, perfect knot, and hair neatly styled. He looks the same. Okay, better if that's possible, but ... "You don't seem the type for a self-fulfilling prophecy."

"I'm not." He doesn't hesitate to answer. "But I can't worry about the consequences. I've got to figure out if everything at Zentello operates properly and follows the rules. People will suffer if corners have been cut or a drug has been rushed through trials. I don't want anyone to get hurt. That includes Nate Lowe."

The underlying edge to Sam's voice is something I don't remember hearing before. But none of this computes. The two things I know about Sam Grant are how logical he is and how he doesn't take risks. He's always been risk-averse. That's why he took the stable government job after his postdoc when he could have worked in the commercial sector. A couple of start-ups wanted to hire him back then.

Nothing he's doing right now fits with how he's acted in the past. I don't get it. "You're a scientist, not a superhero."

"Someone has to do it."

He sounds fucking righteous, and it's so damn attractive. My pulse kicks up, and I find myself moving closer to him. I want to throw myself at him, which would be a bad idea. I need answers to make sense of the senseless.

I cross my arms over my chest, if only to rein myself in. "And you're that someone."

It's not a question, yet he nods. "Something's up."

He's lost me. "With Zentello?"

Sam rubs his chin. "Don't you think it's odd that so many articles written about Zentello suggest something is wrong or there's trouble brewing at the company? And the hard-hitting ones didn't really start until the project that evolved into Orchid began?"

"It's a competitive industry." I remember the articles I've reviewed with Sam and on my own. "But some of the gossipier pieces are strange."

"Nate's known as the golden boy of pharmacology, but he's pissed off a lot of people."

"Including us," I quip. "And who even knows what's going on with Mr. Z?"

Nodding, Sam reaches for his cup and takes a long sip. "Yeah, a couple of journalists even thought that Bradley was Mr. Z."

I scoff. Bradley is a sweet soul who's too good for this planet. I've always liked him. He's a gamer geek, but a nice guy. His fiancée, who I've yet to meet, hit the jackpot. "He works well with Nate, but Bradley's too much of a nerd to be a co-CEO."

"I agree. It's not Bradley, but that raises more questions. Does it make sense for a company like Zentello to have a silent, unseen CEO? We both know Nate lives for the spotlight. But who would give up all that? Makes me wonder if Mr. Z even exists, or maybe he's some shady dude, and that's why he keeps to the shadows."

"Valid points. As is what you said about the timing of the articles." I try to run through all the evidence so far. Too bad we have nothing concrete. "What if the articles have nothing to do with the running of Zentello and everything to do with someone who has it out for the company?"

"That's a strong possibility," he admits.

I have to ask … "Have you found anything suspicious going on?"

"Not really. But all it takes is one person not doing what they're supposed to do and…" His voice is quiet but full of emotion.

I see something behind his eyes that looks like pain. I've seen that look before—the time when he asked me to come home and I wouldn't.

I touch his arm, wanting him to know he's not alone. "Sam?"

He takes a shaky breath. "There's something else I never told you."

Again, I'm not surprised, given how much he kept to himself, but knowing there's more hurts nonetheless. This, however, shouldn't be about me. I know that deep in my bones. "I'm listening."

He closes his eyes and then opens them. He's hunched slightly, telling me what he has to say will be hard for him.

I give him a squeeze. "Take your time."

"Our house burned down because the final electrical inspection was rushed." The words fly out of his mouth as if the sooner he finishes, the faster he can put this behind him. "The inspector got a phone call. Some emergency. He was distracted and rushed off the job, but he missed a critical issue with the wiring and signed off on the house. That problem is what caused the fire that killed my parents and changed my life."

And suddenly, I understand. Sam's report is personal. It has nothing to do with his feelings toward Nate or even the company itself. "You don't want any other kids to lose their parents through someone's carelessness."

"Carelessness or willfulness. The result's the same."

Shit. I want to take a shower to wash off the ickiness creeping over me. Not from anything Sam's saying or doing, but because of what I've done, trying to weaponize sex against him to make him tell me what was going on.

He deserves so much better.

I wrap my arms around him and kiss him hard, putting everything I have into the kiss. I can never make up for him losing his parents or growing up the way he had or me leaving him or Nate lying to him, but I can kiss him now and hope he can feel how much I care.

Because I do.

I care.

I care a lot.

So much it frightens me. And not much has scared me since I left Seattle and Sam.

He's the one who draws the kiss to an end, and I feel bereft. That's a big problem. This man is only in my life temporarily. I'm on my way to a new job, a new continent, a new start.

I need to get things back on an even keel before I forget all that. "What exactly is the report about? All of Zentello or just Orchid?"

"It started out just about Orchid."

"Because you're on the project."

He shakes his head. "I don't want to be associated with a sketchy company, but with Orchid, it's important because the product is for you and women like you."

I'm confused again. "What do you mean, about me?"

"Not you, per se. About your safety, baby." Passion fills his voice. "Once Orchid hits the market, millions of women will take it. And it's my job not only to verify all the data, but to make sure the product is safe and not being rushed. Nate might not have hired me for that particular job, but that's what he got."

I listen to him in awe. Sam Grant is one in a million.

"I'm not letting anything in the project get glossed over in the name of profit to have someone hurt. Not just someone, but a woman," he continues. "A woman who is a mom or grandmother, a sister or cousin or aunt, or a friend or a teacher. That's how it started out—to ensure what we put in the market is safe for all women to take—but because of the articles, I'm looking deeper at the rest of Zentello. I've tried to follow up on everything published. The conditions, the animal testing, you name it. If processes and procedures need to change based on my findings, so be it."

My heart thuds. "You wouldn't want to be connected to that sort of company, especially if it puts people at risk."

"I wouldn't."

My heart swells with affection.

"You're full of surprises," he says.

I know I can be at times, but I'm not sure how I am at the moment. "What do you mean?"

Sam smiles, almost serenely, like he just stepped into one of those hot baths he loves so much. "You believe in me."

His words make me feel all squishy inside. "I do."

"Thank you, but there is one problem." He takes a sip of

his coffee. "I'm not sure if it's serious. It could be just a coincidence. But I find myself in the old which-came-first-the-chicken-or-the-egg dilemma because one of the articles two weeks ago was the same topic as my notes."

A chill runs down my spine. "Sam ..."

"I know, so it could just be a coincidence that the mole found the same thing I did."

"Or the mole got ahold of your notes."

"Yes, but I don't see how that's possible."

I have a thought. One I know he won't like, but I have to say it. He's trying to do good here, and I'd hate to see him be the one hurt if someone's selling his material to the reporter. "What about your hot Little Biker Girl? Could she have passed the report to someone?"

Sam flinches. "*My* hot Little Biker Girl?"

"What?" I can't believe he sounds so surprised. "She is."

He shakes his head. "Geraldine's also a kid, a good kid, so like *I* said, she wouldn't give up that information."

"She might not understand the consequences of her actions."

"If anyone understands consequences, it's her." He sounds absolutely certain.

"How do you know that for sure?"

"She's nineteen with a two-year-old son and wants to go to college but has been torn because her boyfriend, who happens to be a great dad for a kid his age, has a well-paying job here."

"She can still go to school." I suddenly find myself going all in on team Little Biker Girl. "Is the baby daddy holding her back?"

Sam shakes his head and laughs. "No, the baby daddy, who I've met several times and is a good guy, has been her boyfriend for years. He's encouraged her to go to college, and it's taken her this long to have the means to do so. She's leaning toward Pennsylvania because he can transfer with his job. I gave her some advice on which colleges to check out, and I'll help her with the application process."

I place a hand against my heart, feeling bad for every mean thought I've had about Little Biker Girl. Geraldine's just a single mom trying to improve the life of herself and her family like my younger sister Mathilda is trying to do for Flynn. Logical or not, I feel the need to trust Sam's judgment about her. "You're a good man."

"Thank you. That means a lot, but ..."

"That one article bothers you."

"So much." He pulls out a roll of the tamper-proof tape. "When it happened, I checked with Toby, who puts my notes into code. I asked him if the tape has ever been tampered with, and he's been adamant everything is okay. A number shows once the tape is removed, and he said the tape has always been intact. He even confirmed with that specific delivery, and his number matches what I'd written down."

"Wow," I say, though I shouldn't be so surprised. "You really are conscientious about security. What happens when Toby finishes with your notes? Could he do something with them then?"

"The information would be meaningless to him. I use my own abbreviations, plus he's only fourteen years old."

"Wait, what?" I couldn't have heard him correctly. "Fourteen?"

"Yes."

"So why get him to code them at all?"

"I used to work with his dad. Toby's into cybersecurity and stuff like that. He told me he could write a code no one would crack, so I challenged him. The reporter was publishing his crap, and Toby delivered, so I decided to use him. I'm asking an independent adviser to read everything over and determine whether anything needs to be brought to Nate and the board of directors' attention."

"They won't be happy you've gone about this in secret, but your motivation is understandable. And in the end, it'll only help Orchid and Zentello."

"I hope so because this is important."

"You need a cape."

Sam's grin is cheeky and cute and makes my stomach flip. "If you're offering."

Yes, he needs a cape. And I'd love to see him in one and only wearing that. Desire ignites in my stomach.

Sam stands and glances at his computer. "I have more data to review."

"I have something for you first."

He stares at me expectantly. A beat passes. I'm not sure what's driving me, but I know what I want—more of what we'd had before he pulled away from me. I launch myself at Sam and kiss him. I never want to stop kissing him.

CHAPTER 23

SAM

As Hildy kisses me, she wraps her arms around me, holding on like she never wants to let go. Her kiss isn't hot and heavy. It's sweet and meaningful as if this is so much more than a kiss. I relish the feel of her. Her taste and scent intoxicate me. I backed away from the last kiss, so I let her end this one.

She finally pulls away and stares at me, her breathing ragged. Her hand goes to her mouth, and she touches her lips.

"What was that for?" I ask.

She shrugs, not meeting my eyes. "No reason."

"That wasn't a 'I feel hot for you' kiss. It's nothing like the ones we've been sharing."

Hildy blushes, which is the most unlike Hildy thing she's done. The woman is the definition of commanding and confident.

"What?" I press.

She flips her hair. "It's nothing."

It most definitely is something. She's getting all girly on me. Fuck. That's as much of a turn-on as when she used to berate me. I'm sick of being cautious around her. Sick of feeling the bitterness I've felt for the last five years, and I'm also turned on beyond belief by my ex-wife.

When she turns to walk away from me, I won't let her do that. Not again.

I grab her hand and pull her against me. "Baby. All bets are off."

She leans back to look up at me. "What?"

"I'm going to fuck you now, okay?"

Wordlessly, Hildy nods and drops her hands to her sides, giving me clear access to her blouse. The fabric stretches tight over her breasts. Her chest is heaving with each breath, up-down, up-down, the movement getting faster the longer I admire her. The buds of her nipples are clearly hard, making me want to just rip her shirt off, but I know better.

Instead, I slowly undo her shirt, button by button, getting more excited with each revelation of honey-toned skin and a red bra the same color as her blouse. I have no doubt her panties will match.

As her shirt hangs open, I push it off her shoulders and drop my mouth to her collarbone, kissing all the way up her neck to behind her ear. I swipe my tongue around her earlobe.

I raise my lips a millimeter, my breath ghosting her skin. "You taste so good, Hildy."

A moan escapes her mouth, and she arches her back. Her tits press against my chest, which feels too tight, too constricted in the white cotton button-down shirt I'm wearing.

As if reading my mind, Hildy tugs at my tie until it's loose enough to pull over my head and tosses the thing over her shoulder. She unbuttons my shirt, but she's much quicker than

I was with hers, only not nearly as careful. One button pings across the office because she's so forceful. As she watches its trajectory, she giggles, the sound making me even harder.

I reach down for the hem of her skirt and push it up until the fabric bunches over her thighs. When my hand brushes her thigh-highs held up by a garter belt, I know I won't last long when I finally have her.

"You're so fucking sexy." I trail a finger over the satin of her panties and rub her clit through the fabric. I love how she squirms against me. "And so damn wet."

Needing to feel that wetness, I stick my finger underneath the fabric. She's ... soaking, and I go to work on her clit.

Hildy parts her legs to give me better access. That's the only invitation I need. I push two fingers inside her. Fuck. She's soft and warm.

Her mouth parts, and she makes a little gasp. I pump three times before hooking my fingers and finding her sweet spot. She moans.

"Sam, please," she says breathlessly. "I love foreplay, and you're the best at it. But please, just fuck me."

How can I refuse such a polite request? "Whatever you want, baby."

I guide her backward toward her desk, and my arm sweeps the papers on top to the floor. The only thing I carefully put aside is her laptop because ... data. We still have a job to do for Orchid.

I place Hildy onto the desk so she's on her back and bring her legs up. Seeing her heels dangling in the air looks so damn sexy. She's still wearing her panties—and yes, they match her red bra. I push the wisp of fabric aside so I can see her.

Fuck, her pussy's calling out to me.

Hildy leans up on her elbows and looks at me lazily with sultry eyes. As she watches me, I take off my unbuttoned shirt and undo my belt and zipper. Everything feels heightened. The electricity surging between us feels like it will ignite at any moment.

When I drop my pants and push against Hildy's knees to widen her legs, she inhales sharply. I hope it's in anticipation because that's how I'm feeling. She cups a breast and squeezes it.

Fuck. I can't wait any longer. I plunge inside her with such force, she moves up the desk and knocks over a cup of pens I hadn't gotten out of the way. They tumble to the floor.

She grunts. "More, Sam, please."

"You want it harder, baby?"

"Yes," she pants. "Harder."

Never one to disappoint, I pull out all the way and thrust back in hard. Her head drops back, and she tightens her legs around my hips. The heels of her shoes dig into my ass, and the pinch of them pushing against my skin urges me on.

Like a champion, Hildy's hips match my rhythm, and we fuck on her desk with passionate abandon, both of us gasping for breath and gripping each other like we'll lose our lives if we let go.

When I pull out of Hildy, she grabs my hand. I lean forward and lift her, gripping her ass.

"I'm going to pin you against that wall and drill you until you scream," I whisper in her ear.

I'm lucky I have three proper walls in my office, whereas most others at Zentello are all glass. I also keep the privacy glass permanently on the glass wall because I hate working in a glass cage where everyone can watch my every move. I'd been given the choice between two offices, and the solid walls in this one influenced my decision.

Speaking of walls ... I slam Hildy against the one with a door and push back inside her. I continue to fuck her senseless. As I push in and out of her, the door near us rattles.

As I thrust again, she moans, "People will hear us."

"Who the hell cares?" I certainly don't. Ask me again once I come down from my impending orgasm.

"Not me."

I place her on her feet, turn her around, and push back inside her.

I reach around to rub her clit. Hildy slaps her hands against the wall. "Oh my fucking God."

"Hello?" a male voice says. "Is everything okay in there?"

Hildy gasps. We both still. Whoever stands on the other side of the door knocks twice.

She giggles, and I cover her mouth with my hand. But as her shoulders jiggle, making her tits bounce, I laugh.

"Hello?"

I don't recognize the voice so I guess it might be a new intern or someone from another floor. "It's all good, thanks."

"Okay," he says from the other side of the door. "I was ... I was passing and heard yelling."

"Yeah, I, erm ..." What the hell do I say?

"Tell him you're watching porn." Hildy giggles again.

"Sorry for concerning you. I'm watching porn," I say.

Hildy snorts. "I didn't mean it, you idiot."

"I had nothing else," I whisper.

"Oh, wow, okay," the guy says.

"It's to select samples for the next clinical trial," I add. That's totally plausible, right?

"I, erm … I'll … I'll go make my other deliveries." The guy's voice cracks. "I'll come back with your mail another time, Dr. Grant."

"Okay, thanks," I squeak out.

Footsteps retreat, and within seconds, Hildy bursts into peals of laughter. Rocking underneath me with my dick still inside her.

"Quiet," I chide, with a little laughter. "It's not funny."

"Oh, it is fucking hilarious." She glances over her shoulder at me and looks so damn sexy my dick instantly hardens again.

Fuck. I'll never get enough of her. "We need to finish something, don't we?"

As I move my hips, she sucks in a breath. "Yeah, we definitely do."

We are much quieter this time, but it's just as damn good.

HILDY

"Can you pass me that textbook, please?" Sam asks, standing at the workbench in the lab. He's bent over, staring into his microscope, and the view is spectacular. His pants are pulled across his tight ass. Each cheek is probably marked by my heels.

My smile widens. I doubt I'll stop smiling for days. Though, we've been all business since our sex session earlier, except for when the mailroom guy returned after lunch. Sam hid under his desk while I tried hard not to laugh and pretend it hadn't been me who was drilled against the wall on his last visit. The poor guy, a young man with an eye patch—named Ryan Matthews, according to his lanyard—acted even more embarrassed. Probably because of his age. I hope we didn't cause long-lasting damage.

I pass the book to Sam, letting my hand brush against his. "Here you go."

He doesn't look up from the microscope, but I see the hint of a smile. Other than crawling under his desk for a few minutes, he went back to being professional the moment we put our clothes back on.

"What are you looking at?" I ask.

"A blood sample from one of the trial participants. She's been experiencing nausea and is midway through her cycle. I want to check if anything shows in her blood work."

As he continues studying the slide, he's making me feel hot and bothered all over again. I know his dedication to his job drove us apart, but something is sexy about a hardworking man who wants to help others. "Anything?"

Sam straightens and frowns. "No. She's taking daily contraceptive pills, so maybe it's something to do with that."

He thumbs through the textbook until he finds whatever he's looking for and proceeds to read the section.

"She's not the only one." I go over to the computer in the lab and pull up a list on the screen. "We have ... one, two ... nine participants using the contraceptive pill, and of those nine, they're split into four groups. What's her name?"

Sam turns his attention to a document on the workbench. "Rosie Jackson. Age thirty-two."

I refer to my notes. "One child, age two. Morgan Richards takes the same pill and also has one child. The other person in their contraceptive group is Audrey Johnson, and she has no children. Neither has mentioned nausea or any other type of side effect."

Picking up the book, Sam goes to the other desk. He removes his glasses and throws them onto the textbook. Pinching the bridge of his nose, he sighs. "I can't determine what it might be, and I don't want to pull her from the trial, but if we can't figure it out, I might have to."

"No one else has this symptom?" I ask.

Sam shakes his head. "I've triple-checked."

"It's manageable though, right?"

"She says so. She said it lasts for a couple of hours in the morning but is gone by the time she goes to the café across the street from her job for the coffee order."

I frown, but something he said ...

"What?" Sam asks. "What are you thinking?"

"Does her nausea subside before or after the coffee?"

Sam raises an eyebrow. "Not sure, but I'll make a note for Macie to give her a call. If it's after, then it could mean caffeine combined with Orchid is a preventive for nausea. If that's the case, it can't be anything too dangerous to her."

"Exactly," I agree. "Which means she won't need to be removed from the trial."

Sam smiles. "I'll need to organize more tests, but that would be the top and bottom of it. I hate removing people, especially when it's a great source of income for them."

God, this man. He's so caring, even if he is a bullheaded idiot at times.

I wiggle my eyebrows. "With that mystery solved, what's next?"

"Well, not that." Sam smirks. "We've had enough excitement for one day."

"You never used to say that." I pout. "I remember lots of times when we'd play hooky and meet up back home for some fun."

"Unfortunately, I wasn't a lead scientist then. Maybe we can put a pin in it, though?"

His expression is so cute and hopeful; who am I to spoil a man's sex fantasy? "We can arrange that. Anyway, I have something to tell you."

Sam's forehead creases.

"No need to look worried," I say.

That doesn't seem to comfort him. He leans his forearms on his desk. "What is it, then?"

"We're going for drinks after work," I announce, feeling extremely proud of myself. "With the Orchid team."

Sam's face falls. That's not the enthusiasm I'd been hoping for. "You're joking, right?"

My smile doesn't seem to change his mind. "No, I'm not."

"Why would you do that?" He sounds genuinely stunned.

"Because it's a great opportunity." I try to keep my shoulders from sagging with disappointment. I thought he'd be okay with it. I haven't told him why I wanted to do this yet, but I kind of hoped he'd see it as a way of people seeing us together. As a couple. I obviously overthought things as usual.

"What's it an opportunity for? You know how I hate small talk with people I don't really know."

"They're your team, Sam. You should know them and for more reasons than just working together. You're the boss of this part of the trial."

His brow furrows, and I can see he has no inkling of what I'm trying to say.

"For Pete's sake, Sam." I roll my eyes. "We'll have everyone from the Orchid team in the same room, and we'll be able to talk to them and hopefully find out who the hell our mole is."

Even though we'd initially thought it couldn't be one of the team members, we kept coming back to the mole being someone with access to inside information. Someone with the ability to get into this lab, too. Maybe only with permission, but that didn't mean they couldn't sneak in if Sam was in the lab and not the office.

Finally, a light seems to dawn, and Sam seems to allow himself a small smile. "I see how that might work. Although I can't say I'm happy about spending time with them in a nonwork setting. Like I said, small talk isn't my thing."

That's true. He's never been one who could chitchat comfortably. He's always straight to the point—short and sweet.

"I know it'll be torture for you, but—"

"Hildy, baby, it's fine." He holds up his hand. "I'll go for drinks and see what we can find out, but one thing."

I grin. "Yes. What's that?"

"We do not make this a regular team event. No matter how drunk you get, don't even suggest it, okay?"

I frown. "Not just once more?"

"No," he snaps and then flashes me a beautiful, crinkled-eye smile that melts my heart.

CHAPTER 24

HILDY

We've been in the bar with the Orchid team for almost two hours. I've met a few new people, but I'm none the wiser as to who our mole might be. Bradley introduced me to his fiancée, Christina, who gave me a bottle of perfume called Joyous that she created. She entered it into a prestigious fragrance competition and won. She's younger than Bradley, but he's smitten, and they seem to make a great couple. I glance their way and notice them now talking to Macie and her fiancé, who is a lawyer.

"Here you go, Hildy." Max hands Sophie and me each a glass of wine. "We're glad you could drag Sam out. This is the first time he's come out with all of us. Though he'll join Bradley and me occasionally."

I must admit I'm smitten with the scientist's incredibly sexy British accent, but the way Max never stops touching his wife, Sophie, is the definition of adorable. Sam told me the couple has only been married a month, and they are definitely acting like newlyweds who can't get enough of each other.

And I'll be totally honest—I'm jealous. Still, I smile. "It's good for Sam."

Sophie grins. "We need to get Sam up on stage at Randy's."

Her enthusiasm is contagious. She's beautiful and smart, recently received her PhD in biochemistry, and is starting a postdoc at the local university soon.

"What's Randy's?" I ask.

Sophie practically bounces with excitement. "A local karaoke place."

"A dive bar, but we enjoy it," Max adds.

"My friend Jules and I perform there all the time. You should join us." Sophie gives me a once-over. "The crowd would love you."

I laugh. "Thanks, but I can't sing."

"Neither can she," Max jokes.

"I can't," Sophie agrees. "But I don't let that stop me."

I like these two, and can imagine getting to know them better and going on double dates with them, only ... My chest tightens. I won't be in Seattle for much longer. I might never speak to Sophie again after tonight. And what about Sam? No, I can't think about the future, or I'll ruin tonight. "Maybe I can see you perform sometime."

Sophie shimmies her shoulders. "I'll have Max tell you when the next Gurl Power night is."

"Do." I glance over at Sam. He's still talking to Lauren, a pretty woman who happens to be one of Bradley's research assistants. The two have been chatting for almost twenty minutes. Not that I'm counting.

Sam laughs.

What the fuck? He should be mingling, not letting some young twenty-something flirt and monopolize him. Worse, he doesn't even notice I'm staring at him.

Well, two can play that game.

"I'll talk to you later," I say to Max and Sophie. "Let me know about karaoke."

I'm sure the thought of going to something like that will mortify Sam, but he needs to get out more. At least Lauren doesn't seem like the karaoke type.

I make my way over to Daniel, who also works on the Orchid project. The young scientist is cute, but he seems shy. He's nursed the same drink while sitting in the same place since we arrived.

I sit next to him, scooting closer until our thighs touch. "So tell me what you do in your spare time. Do you like to spend time outdoors?"

He's pale, which isn't odd during the winter in Seattle, but it's summertime. I wonder if he ever sees sunlight.

A blush travels up his neck. "I play a lot of Dungeons & Dragons."

I'm not a gamer, but I gush with excitement. "Oh my goodness. That's fantastic. How interesting."

He looks perplexed. "It is?"

"It really is." I playfully tap his knee. "I'm super excited for you."

I sneak a glance at Sam, who's looking my way. Bingo. A few seconds later, though, Sam's head drops back. He laughs again at something Lauren said.

I turn my attention back to Daniel. "And apart from Dungeons & Monsters?"

"Dragons," Daniel corrects me. "It's Dungeons & Dragons."

"Sorry, Dragons." A glance at Sam shows me he's also glancing at me. "Apart from that, what do you do?"

"I like to watch old 60s comedy shows too."

"You do, wow." It's my turn to laugh—loudly.

Daniel laughs nervously and takes a gulp of his drink. "Do you know why Dr. Grant ... Sam is here? Is he looking to get rid of people from the project? I kind of figured you'd know since you work so closely with him."

I glance over at Sam. "No, why would you think that?"

"He never goes out with us for team stuff." Daniel keeps his voice low. "He's never once taken us out for drinks since he took over the project. Everyone's wondering if he's cutting the staff, and this is some kind of bon voyage going-away shindig."

"God no, he's not doing that. I promise." I need to do some damage control. The guy sounds really worried. "I persuaded him to come out tonight. I thought it might be nice if he thanked the team for their hard work with a few drinks."

"You sure?" He glances around, appearing even more nervous. "Because I'm the last person to join the project, and I figure I'll be the first out if they need to cut costs."

"I promise you, Daniel." Goose bumps erupt over my skin, and I know Sam stands behind me. When I glance over my shoulder, he's smiling. "Ah, Sam. Daniel and I have been talking about you."

"Really. Is it good or bad?" No one can see because of the way we're standing, but Sam's finger ghosts up and down my back.

"All good. Daniel asked if you're cutting people from the project. I've been assuring him that's not happening."

Sam gets a concerned expression. "Nothing like that's happening, Daniel. You're doing an amazing job with the participants and the trial. You've nothing to worry about. But do you think that I can steal Hildy away from you for a couple of minutes?"

Daniel's face turns beet red. "Oh, she's not with me. We're just talking, Dr. Grant. I mean, Sam."

"It's fine, Daniel. I think Sam knows that." I smile at Daniel and then follow Sam to a quieter part of the bar.

"Hey," Sam says once we're away from everyone. "Can we call it a night yet?"

"Did you find out anything?" I ask, hopeful.

Sam shakes his head. "Not a thing, unless you count the fact that Lauren has three bunnies."

I roll my eyes. "I'm not interested in Lauren's bunnies."

Sam shrugs. "So can we go?"

"I guess so." But I feel myself sag. "We don't have anything to give Nate on the mole, do we?"

"No." He glances around the bar, and everyone is occupied drinking and talking. Sam runs a finger down my cheek. "*We* do have something, though."

I lean into his touch. "What's that?"

"Chemistry."

I grin. "Really, and here's me thinking biology's more our specialty."

Sam laughs. "Come on, I'll see you home."

As he leads me out of the bar, I can't help but hope him seeing me home leads to something more like a trip to my bed, because I can't get enough of him.

I have no doubt Sam Grant will break my heart again, but I don't care. Soon, I'll be far away, leading my own team, and I'll be busy enough I won't even have time to miss him.

At least that's what I'm going to keep telling myself.

SAM

I want nothing more than to go inside Hildy's apartment tonight and take her to bed. I can tell by the way she keeps glancing at my crotch that's what she wants too, but seeing her interacting with the team did something to me.

Her trying to make me jealous by speaking to Daniel was typical Hildy. She probably made the young man's year with her attention. But watching her with Bradley and Christina and Max and Sophie turned everything I thought I knew inside out.

At the bar with her interacting with my coworkers, I can see us as much of a couple as they are. And the two pairs are about the sugary, sweetest, gag-me happy couples I've ever come across, and yes, I've been jealous as hell of them. I'd never even hoped to come close to that, given my lack of interest in dating. And that scares me.

We reach her door, and she pulls out her keys. The metal jingles in her hand. "Coming inside?"

Her tone is suggestive, and I'm so tempted. Going inside and staying the night would be so easy. It's what she wants. Who am I kidding? I want it too, but …

Something inside me tells me I need to leave. It's not that

I don't want to stay. God, I want that more than anything, but I want us to be more than just sex. That's always worked between us. Everything else turned things into a shit show, which is why I want to be more careful this time. I don't want to repeat past mistakes. We might not get another chance if we screw up like we did the last time.

And I want Hildy to know that.

I take a breath. "Not tonight."

Her face falls. "Oh."

"It's not what you think. I want you. God, how I want you. I just think things have been happening fast. And I don't want us to rush when we should be taking things slower."

"So is this where you say it's you, not me?" If she's trying to make a joke, there's no humor in her voice.

"I'm ... confused about what this"—I point at her and then back to me—"is."

"Hot sex isn't enough?"

"Yes, but that's never been a problem with us."

She sighs. "No, it hasn't."

"What if I told you I wanted more than hot sex?"

Hildy tilts her head. "Hypothetically?"

"We can go with that."

"I'd say, hypothetically, that sounds good to me too."

Okay. I release the breath I've been holding. For once, I made a logical decision where she's concerned. Maybe there's hope we can be more ... "That's good to know. Hypothetically."

She nods. "So are you coming in now?"

"Not tonight. Get some sleep," I say, knowing it's the right move if we're meant to have a future, even if my dick would disagree fully. "I'll see you at the office."

I kiss her on the lips. More of a peck than a full-on kiss. And it's not nearly enough.

She stares up at me with questions in her eyes. "Are you going straight home?"

"Yes."

"Okay."

Her question confuses me. She's implying something. I should just ask. That's what Bradley would tell me to do. "Where else would I go?"

"To see Lauren's bunnies."

I want to laugh, but I get the feeling Hildy's serious. Her eyes haven't turned green, but she's jealous. And she has no reason to worry. She's been the only woman who's ever touched my heart. "If I went anywhere except home, it would be to your bed. I promise you."

"That's the right answer." Hildy opens the door. "Thanks."

"Thank you for organizing the team drinks tonight." I hope she can hear how grateful I am for what she did. "I tend to get stuck in my ways, and I need to be less of a hermit."

"I'm happy you see that. Just remember, a little socialization goes a long way."

I nod. "Don't forget to lock the door, baby."

She smirks. "Getting into a daddy kink?"

"No." I laugh. "Get inside. But you'd better be a good girl for me, or you'll get a spanking."

It's her turn to laugh. "Promises, promises."

She enters her apartment with an extra sway to her hips, closes the door, and locks it. A part of me wants to knock on the door and tell her I've changed my mind so I can fuck her all night long, but I know walking away tonight is for the best. Even if it sucks.

The following day, we sit at my desk, eating the lunch I'd prepared for us. Do I usually pack my lunch? Not unless I have enough leftovers, which I didn't this morning, but on my way in to work, I passed a nice grocery store with a great deli. After all the meals she cooked for me over the years, this is the least I can do. I handled the cleaning, but cooking was never my thing. I'd never been taught properly, so I got by with heating things up. Anything else was a stretch.

"This is delicious," she says between mouthfuls of quinoa salad. "Did you buy it or make it?"

I lift a finger to wipe the side of her mouth. "Bought it. I've changed over the past five years and learned to cook. But I still live off leftovers from takeout most of the time. I prefer the easy life."

"Yet you married me." Hildy winks at me.

My stomach does a backflip. It's amazing she still has that effect on me. Admittedly, what's happening between us feels more like a new relationship than one starting over, but it still doesn't alter the fact that being with Hildy again is the best thing to ever happen to me. I don't want it to end.

"Did Macie schedule the new tests for Rosie Jackson?" Hildy asks.

"She did. Rosie's coming in on Wednesday. Hopefully,

further tests will help us determine the problem." I take a piece of chicken from Hildy's plate and earn myself a tap on the knuckles with her fork. "Thanks to Zelda, I've also gotten approval to continue to pay Rosie if we have to remove her from the trial."

Hildy gasps and then pulls me into her arms and hugs me hard. "That's wonderful."

I surreptitiously inhale her scent. I recognize it as Christina's latest. Bradley had passed some bottles out to members of the team earlier in the year. The fragrance goes straight to my dick, which perks up. "What?"

"Continuing to pay Rosie. You're such a good man," Hildy whispers. "So good."

After at least a full minute of hugging, she lets me go and kisses my cheek before returning to her salad.

"We should discuss our supersecret sleuthing project," Hildy says.

"You mean ferreting out the mole?"

She nods. "We can examine our list of suspects. What we need is a person of interest."

I laugh. "Now you sound like a cop."

"Super Sleuth Scientists to the rescue." She wiggles her eyebrows. "We can find anything."

"You could maybe." I push my plate away. After Hildy does the same, I take her hand in mine. "You're so smart, baby. Your brain is spectacular. Everything you do, you give a thousand percent."

She chews on her lip, and her gorgeous eyes shine with a brightness that is one hundred percent her. Only Hildy. She's a six sigma, always has been. I'd loved this woman beyond anything, she was my world. Now, I feel like the same thing is happening as it did years ago, but I don't mind one bit.

I pull her closer. "I'm going to kiss you now."

"You are?" she asks softly.

"Yes, baby, I am."

I lower my mouth to hers. Her lips are soft and gentle. When she threads her fingers through my hair, a feeling of pure joy envelops me. This isn't the sort of kiss that leads to sex. No, this one is gentle and romantic, not hurried, and it tells me so much about what we could be and makes me wonder if maybe there's hope for a future together.

I still have work to do on myself, but a part of me wants her to stay with me instead of going to New Zealand. I know that's too selfish to ask of her, but I love being with her again. I want to be by her side if she'll let me, though I have no idea what that would look like or what that means. I know what I did wrong before, and I won't do that again. I trust her with my heart, and that's something I never imagined doing again.

To move forward, I know I need to put the past behind me. That means clearing the air with Nate. I don't look forward to that conversation, but I still need to work here to finish the Orchid analysis, and if Hildy stays in Seattle, she'll need a job. Zentello is a perfect fit for her. I just hope she thinks I'm a perfect fit for her too.

After lunch, I listen to Hildy as she reads over the suspect list she's made from the spreadsheet with all the Orchid team's information. She doesn't want to leave off anyone. Even though it feels like we're making no progress, we keep going. I appreciate her wanting to get to the bottom of this so Nate can't use his suspicions to fire me.

Hildy points at Daniel's name on the spreadsheet. "What about this guy? Daniel told me he enjoys playing a Dungeons and something game. That might give him some special skills for spying."

I laugh. Daniel would be at the bottom of my list. The guy is smart as hell. He's been wonderful in the way he's interacting and interviewing trial participants but shy outside of the lab. "Bradley plays that game too. That doesn't make him our mole."

We lean closer to the computer screen, our heads almost touching as we study our list of suspects. I keep inhaling to smell her. Let's just say, this part of our sleuthing doesn't suck. Unfortunately, we're just going over the same people and not making any forward progress.

"If not him ..."

I turn my head as Hildy turns hers. Our lips are so close that I feel her breath on my mouth. I need to kiss her, so I drop a quick smacker on her lips.

"You're thinking out of the box, which is great." I tap the tip of her nose. "But I don't think enjoying role-play games makes Daniel—or Bradley, for that matter—the sort of person who would sell information to the press."

"I suppose." Still, she grimaces, making me grin. "Who's next on the list?"

I see the name and smirk. "Lauren Waters."

"Oh, yes!" Hildy yells. "It's definitely her."

I know where this is going, but I want to play along. "Why?"

"Gut instinct."

Only if it's green colored. I recall the looks Hildy tossed my way when I spoke to Lauren at the bar last night. "You aren't jealous of her at all?"

Hildy shakes her head. "Why would I be?"

"No reason." I kiss the side of her head and earn a beautiful, soft smile. "Okay, so what actual reasons do you have for thinking it's Lauren?"

Hildy's quiet and then glances at the ceiling. She blows out a breath. "I've got nothing. Okay, who's next?"

We continue going over names for the next half hour and come up empty again. It's almost six thirty. Time to call it.

"Why don't we go home?" I stretch my arms above my head. "We've got a few names left to review, but it's late. We can review them tomorrow."

Hildy yawns. "Are you sure?"

I don't like that she's so tired. It's been a long day, but she needs to not work so hard. "Yes, absolutely."

"Want to come over for dinner?" Hildy asks. "We can get takeout."

I take her hand in mine and kiss it. "I'd love to, baby, but I still have work to finish. I also know tonight is when that show you like to watch is on." I kiss her wrist if only to smell her one more time. "Go home, and I'll come over in the morning. We can stop for breakfast on the way in to work."

She pouts but then finally nods. "Okay. But I want to go to a diner where I can get a real breakfast. Hashbrowns and bacon, the works. Pleeeaaase." She flutters her eyelashes, and I can't resist.

The truth is I can't resist her. "I know just the place. Everything is served with ketchup or hot sauce. You can wipe grease off the walls."

"Sounds perfect. Thank you." She kisses my right cheek. "Thank you." A kiss to my left cheek. "Thank you." A kiss to my lips and then she stands.

"See you at seven?" I ask.

"Perfect." Hildy grabs her bag and heads to the door. As she places her hand to the panel to unlock it—yes, we always lock the door now after the mailroom guy incident—she glances over her shoulder at me. "If you change your mind about coming over tonight, I can watch the show another night. One of the joys of streaming."

Her invitation is tempting. But I've spent so much time looking for the mole, I do have data to go through. Still, I grin. "Get out of here, and I'll see you tomorrow."

Half an hour later, I finish what has to be done. I decide there's no time like the present to clear the air with Nate. It's not that late, so there's a good chance he's still in his office. Occasionally, he'll go out to dinner with Ashton, his younger brother who is the VP of marketing, and Bradley. I'm always invited, but I'd rather starve than sit at the same table and break bread with Nate Lowe.

Tonight, I have some files for him to look at—the current updates on Orchid. That gives me a good excuse to go see him and bring up the subject of his stupid lies. If he's not in his office, I can leave the files and try again another day.

I put on my suit jacket to look more presentable and gather the files.

Do I ever plan on being friends with Nate again? Nope. But he's my boss, so I need to get to a place where I can sit in a meeting or see him in the building without wanting to attack him. Verbally, that is. Though more than once, I've really wanted to hit him, and I'm not a violent type. And in full transparency, wanting to attack has led me to assaulting him with as many barbs and sarcastic comments as possible since I started working here, and after learning more about what he's done, I fear I'll react worse, which would likely lead to me getting fired.

Once I have my bonus, Nate and Mr. Z can do whatever they want to me, but I want that money and will do everything in my power to get it. Even if it means playing—not nice—indifferent to the fucking asshole.

When I reach the twenty-second floor, it's quieter than usual. That isn't unusual at this hour. Zelda isn't in her office—strange because she usually stays until Nate leaves—but his door is open. For all I know, he saw me coming through a camera and awaits my arrival. That seems like a very Nate thing to do. He always said he likes to stay at least three steps ahead of everyone else, which explains Zentello's success.

Taking a deep breath, I brace myself for a conversation I'm not sure I'm ready to have. I hold the files in front of me like a shield. They won't offer much protection, but mentally, it helps. I'm older than Nate, but I still feel like a child learning to read when I'm around him. He's always been faster and so much smarter. I didn't mind so much when he was my friend. Now ... he's just an arrogant prick.

When I get closer to the doorway, I see him leaning against the edge of his desk, only...

I freeze. It can't be ...

I blink and then refocus and still see ... her.

My heart drops and falls straight through the liquid nickel and iron to the earth's core. This can't be happening. Not again. Every muscle bunches.

Nate stands right in front of Hildy. Her legs might even be between his. I can't tell from this position, but they're close. Too close.

What the fuck? She told me she hated him as much as I did. If that's true, what's Hildy doing here when she should be home watching TV?

I'm not sure what I've walked into, and I don't care. My blood runs cold. My legs turn leaden. I couldn't move farther into the office if I wanted to. Bile swills in my gut and rises to my throat.

"... Sam is the mole," Hildy says. "Do you believe me now?"

"That's why I brought you to Zentello," Nate says with no hesitation. He sounds cockier than usual. "To get close to Sam and find out for certain. I hired you because I knew you were the perfect woman for the job. I'm sure you can't wait to get to New Zealand and leave all this behind you."

"Well, it's a chance of a lifetime." I can't see Hildy's face, but I can hear her anticipation—her excitement—and both cut deep. She can't wait to leave Seattle and ... me.

I'm gutted. A deep growl starts from the bottom of my lungs and emits from my mouth. It sounds raw and inhuman, exactly the way I feel. She's done it again.

She's fucking done it again.

Hildy and Nate turn to stare at me.

She gasps, and her eyes go wide. "Sam?"

Nate groans and scrubs a hand down his face. "Ah, fuck."

"Yeah, I guess fuck just about covers it." I step into his office and toss the files on the floor. "There's your latest update on Orchid, and just so you know, I quit."

No, I don't have another job lined up, and I'll be walking away from my bonus. But I can't stay.

Neither says a word, which gives me time to get out of there.

As I walk away, my heart shatters, fragmenting into minuscule pieces. The worst part is Hildy has done this to me yet again. The same thing is happening to me over the same woman. Only now I'm struck by a cruel realization. This time, what she's done hurts more.

CHAPTER 25

HILDY

What the hell just happened? I sit stunned, trying to figure it out. One minute, I'm telling Nate how ridiculous it is that he ever thought Sam could be the mole, and the next, Sam is throwing something onto the floor in Nate's office and shouting he quits.

"What the hell?" I jump to my feet to chase after Sam, but Nate grabs my hand.

"Hildy, let him cool down."

I pull free. Letting Sam cool down is the wrong move. Something I learned the first time we split up. "No, I need to find him. I have no idea what he heard or thinks he heard, but he'll twist whatever it is into something that'll hurt him. I can't hurt him again. I've hurt him enough and so have you."

Nate raises an eyebrow.

Before he can say a word, I bolt from his office. As I run down the hallway, I mentally slap myself for going to see Nate instead of heading home as Sam suggested. I'd wanted to tell Nate I hadn't found the mole yet, and that I'm running out of time, which I did. I also added if he wants this accomplished before I leave, I need extra help to expand the search beyond the Orchid team. I don't want this final week in Seattle to be all about mole hunting. I want to spend it with Sam and tell him how I'm falling for him all over again.

Well, that's not really true.

I've already fallen for Sam Grant. Hard.

Now, he probably thinks I've been trying to get close to spy on him. A pain in my chest sharpens. I hope I'm wrong. I really hope I'm wrong.

I jab the down button on the elevator. If luck is on my side, the doors will open in seconds.

They don't.

Shit. I press the button again and again.

Nothing.

The car finally arrives, and I jump in. I can't help but count each floor until I reach the biochemistry floor. My heart pounds, but that doesn't stop me from running to Sam's office. I open the door with my palm, trying to catch my breath, and

...

He's sitting at his desk—working.

As usual.

It appears nothing is wrong.

I nearly deflate with relief. I've been so worried these past three, maybe five, minutes.

Seeing him like this, doing exactly what he's always done, pisses me off. Don't get me wrong. I'd rather he be here than storming out of the building onto the streets of Seattle in some misguided rage. But ...

Work was at the center of all our problems when we were married. Yes, he explained why, due to his past and wanting to make something of himself for us, but he also told me he's changed. Yet here he is, working, acting like nothing just happened in Nate's office.

I don't get it.

I know Sam heard something hurtful, and he thinks I've betrayed him yet again, but I thought I meant something to him, something worth at least discussing if he wants to have a relationship going forward. But he hasn't even glanced my way. There's no way he missed the sound of the door opening or my steps across the floor or my stupid panting from being out of shape.

Or maybe whatever's between us is just hot sex.

The way it had been during our marriage.

And his reaction upstairs was all he needed to move on.

As realization washes over me, my stomach knots.

I guess I thought things would be different this time, yet here we are in the same place. He was losing himself in his job, and I was upset about it.

I cross my arms over my chest. "I thought you quit."

He doesn't look at me but continues to type on the keyboard. So typical of him.

He'd rather keep working than fight.

"Are you going to answer me?" I force myself to move closer to his desk even though a part of me would rather keep my distance. I know I'm to blame here. Going to see Nate was a mistake. I should have told Sam my plan so he wouldn't get the wrong idea. But damn, I don't even know if that's the case, given how he's acting.

My body feels tense as if coiled like a spring ready to pop.

I'm good at leaving, but something makes me want to stay this time, even if I can feel my temper spiraling out of control. "Or, as usual, are you going to ignore the situation and continue working?"

His gaze remains focused on the screen. "I quit."

"Yet you're still at your computer, working." I sound like a bitch. Oh well …

"You know me, Hildegard. I'm Mr. Professional. I like to make sure nothing is left unfinished. I'm going to finish this, and then I'm out."

Damn, this man infuriates me. His quitting tells me that he's affected by what happened in Nate's office. The only thing Sam's ever quit is our marriage, but I hate the way he processes being hurt, shutting down and trying to appear totally unaffected by it when his insides must be reeling like mine are.

God, I want things to be different, yet he sits there tapping away at his computer with his damn sexy black glasses perched on his nose. I stand next to him, wanting to discuss what happened, but Sam ignores me like I'm not even here.

If he thinks I'll accept being invisible to him, he's wrong. I slam my hands on his desk and wait for him to respond.

He doesn't even flinch.

Unbelievable. The last time I left him some might say I ran away from Sam. That's not happening this time. If he doesn't like that, fuck him. "Don't you think that we should talk?"

After what seems like hours but is only seconds, maybe a minute, he finally looks up. "What's there to discuss? You're here to try to prove I'm the Zentello mole. You've told Nate I am, so your job's done. Now you can go to New Zealand to start your new life."

At least I know what he heard, and as I suspected, he got it completely wrong. "That isn't what I was telling Nate. Quite the opposite, in fact."

"It didn't sound that way to me."

"Well, it was." My voice rises an octave, maybe two. I don't care. "I was expressing how stupid it was of him to think you were the mole."

"That isn't the issue," Sam says through clenched teeth. If he tightens his jaw any more, he might crack a molar. "The issue is Nate hired you to spy on me, and you started a sexual relationship with me so you could get information on me."

My chest thuds, and my palms sweat. I can't deny what Nate did, but that isn't why I had sex with him. My heart sinks. I thought Sam wouldn't think the worst of me and knows me better than this. But he only sees what he wants to see in his narrow world, where everything, each decision is binary—black or white, yes or no. He's always been that way, but he said he'd changed, and I believe him. Only he hasn't. What I thought we had and shared is nothing more than a fairy tale. It isn't real, nor will it ever be.

The realization pushes me over the edge.

"How dare you." My voice breaks as anger takes over. "I would never, ever sleep with someone to get information. I especially wouldn't do it because my boss asked me to."

"Boss or fake fiancé ... Either way, it smacks of something unpleasant."

I dig my fingernails into my palms, not caring if it hurts or I draw blood. "What does that mean?"

Sam's eyes harden behind his glasses. All their usual

brightness has dimmed. "You're a clever woman, Hildy. I'm sure you can figure it out."

Something inside me wants to try one more time. It might be futile, but ... "I only went to Nate to confirm the mole isn't you and ask for more resources to look beyond the Orchid team."

Feeling Sam slip away, I pace to the other side of the office. My breathing comes faster, the tightness in my chest becoming almost unbearable. I try to take deep breaths, but it's not helping. My eyes sting, and a massive lump forms in my throat. It burns.

No, no, no.

I can't look at him because I don't want him to see me on the verge of tears. "I asked Nate for help because we can't investigate all of Zentello on our own."

I hear rustling, so I turn around to see he's now standing and holding a pile of papers in his hand.

I thrust my hands on my hips. "Are you leaving?"

"There's nothing left for us to discuss." He gives a dismissive shake of his head. "You did what you did. It's done, and everything is over."

Everything ...

He means us.

Fuck. I throw my hands into the air. "Just like that. You're going to walk out of here and not look back at what we've shared, what we could have together?"

Sam drops his head back and inhales deeply and then brings his gaze back to me.

"Can you appreciate how much all of this hurts?" he asks,

and I glimpse the breathing, feeling human inside the shell he's been presenting. "Or how hard it was for me to let myself fall back into some sort of relationship with you, no matter how false it turned out to be?"

"It isn't false." My eyes sting. Shit. I really don't want to cry, so I blink. "I would never do that to you."

"Yet you did." The pure venom in his voice and pain in his eyes tell me how hurt he is.

I'm hurt too because he thinks I hurt him. He can't understand that's the last thing I would ever do to him. I get he's only protecting himself, but he's not seeing me and how much he means to me. He's only seeing one outcome, not realizing the equation has other solutions.

"Sam ..."

His nostrils flare, and he doesn't say a word.

I blink again, trying to hold myself together. "Whatever you think you heard, or however you're analyzing what just went down, I didn't betray you. I would never do that."

Sam's jaw tightens, but he says nothing.

Keep calm. Not easy to do with my insides trembling. It's probably too late to save this, but I have to shoot my shot. "I know you're speaking out of anger, trying to protect yourself, but what you think—"

"Save it for someone who cares."

"You care." The words shoot out. My lower lip quivers, but this isn't the time to appear vulnerable. I need to be strong and fight for what I want, fight for him. "If you didn't care, if you weren't so upset, you would've never quit and left your bonus on the table because I know how much that money means to you."

A beat passes and another. "You know nothing about me. I'm just burying myself in work and ignoring the situation. As usual."

No. I don't believe him. My heart races so fast I'm surprised I'm still standing and not passed out flat on the ground. No matter how he's acting, I'm not giving up on us.

"As I told you, I went to Nate's office to help you. I wanted him to see how much you care about Zentello and the people who work on the Orchid team. But we still need to find the mole. That means looking deeper than we've been doing. Something we can't do ourselves efficiently."

I'm saying the same thing over again, but maybe he'll finally hear it this time. Otherwise ...

He scoffs, and the sound cuts deep. "This whole science sleuthing is just a game to you. Why don't you leave for New Zealand now? Nothing is keeping you in Seattle."

His words hit me like a punch to my gut. "Fuck you, Sam."

He winks at me, but his gesture isn't playful. It's full of disdain—hate. "Yeah, already did that, baby."

My heart splinters. This is what we've come to, hurling painful words at one another. I can't take any more of it. I thought we had a chance, but he clearly believes I'll whore myself out for information. No doubt shows in his voice or his expression. And if that's what he thinks ...

Tears blur my vision, and I glance at the ceiling in hopes of keeping them from falling.

A realization hits me hard, and I can't ignore the truth any longer.

Sam has always been right when he said we couldn't work.

We'll never work out. No matter how much I might want us to.

I inhale a shaky breath. "Sometimes I really hate you."

I turn on my heels and head out of the office. As the door slides open, someone runs away. Uh-oh. I think they were listening to us. Screw that. I'm going to rip whoever that was a new one if they think it's okay to eavesdrop on a personal conversation—well, fight.

I take off after them.

SAM

Dammit.

I pinch my eyes closed and hope the past few minutes have been nothing more than a fucking nightmare. I'm sick to my stomach, and I know I should go after Hildy to sort things out. I should find her and tell her that she means everything to me. I should tell her the thought of being without her again makes my heart wither and die, but I can't.

Instead, I decide to do what I do best and work.

Hildy's right. I haven't changed. Not one fucking bit.

Ten minutes later, I can't stand it any longer. The need to find Hildy is overwhelming—all-consuming. I need to do the biggest one-eighty I've ever done in my life, and if I want the woman I love, I must swallow my pride and just do it.

First, I need to check if she's still in the building. It's pointless to go all the way to her apartment if she hasn't left Zentello. For all I know, she's back in Nate's office.

Ugh. And doesn't that burn.

Tapping a few buttons on my keyboard, I bring up the control monitor that all leads can access. I'd forgotten about that until this moment because I never felt the need to micromanage my team, but remembering that would have cleared the Orchid team sooner. At least for whomever had gotten onto my computer. The monitor shows the comings and goings of each team member, and if they're still in the building, their whereabouts.

I enter Hildy's name and a list of places she's been in the past twelve hours show on the display. Glowing like a beacon is the access panel to Nate's office. I skim over that one and this office and skip to the bottom of the list to see she's still here. Only she's in ... the *mailroom.*

What the hell is she doing there?

I guess I'm about to find out. I stride purposely out of my office, stopping only long enough to make sure I've locked everything down.

Lesson learned.

The mailroom isn't in the basement of the building like some companies. Nate and Mr. Z believe the mail people deserve the same sort of office or lab as everyone else at Zentello. That's why the mailroom is open and bright with glass walls.

It still takes me ten minutes to get there, and I'm afraid she'll be gone.

When I walk in, the lights are off. Not surprising, given the hour. It takes me a couple of seconds for my vision to adjust to the semi-darkness after the bright lights of my office, but once I can see again, I spot Hildy.

I squint to get a better look at her.

What the hell is she doing?

She crouches behind a line of mail carts, occasionally popping up her head to peer over them. I can't tell what she's looking at, but she appears to be watching someone or something.

I assume—and it's a big assumption under the circumstances—she's trying to stay hidden. That means I don't want to blow her cover per se. The only thing I can do is crouch and sneak across the room to where she's hiding.

"Of all the mailrooms in all the world, I find you in this one," I whisper behind her, making her jump.

"Fuck, Sam." She slaps her hand to her chest and keeps her voice low. "You almost gave me a heart attack."

"What the hell are you doing here?"

She glances above the parapet of carts and waves her hand to tell me to keep it down. "It's the mail guy."

"Well, we are in the mailroom, so I'd expect a mail guy or woman to be here." I glance at my watch. "Although not necessarily at eight o'clock in the evening."

Hildy blows out a breath. "I know he works here, but why is he hanging around outside your office and listening to us talk after hours?"

I shrug. "He's nosy?"

She shakes her head. "He was standing at the door listening when I went to leave tonight. And then he ran away. Why didn't he just apologize? I also think it's the same guy from the other day." She swallows hard. "When we were having sex in your office."

Her words sting because that's the day I believed things changed for us.

"The one who came back later," she continues. "The young guy with the eye patch."

"He could just be a voyeur. What else makes you think he's the mole?"

Hildy drops onto her ass. "I followed him because I wanted to lay into him for eavesdropping, but then when he came in here, he rifled through one of the internal mail carts and grabbed a pile of letters. He took one envelope, made a copy of what was in it, and then returned it. And then, he went to the external mail cart and did the same thing. Whatever he copied, he shoved in his pocket."

That sounds sketchy. "What do you think he's doing?"

"I don't know. But I know which carts they are, so I figure once he leaves, I'll check the bundles to figure out what he's taken out."

"What if there's more than one bundle?"

She shakes her head. "Do you know anything about the workings of a mailroom?"

"They deliver mail."

Hildy doesn't roll her eyes, but I have a feeling she's tempted, given the way her eyelashes flutter. "Each bundle has a colored band, depending on which department sent them. The bundles he rifled through had a purple band, which is HR. Orchid has a red band."

The woman proves how smart she is every day. I stare at her, dumbfounded. "How in the hell do you know this shit?"

"Chatting with people gets you information." She focuses

on the mail guy. "You should try it sometime."

This woman amazes me. It's no wonder she has my fucking heart. I don't understand how we can be arguing and spewing hate one minute and then sitting on the mailroom floor together chatting about a nosy mailman the next.

"Shh," she hisses. "He's leaving."

The guy slings his jacket over his shoulder like he doesn't have a care in the world. He sings a song, maybe something from Wham or The Backstreet Boys, and he's actually got a really good singing voice, which I'm surprised I notice, but that's how talented he is. He lets himself out of the mailroom.

After waiting a few more minutes, Hildy nudges me in the ribs. "Go, go, go."

"We're not Crocket and Tubbs, baby."

"Who?"

"*Miami Vice*, an 80s classic?" I hold up my hands, totally shocked the woman I loved, have loved, probably still love has no clue about it. "Did your parents not tell you about the show? Mine did."

She stares at me as if I've lost my mind. "You've met my parents. Do you really think my mom and dad would ever discuss an 80s TV show with me?"

I laugh. "Good point."

We stand, and Hildy leads me to the mailcarts and the bundles of mail the guy tampered with.

Hildy passes me a letter from HR, and I read it. "Dammit. This talks about the alteration of pay scales. Fuck, if this gets out, it could cause bad publicity for Zentello."

She peers over my shoulder. "There's nothing too bad. No

salaries or anything specific mentioned."

"It's not the numbers that are the problem," I explain. "The implication of pay cuts suggests quarterly earnings might not meet expectations. That'll cause trouble. What's the other letter?"

The envelope flap is pressed down but no longer sealed. She removes the letter and reads it. "It's telling trial participants about the date for the next round of blood tests."

I exhale in relief. "Nothing too bad."

"Not this time." Hildy rubs her neck. "We need to set him up. Send something from Orchid to prove he's the mole."

The idea makes sense, but ... "How do we do that?"

She chews on her thumbnail and then slaps her hands together. "Okay. I have a plan, but it'll mean us working together, and we might have to work late into the night, and you'll need to be here tomorrow."

Ah, fuck.

Well, I'll have to pack up my office at some point and make sure Bradley and Max know where things stand with the data verification. Someone will have to take that over ... and the realization makes me itch. I might be leaving the project without finishing, but the least I can do is help with the transition. Why not get that all done tomorrow?

I give a single nod. "Okay, lay it on me."

PHARMA LAB NOTES #271

BY ANDY CHEKOV

Inside sources claim a certain mysterious co-CEO is attempting to make up for overspending on his flowery product in development by altering the salary schedule for his employees. The longer his identity remains a mystery, the sketchier his past begins to look. Could the budget problems stem from something else—like skimming money? No one knows his identity other than the letter Z, so anything is fair game.

As for the salary level adjustments, the exact percentages of these cuts are unknown. But they must be cuts because do you know any big pharmaceutical company that would willingly increase salaries except for a yearly cost-of-living adjustment?

We feel sorry for the hardworking men and women at Zentello. Will employees be fair game for recruiters now? Only time will tell. Our inquiries to the company have yet to be answered. We'd love to hear from anyone at the company who can provide more information.

CHAPTER 26

SAM

Just as I told Hildy I would be last night, I'm in my office the following morning, but it's the last place I want to be. I hope it won't be for long, though I've had no time to pack my things or talk to Bradley and Max yet. Her "plan" to catch the mole has taken all my attention.

The tension between us hangs heavy in the air, yet all I can do is ignore it. I'm just trying to get through this day to put her, Nate, and Zentello behind me. After sleeping on everything that happened, I realized Hildy would still go to New Zealand. No matter how I feel, I don't fit into her plans. So I need to make some of my own. I've already emailed the recruiter who had a job opportunity I turned down because of my commitment to Zentello. Maybe the position is still open. If not, I hope he knows of others.

Hildy glances down the hallway, steps back into the office, and closes the door. "You ready? He's coming."

I nod. The sooner this is over, the better. I glance at the empty copier paper boxes I snagged from a supply closet on the fourth floor. "Yes, I'm ready."

We'd stayed in the office until midnight setting up "the

sting," as Hildy calls her plan. That entails a fake meeting notice for a nonexistent trial participant to advise them they'll be paid for falsifying their results. It's the kind of thing that can ruin trials, reputations, and careers. I spent hours creating a list of the results we want "Courtney Hernandez" to falsify. The meeting with me is supposed to be "top secret." The two words are even stamped on the envelope. This isn't a time for subtlety, according to Hildy, and she's right.

"Knock, knock." A voice comes over the intercom at the door. "Someone called with urgent outgoing mail?"

"Showtime," Hildy whispers. Her voice might be quiet, but her body hums with anticipation. I don't know why catching this guy has become a personal vendetta for her. I guess she really wants to go to New Zealand and not have anything tying her to Zentello.

I pick up the envelope and walk closer to the door as it slides open. "Hey."

The mail guy—Ryan Matthews, I confirm the name on his badge—steps into the doorway. He's wearing the eye patch again. "Outgoing mail?"

"I have something." I shoot Hildy, working at her desk, a furtive look, which I hope isn't too obvious or overdramatic. "Though I need a personal delivery offsite. Can you handle that?"

Ryan's breath comes faster. "Of course. I can take care of it myself for you, Dr. Grant."

I hear Hildy's chair roll but don't look her way. She's implementing the next part of her plan.

"This is between us," I whisper to Ryan and hand him two

twenty-dollar bills. I know I'll never see the money back, so it's just the price of my freedom. "There should be enough cash for a ride. Confidential, remember?"

Ryan nods. "Absolutely, Dr. Grant."

Ryan doesn't know that he's delivering the letter to an old friend of Hildy's named Allison, who lives in Ballard with her husband and two kids.

"I'm going to get a coffee. Want one?" Hildy walks right into Ryan. "Oops, sorry. I thought I had more room to get by."

"No problem." As she leaves the office, Ryan smiles at her and takes the letter from me. He raises it to show me he's grasping it tightly, salutes, and then hurries toward the elevator.

I check the hallway to make sure he's gone and wait for Hildy to return. Five minutes later, she's back.

She taps on her phone. "I slipped the tracker into his jacket pocket when I bumped into him, and it's connected to my phone. He's in the mailroom."

"Probably making a copy."

"The plan is working." She beams at me.

I hope she's only happy about our mission to catch the mole working. My bruised heart isn't up for more pain, so I won't bring up last night when we still have stuff to do.

Who am I kidding? I'm not sure I'll ever be ready for that discussion. Why, when we have no future?

She keeps staring at her phone. "He's leaving Zentello."

"Okay, let's go." She grabs her bag and heads toward the door.

I follow her out of the office. "Super Sleuth Scientists strike again."

I'm being sarcastic, but she grins. Whatever.

Inside the elevator, I press the button for the lobby. Hildy glances at her shoes, which are sunshine-yellow heels. Not exactly suitable for being incognito, but who knows why she does what she does?

"Should we talk about everything?" she asks, reaffirming the thought I'd just had about her.

Should we? I want to say no, given everything I've been thinking this morning, but the truth is I have no idea. My answer should be *probably* because I'd been willing to discuss it when I looked for her last night. Now ... Oh, fuck it. "Yes, we probably should, but let's get the mole first so we give that discussion our full attention. Okay?"

She clears her throat. "Okay."

Her voice doesn't sound okay. That only makes me feel worse. It's all I can do not to hold her hand to reassure her. But I ... can't. Not right now. I need to protect myself and...

We have the mole to capture. Well, trap.

On the sidewalk, I keep my distance from Hildy, and we both hang back from Ryan so he doesn't notice us. The guy's taking his sweet time reaching his destination.

"There he is." Hildy puts an arm across my stomach to stop me from walking into view.

I peer ahead of her to see Ryan, ironically hanging around outside a greasy diner, our planned breakfast venue. That just tells me fate has a cruel sense of humor.

Ryan looks up and down the street.

"He's certainly acting shifty." I try to act nonchalant so he doesn't notice us. "If a cop sees him, he'll probably ask him what he's up to."

Hildy sighs. "Let's hope no one does. Otherwise, this will all have been for nothing."

"In all seriousness ..." I shouldn't, but I move closer to her and get a better sniff of her perfume. I might have to buy a bottle from Christina just to have it after Hildy leaves for New Zealand. "You're good at this. I would never have thought of putting a tracker in Ryan's pocket. I'd have followed him and given the game away."

She glances over her shoulder at me. "I watch and listen to a lot of true crime stuff."

"I thought that sort of stuff scared you. You used to hate anything like that when we were married."

She shrugs. "I guess I grew brave. When you're on your own, you have to be brave about a lot of things."

The thought of her being scared by anything fills me with dread and regret. A helluva lot of regret. Fear is one of the worst emotions to have and what I felt every day after Mom and Dad died. At one point, fear became a constant companion. I don't want that for her or anyone.

"I even had to learn not to be scared of spiders. When there's no one else to get rid of those for you, you have to face your fear." She shudders, telling me she's still not totally at ease with them.

I wonder how much the divorce forced her to change. At first, I hated living alone, and having my own place was a huge adjustment, but I found solace in the solitude and my hermitic ways.

Hildy hisses. "Someone's coming."

A guy wearing a baseball cap with a laptop bag strapped to his shoulder stops beside Ryan. As the two men speak, Hildy takes a photo of them with her cell phone. She's so good at this. I hadn't thought of taking pictures.

Ryan glances at his wrist as if checking the time, but even from this distance, I can see he's not wearing a watch. The guy in the cap crosses the street and goes into a bookstore. Ryan remains where he is.

Something feels off. I wonder if we've gotten it all wrong. "That can't have been him."

"I don't know. Did you see the way the other guy kept glancing around? That's suspicious as hell."

"Maybe."

"Do you think we're barking up the wrong tree?" she asks.

"I don't know." And I hate that. "I hope not. Otherwise, we've wasted hours of effort and money."

"The tracker was inexpensive compared to the cash you gave the guy." She holds up her phone. "I'm going to see if Veronica has a printout for us yet."

I nod, my eyes on Ryan, clueless that he's being tracked. Veronica is the supervisor in the mailroom, and Hildy wants to get a copy of the log from that morning with the usernames who'd accessed the copier. "Did you ask her for one already?"

"Yes, right before we left the building."

Ryan had returned to the mailroom after getting the delivery, and we hope he copied the letter like he did last night.

The log would tell us if he made a copy of something and what that happened to be before leaving the building. All the printers and copiers in Zentello had the ability to print a log as a security feature in case, as what might be happening here, someone copies confidential information. Every department head is supposed to print off the history log at least once a week, but I'm lax doing it and so are others. Which is why Hildy is the one who gleaned that information when she'd spoken to the staff, proving to me once again that chatting to others is a useful activity.

"Hi, Veronica," Hildy says in a quiet voice, not that we're close enough for Ryan to hear her. "Did you get it? ... Yes ... Perfect ... Yes, that's it. Thank you. I'll pick it up later ... Yes, bye."

"Sounds like the printout has what we wanted?"

"Yes." The corners of her mouth curl. "The letter was copied by Ryan Matthews. So I'm guessing that's what he's giving to his contact."

"Hey." I point across the street. "The guy with the baseball cap is coming back."

The cap guy stands next to Ryan.

"Take pictures, Sam. We need as many as we can get," Hildy says as she takes more. "As close up as you can. So we can see his face."

As Ryan pulls out an envelope from his messenger bag, I snap photos with my phone. I take more as he speaks to the man in the cap. The other guy appears to be recording him as he's holding his phone close to Ryan's mouth. Finally, the other man nods, takes the envelope from Ryan, puts it into his laptop bag, then pulls out a smaller envelope which bulges slightly.

"Do you think that's full of cash?" Hildy asks, snapping photos.

"I'd bet my house on it."

The guy removes his cap and wipes his brow. Before he puts it back on, I get a clear shot of his face.

Finally, Ryan and his contact walk away in different directions. The cap guy approaches us. I grab Hildy and turn her so she's facing a bakery's window.

Behind us, coming closer, the footsteps get louder. I see his reflection in the window.

Hildy and I stand silent as if holding our breath, waiting for the other shoe to drop. I don't care about the cakes or breads in the display. I just want this guy not to notice us.

The guy passes without glancing at us.

I take a breath. "It appears your plan worked perfectly."

"We have one more thing to do," Hildy finally says.

Her words surprise me. We have the mole's identity, which was the purpose of all that. "What's that?"

"To discover who the journalist is. I thought the guy might be a courier, but it looks like he asked Ryan questions and recorded him. That screams reporter to me. Maybe he's one of the journalists who bothered Bradley and Christina. If we can identify him, that'll be the final piece of the puzzle."

"Why don't you do that while I figure out how Ryan got into my office to look at my files without his entry appearing on the log?"

She faces me and gives me a small smile. "Sure, and then I'll be out of your hair."

As she walks past me, a cold shiver runs through me. If that's true, I hope our plan fails.

And whatever happened to us discussing things once we found the mole? Did she change her mind?

CHAPTER 27

HILDY

I still can't believe it. Sam and I pulled off our sting. Ryan Matthews fell for our plan, and after passing over what we assume to be a copy of the letter in exchange for a bundle of cash, he delivered the real fake to Allison. But to make sure the "fake news" doesn't get printed, we let Ashton Lowe, the VP of marketing, know that he needs to stop that from being published. If the magazine goes ahead with the story, the Zentello law team is ready to pounce.

Yes, Sam and Zentello's reputation is on the line, but Ashton knows how to play hardball with the best of them. Something tells me he was on top of this as soon as we told him what had happened.

Only one other Lowe needs to be told. I must admit I'm not looking forward to this. I'm worried about how Sam will react with Nate. But it must be done.

We have all the evidence Nate wanted. All we have to do is show him what we did and let the authorities take over. And then ...

I shiver.

I'm not ready to think about Sam and me. The thought of what might or might not happen scares me.

As Sam walks next to me on the way to Nate's office, I glance his way. "You have the pictures?"

"Everything is in the folder." He smiles at me. "How you knew it was the mail guy and one of the reporters, I'll never know."

I shrug, but pride flows through me that my hunch has been proven right. I clear my throat. "Instinct, I guess. We make a good team."

"We do, however temporary."

And doesn't that hurt. I ignore the sting, the way I've pretended everything is fine since last night. When Sam came looking for me in the mailroom, I thought he wanted to figure things out between us. Then he said we'd talk after we got the evidence about the mole, but he still hasn't broached the subject.

After I'd called in a couple of favors and found out who Ryan Matthews had given the copy of the letter to, Sam had quickly hugged me and then clammed up. We've barely spoken since. He's been too busy working on the trial data, which is strange, given he quit and the boxes he planned to use for packing are still empty. Unless he plans to wait until later and just wants to finish what he started. I can see him doing that.

Or …

Does that mean he changed his mind about leaving? I need to know. "Sam …"

We come to Zelda's office first. He looks my way. "Let's get this over with."

I enter her office, and he follows me in. Zelda sits behind her desk. She sees us and frowns. "Nate doesn't have an appointment with you."

"We don't have one," Sam says, "but it's urgent."

"Let me see if he has time to speak to you." She leaves us in her office and goes into Nate's.

"What do you think Nate will do about it?" I ask.

"He'll fire Ryan. As for the journalist, I'm not sure." Sam gives a straight answer with no eye contact, exactly how he acted while we put together our discovery for Nate. "Your friend is certain about the guy's name?"

"Positive. Brian said he recognized the guy from various networking events." My ex-neighbor from when I was a kid is a journalist. It had been a long shot, but I sent him the guy's picture, and as luck would have it, Brian knew him. He was surprised to hear the guy might be involved in something shady. Supposedly, the guy's very much above board.

"At least this gives Zentello something to work with."

Wow, Sam is all business. It'll make his leaving the company and me easier. Well, I hope it will.

Zelda reappears. "You can go in. Nate has ten minutes."

"This won't take long." I flash a fortifying smile at Sam and follow him into Nate's office.

"Well." Nate sits back in his chair. "I didn't expect to see either of you in here after last night."

"I bet you didn't," Sam mutters under his breath.

"Chill, Sam," Nate says, keeping his tone lighthearted. "What can I help you with?"

I step forward and place a copy of the letter we sent to

"Courtney Hernandez" on Nate's desk. "This is what we used to catch your mole."

Nate frowns at the letter, picks it up, and reads it. "I'm not sure I follow."

Sam exhales. "We sent this letter containing false information to a fake trial participant and asked our suspected mole to deliver it by hand. We took a chance he'd make a copy, and we were right."

"Sam has pictures of the handoff of the letter in the file," I say.

Nate looks up, slightly startled. "So we have our mole?"

"Enough evidence for however you want to deal with this. Ashton is already aware and prepared to do what it takes for any necessary damage control." I go to say more, but Sam steps forward and throws two files onto Nate's desk. They thud, and all I can think is *mic drop*. Honestly, that's more my style than Sam's, but given his issues with Nate, I don't blame him.

"The pictures show Ryan Matthews from the mailroom handing over the letter." His voice is gruff.

Nate's brows knot. "Ryan Matthews is the mole?"

"Yes, do you know him?" I ask.

Nate nods. "His mother has caused trouble here in the past. With my sister-in-law, Chloe, and with Sophie, Max's wife."

Sam's jaw drops. "The mole is Bitter Belinda's son?"

Oh, that's the woman Zelda had mentioned. "Zelda warned me to keep my distance from the woman."

Sam nods. "Good advice from Zelda."

"Damn." Sam rubs his chin. "Belinda worked for the

scientist who had my lab and office before I was hired. I wonder if her badge still opens the door but somehow bypasses the system, and she let her son use it."

"That would explain how someone got in to look at your computer." That's the only thing we haven't been able to figure out.

Nate skims through the photographs. He tilts his head. "How are we sure a handoff of information is happening?"

"After he left the building, I asked Veronica, the mailroom supervisor, to access the copier history and print off this morning's copies," I explain. "The letter was one of them, and it was copied with Ryan Matthews's access code."

Nate taps the second folder. "And this one?"

"That's something different," Sam says proudly. "It's a report I've compiled about Zentello and Orchid. I wanted to ensure I was putting my name on something good. This is the result."

Nate's jaw tenses. "What made you decide to do this?"

"Like I said," Sam replies with zero emotion. "I wanted to be sure I'm not working for some crap company that takes shortcuts and risks with people's lives."

Nate stares at him, not even blinking. "And?"

"You're in the clear," Sam says. "You have a good company with solid procedures and good ethics, aside from a couple of misogynistic bastards on the board." Nate clears his throat, but Sam continues. "Orchid is a great product, and I'm confident it'll make you a lot of money. A copy has been sent to an independent pharmaceutical adviser to get an outside opinion on what I've covered. He'll also let me know if the report will pass peer review so it can be published should any journalists decide to discredit Zentello again."

Nate pulls out the report. "It's thick."

"Yes." Sam tugs on his tie, which he'd loosened as soon as he'd walked into the office this morning. "I've been compiling it for some time and have gone to great lengths to ensure no one can ever get ahold of it or understand what I've written if they do."

"It's all in code," I offer.

Nate's gaze swings to me. "You seem pretty agreeable about this."

"I agree with Sam writing the report." I meet Nate's eyes straight on. "What he's researched is a good thing."

Nate flips open the report's cover. "Will I be able to read it?"

"Yes. I transcribed everything into something you can understand. My independent adviser has the code so there's no chance of anyone else understanding it." Sam exhales slowly. "Before you ask, he's extremely trustworthy and would never use the information against Zentello. Not that there's anything to use anyway. Like I said, you run a tight ship here."

Nate steeples his fingers under his chin. "Okay. Is that it?"

"As far as the report goes, yes." Sam raises his chin. "There's one more thing."

My head whips toward him. He's caught me off guard. I thought we've covered everything.

"What's that?" Nate asks.

"I still quit," he says without any hesitation.

"You do?" Nate doesn't appear the least bit surprised. In

fact, he's smiling as though he thinks Sam's joking. "Okay, then."

Sam nods. "Okay."

He glances at me briefly, but then he turns and stalks out of Nate's office. It's at that moment, watching his back, I hear my heart crack open.

He can't go. We haven't talked. We haven't ironed things out and fixed things.

Fixed us.

"Sam," Nate stands and calls after him. "Don't be an idiot."

Air rushes from my lungs. I gasp for air. "Oh my God. Please don't leave, Sam."

Sam stops walking and turns around. For one moment, he appears as if he might storm over and lift me over his shoulder to carry me out of there. But he doesn't.

Instead, Sam walks straight up to Nate and punches him in the face. He hits Nate so hard he stumbles backward, grabbing ahold of his desk so he doesn't fall on his ass.

As Nate backpedals until he collides with his chair, he groans. "Fucker."

"Sam!" I glance between him and Nate, the adrenaline in my body going crazy.

Sam points at Nate, who cradles his jaw and looks like he might punch back. "That's for what you put me through five years ago. You also told others you slept with Hildy. Don't mess with a woman's reputation. That's tacky as hell, bro."

Nate laughs. Actually, he's cackling. My hate level for the man soars exponentially.

"I'm glad you think it's funny, Lowe," Sam growls.

"Because I fucking don't. You messed up everything, and I have no idea why."

Nate throws his hands in the air. "Because you two are a pair of dumbasses who can't work anything out yourselves, so I played matchmaker."

"Matchmaker," I yell. "Why the hell do we need a matchmaker?"

"What the fuck? The only dumbass is you, Lowe." Sam's voice is gravelly. His hands ball into fists. "What does matchmaking have to do with you lying about doing things with my wife, lying about asking her to marry you, and hiring her to spy on me by telling her I'm the mole?"

I agree completely. The man is whack. "Oh my God, Nate. Why would you do all this?"

"Why?" Nate laughs and then cradles his jaw. "Ooh, that hurts."

"Stop being a baby, Nate." I don't care if he's in pain. He deserves it.

"Thanks for the sympathy," he says flippantly. When I sigh impatiently, he continues. "Five years ago, you didn't see Sam like I did. I hated that my best friend was a shadow of the man he'd been, all because of you. He'd given up on everything. I'd made the same mistake with Zelda, and I didn't want Sam to suffer like I had. I wanted him to fight for you."

"That doesn't change the fact you interfered in Sam's and my life," I say. "Then and now."

"And you thought telling me you'd fucked my wife would help?" Sam yells as he shrugs in disbelief. "Are you stupid? Actually, don't bother answering that. I know the answer."

"I needed to see some emotion from you, Sam, and hatred of me was better than nothing. I needed to force you to do something before it was too late." Nate points at me. "As for you, I tried to reason with you and tell you to talk to him. Begged you to reconsider what you'd left behind, but you were too stubborn and pigheaded to listen to anyone. Sam can vouch for that."

I turn to Sam, who tilts his head, thinking about it.

I poke him in the side. "Samuel."

Sam shrugs. "He has a point."

I poke him again.

"Listen to you both." Nate wags his fingers. "You're like a married couple even now. You loved each other. You told me you did but were both too stubborn to do anything about it. You still fucking love each other."

I look at Sam. "You told him you still loved me?"

"You know I did. I've never stopped." Sam takes a deep breath. "You told Nate you loved me?"

"Of course I did. I just wanted you to put me first. Then, after you kept asking for another chance, you stopped contacting me, so I thought you'd stopped loving me."

"See?" Nate says. "Dumbasses, both of you. Five fucking years and you're still apart. That's why I lured Sam to Zentello with a job and you with the plan of helping with the data verification. Finding the mole was a bonus. I never expected to have to deal with corporate espionage. But I always knew Sam wasn't the mole. I just couldn't let on, and I knew you'd know that Sam wasn't it as soon as you spent a couple of hours with him. I thought you'd realize what a great man he still is, and he'd realize what an amazing woman you are. Not for one minute did I think you'd carry on being so stubborn, Hildy."

"You're an absolute douche, Nate Lowe," I snap. "Nothing you've done or tried to do makes any sense. Your matchmaking plan has more holes than a Sierpiński Triangle. I've got a good mind not to give you the name of the fucking journalist we found involved with the mail guy."

"Hildy." Sam keeps his voice even, which is more than I can do. "Just give him the name and what you found out so we can get out of here."

I huff, pull a piece of paper from my bra, which earns a groan from Sam, and slap the name against Nate's chest.

"Jack Parker. He's the science reporter who paid off Ryan Matthews. He's one of the journalists using famous writers' names as aliases. There are others who all work for the same magazine and use similar aliases. Someone has it out for Zentello and wants to unmask Mr. Z. But ..." I lean closer to Nate. "That's your problem to deal with. I'm no longer playing Super Sleuth Scientist."

Nate stares at the floor, then at the ceiling, muttering something that sounds like "fuck my life" and then yells for Zelda and rushes out of his office.

Once Nate leaves in a storm of anger and frustration, Sam and I face each other, standing in silence for what feels like forever, neither of us breathing or blinking.

"Why are you quitting?" I ask him. "You never walk away from anything unfinished."

"I don't," he admits. "But the most important thing in my life remains unfinished, and I need to remedy that."

I have no idea what he's talking about. "What's the most important thing?"

"You."

I gasp. "Me?"

He nods. "You and our marriage."

I stare in disbelief.

"I'm quitting Zentello." He gently tucks my hair behind my ear. "But I'm not quitting you, Hildy. I'll never quit you again."

Tears prick at my lashes. "I thought you didn't want me."

Even saying the words is painful. I've made many mistakes by not opening up and communicating with Sam. We lost five years because I'd gotten fed up and left because I'd been so stubborn and taken his working all the time as his rejection of me. To think he might want me again is something out of a dream.

He blows out his cheeks and grins. "I've always wanted you, baby. Never stopped. You should know that." He gives a short laugh. "Although apparently, I'm a dumbass, so maybe not."

I reach for his fingertips and link mine with his. "So what happens next?"

"We go to New Zealand, where that dream job awaits you."

My jaw drops. "What about you? There are fewer jobs there, and you'll need a visa."

"I'm not worried about that. I can try being a stay-at-home husband. I also have that book I outlined. I'd like to write it."

My heart thuds in my chest. "You'd do that for me?"

His smile crinkles the corners of his eyes. "I'd do anything for you. You're stuck with me now, but I promise this time will be different."

My heart beats faster and harder. When he gives me another beautiful smile, it practically dances. "What about your house?"

"The rental market's solid in Seattle. I'm sure I could find someone at Zentello to move in. People here are always looking for places to live. But I'd like to keep it in case we decide to return someday."

"It's where we had sex for the first time in more than five years."

"Lots of good memories."

I nod.

He takes a breath and then straightens. "I'm sorry for what I said to you, what I accused you of doing."

I'm so happy to hear him say this, but I have something to say in return. "I'm sorry if anything I did or said hurt you. I can see why you thought I'd used you, but I would never do that."

"Logically, I know you wouldn't, but ..."

"The heart isn't as logical as the brain." My heart tells me to run to him, but my brain keeps telling me to keep my distance for now.

"Not at all."

Well, both my heart and mind agree on one thing. "I forgive you."

"So you'll take me back, then?" He steps closer and closer, and I meet him halfway. "I know I'm an idiot, but I'll do it right this time."

"Just be you, Sam. That's all I need." I reach out, and he pulls me against him. I go eagerly, happy to be back in his arms. "You, our love, and our trust, and I promise to give you the same. Oh, and not to bottle things up until I burst. I won't take things so personally, and I won't run away again."

"Thank fuck." He kisses me quickly. "You know I love you exactly the way you are. I accept you, too."

"Good." I wink. "So now we can get a dog and have a couple of kids?"

He laughs. "Whatever you want. Even if that's two dogs and half a dozen kids."

"Sounds good to me."

Sam lowers his mouth to mine in a heart-stopping kiss, and I know without a doubt we'll make it this time.

This time, more than chemistry is involved. Our hearts know what's at stake, and we'll do whatever it takes to hold on—forever.

Thanks for reading *Chemistry of the Heart*! I hope you enjoyed Hildy and Sam's story. If want to read the next story in my Romancing the Geek series, featuring Zelda, check out *Love Under the Microscope*.

If you'd like to receive a FREE story, join my newsletter where you'll hear about upcoming releases and other news. To subscribe, go to www.emileonbooks.com/subscribe.

As a new romantic comedy author, I would appreciate your help spreading the word about my stories. If you have friends who might enjoy this steamy rom-com, please let them know, and also, consider leaving a review. Thanks so much!

ABOUT THE AUTHOR

Emi Leon lives in Washington state. She believes love and laughter go hand-in-hand. Nerdy and grumpy heroes are her favorites. The fact she married one has absolutely nothing to do with it. She's a STEM girl turned romance writer, who has a thing for F1 drivers and hockey players and happily ever afters.

Website: www.emileonbooks.com
Facebook: www.facebook.com/emileonbooks
Instagram: www.instagram.com/emileonbooks
TikTok: www.tiktok.com/emileonbooks

BOOKS BY THE AUTHOR

The Wrong Gift: A Christmas Romantic Comedy
A Scrooge of a boss gets more than the wrong Christmas gift when he fires his full-of-sunshine temp …

Hypothesis for Love
A PhD student who wants a recommendation, a scientist who needs an assistant, and a new product that will change people's lives … if the two don't kill each other first.

The Sex Variable
What's a little secret when the chemistry is off the charts? But, like any explosive reaction, the truth invariably comes out … Can a perfumer and a chemist survive the unexpected results of this love equation?

Chemistry of the Heart
The line between love and hate blurs when two exes still sizzle more than a Bunsen burner on full blast.